Readers love
ANDREW GREY

Paint by Number

"This story, like most of Andrew's books is sweet and full of feelings... If you've never read a book from Andrew Grey and even if you have, I highly recommend this one."

—Open Skye Book Reviews

"There is a saying that you can never go home again but this story will prove an exception to that."

—Paranormal Romance Guild

Catch of a Lifetime

"...a salute to Mr. Grey's mastery of gay locution, which added enormously to my reading pleasure."

—Rainbow Book Reviews

Twice Baked

"This a great second chance romance novel... There is loads of charm and romance."

—MM Good Book Reviews

"A fun and flirty story I enjoyed and I believe you will, too."
—Bayou Book Junkie

T0004480

By Andrew Grey

Published by Dreamspinner Press
www.dreamspinneprress.com

Published by DREAMSPINNER PRESS
www.dreamspinnerpress.com

By Andrew Grey

Published by Dreamspinner Press
www.dreamspinnerprress.com

BAD
TO BE GOOD

ANDREW GREY

REAMSPINNER
PRESS

Published by
DREAMSPINNER PRESS

5032 CAPITAL CIRCLE SW, SUITE 2, PMB# 279, TALLAHASSEE,
FL 32305-7886 USA
WWW.DREAMSPINNERPRESS.COM

Bad to Be Good
© 2020 Andrew Grey

Cover Art
© 2020 Kanaxa
Cover content is for illustrative purposes only and any person depicted
on the cover is a model.

Mass Market Paperback ISBN: 978-1-64108-219-8
Trade Paperback ISBN: 978-1-64405-651-6
Digital ISBN: 978-1-64405-650-9
Library of Congress Control Number: 2020938603
Mass Market published February 2021
First Edition
v. 1.0

Printed in the United States of America
∞
This paper meets the requirements of
ANSI/NISO Z39.48-1992 (Permanence of Paper).

To Christi B.—one prologue from you and the ideas flowed.
You're amazing, and you inspired it all.

Chapter 1

RICHARD MARSDEN——yes, that was his name now. It was always at the front of his mind that his old life was over. Everything had been stripped away, and the person and the life he'd had before were gone. And that included his real name. Well, now Marsden was his "real" name. At least it was supposed to be, but it didn't feel like it. Though to be fair, nothing about where he lived and what he did each day felt real to him. He doubted it ever would.

"I ain't never gonna get used to this shit," his brother Terrance grumped as he stalked into the empty bar, looking around. "You know what went down?" He came closer, stomping on the wooden floor. "A customer got in my face 'cause we didn't have the size flange that he needed, and I fucking had to stand there like a dope instead of ripping the fucker's head off."

Richard shot his hand out and smacked Terrance on the back of the head. "No talking about that stuff. Not here—or anywhere, for that matter. And no street talk. Remember that we need to speak *properly* so we don't stand out." He rolled his eyes and then puffed up his chest, glaring hard at his younger, but built like a brick shithouse, brother in spirit. "And no ripping anyone's head off," he added in a hiss just above a whisper. "Sometimes I wonder what the hell is wrong with you."

Terrance inhaled, and anger flared in his eyes but then abated slowly. "At least he isn't dead." That was better.

Richard took a deep breath, inhaling the scent of fish, ocean water, and whatever seasoning the guys in the kitchen were using. The damned stuff had been stoking his appetite since he arrived an hour ago. "What are you doing here instead of being at work?"

"Break. I walked down to cool off," Terrance said.

"Okay. Go on back to the hardware store and finish your shift, because you are not to get fired. And don't draw any extra attention to yourself. Remember the rules." He crooked his finger and lowered his voice. "If you do decide to rip anyone's head off, remember that yours is next. You know I'll do it, and piss down your damned neck. Now go back to work, and no talking about…. Just keep your mouth shut. You know how to do that."

Terrance nodded and turned away, leaving the bar and smacking the door shut with a bang. Richard picked up his tray of glasses, shaking his head as he went back to work stocking the bar for tonight.

It wasn't that Richard didn't understand how Terrance felt—he very much did. Richard had spent the past four months stocking glasses and getting drinks, listening to guys who sat at the bar bellyaching over the fact that they thought their wives were having an affair or that things at work were going to shit. Richard could tell them all about things going to hell. It had happened to them—him and his brothers—and now he was tending bar instead of running an entertainment organization. Now that was the shits of epic proportions.

Richard finished stocking and stepped outside the bar for a breath of fresh air. They didn't open for another half hour, and he was ready.

The sun beat down on the empty parking area, the Florida heat wafting off the blacktop. If he looked carefully across the street and between the houses and palm trees, he could see the Gulf of Mexico, the water sparkling as the waves caught the light. To most people, this would be paradise. Richard knew that, and yet he missed Detroit and his home. Yeah, to most people Detroit was not the kind of place you missed. Richard could understand that. But it was the city he'd grown up in, his home, and he had been somebody there. He thought he was going places, in line for big things, and then everything fucking changed at the drop of a hat, and just like that it was gone.

The familiar white Focus with the ding in the front bumper pulled into the parking area and up next to where he was standing. His youngest friend and brother from a different mother, Gerome, lowered the window. "I saw you standing out here. You out to get sunstroke or something?"

Richard rolled his eyes. "No. Getting some fresh, water-filled air before I go back inside and pretend to be a bartender." That was it—his entire life was pretend. "And we gotta have the 'keep your damn mouth shut' conversation with Terrance... again." He was getting so sick of this. For the millionth time he wondered if anything was ever going to be normal again. The answer that he kept coming back to was that it wasn't.

Richard, Terrance, and Gerome had been friends and a family of their own making since they were twelve years old. They'd survived on the mean streets of depressed inner-city Detroit by their wits and having each other's backs. The three of them joined the Garvic organization of the Italian mafia when they were fourteen and worked their way upward fast. They were tough as hell and none of them took any shit from anyone—or had to—because everyone in the organization knew that to take one of them on was to engage all three of them. They were tough, smart, and feared. Richard liked that.

In the end, the three of them had made a great deal of money for Harold Garvic. Richard ran the gay clubs in Detroit and was the king of the gay mafia... so to speak. He ran the entire enterprise and returned a great deal of money, managing the legitimate club façade while laundering millions in cash. Terrance was the muscle and feared well beyond their group. No one messed with any of them because no one in the Garvic organization wanted to see Terrance come through their door. Gerome was the idea man. He dreamed up new ways to make piles of money, and together the three of them made it happen. Life was fucking sweet.

Then Harold Sr. died, and his prick of a son didn't want to be involved in "their" kind of business. Instead of letting the three of them have their little piece of the empire, he made his first and biggest mistake: Harold

Jr. came after them. Now the Garvic organization was a shadow of what it was, their leaders were doing decades behind bars, and Richard, Terrance, and Gerome had different lives, living on Longboat Key in Florida, abiding by a million rules so the government could keep them safe. They were three brothers in spirit who were now trying to figure things out in a world where they didn't understand the rules.

"All right, I'll talk to him." Gerome nodded, seeming resigned, his words pulling Richard out of his good-old-days fog. Of the three of them, Gerome had had the easiest time. He had been placed at a gift boutique that sold upscale tourist items. The thing was that Gerome could sell anything. He had rearranged the place within the first two weeks, asked about new items, and all of a sudden he was in charge of the sales floor when sales started going through the roof. At least one of them was doing okay. "I'll handle it. See you later." He raised the window and pulled out of the lot.

Richard took a deep breath, pushing away the hurt to his pride that each and every day seemed to bring, and went back inside. He had work to do. He checked that the kitchen was all right, then greeted Andi as she came in through the back door.

"Everything okay?" she asked.

Richard wiped the moroseness off his face, plastering on a professional mask. "Sure. You all set?" He went behind the bar to cut limes and lemons for garnish, taking a second as she wound through the floor of tables that looked as though they had been through one of Florida's tropical storms and come out the other side. The chairs had seen the wear from hundreds of butts, and the walls, darkened with age and constant exposure to humid salt air, were decorated with mounted fish and old buoys, as well as pictures of great catches. The entire place seemed to have soaked up the scent of the sea, fish, and water.

"You know me. I'm always ready." She gave him a little swing of her hips and then turned away. Andi was one of the few people outside of the guys who knew that he was gay. She had made a play for him the first week he'd worked at the bar, and he had turned her down. To tell the truth, she was attractive, with shoulder-length black hair, a great figure, and intense eyes.

"Too bad you never go for a guy who would deserve you," he muttered and returned to work as the first patrons came through the front door.

The bar patrons were a combination of tourists and locals. A few of the people he saw all the time came in and took familiar places at the bar. Richard pulled beers and made drinks, started tabs, and took payment, the cash settling in his hand before going to the register.

That had been one of the hardest things to remember. In Detroit it was expected that he would skim a certain amount off the top. Richard and Gerome were masters of it, and he'd always been conscientious about returning a growing amount to Harold, which had kept him happy.

"Happy Wednesday," Tim, one of the regulars, said, and Richard's mind skipped a track for a second. He had completely forgotten, and now some of the gloom lifted from inside him.

Richard filled an order from Andi and continued his tasks with half an eye on the front door as he worked.

He knew when it was six o'clock because Daniel came into the bar.

Richard had no idea what it was about this slim man with intense brown eyes and surfer-length black hair hanging to just below his ears that drew him, but as long as Daniel was in the bar, Richard knew exactly where he was at all times, even when his back was turned.

Daniel took a place at the bar.

"You want your usual?" He was already pulling Daniel's beer without really thinking about it. Once Daniel nodded, he placed the beer on the scarred bar surface in front of him.

"The fish and chips, please," Daniel said in his soft voice. Then he flashed him a smile. Richard was determined not to allow his heart rate to rise, but the fucking thing did it anyway. He leaned over the bar just a little, almost as though Daniel had a gravity of his own and Richard was caught in it.

"Of course. I'll put your order in right away," Richard said and swallowed hard, licking his lips as their gazes locked for the fraction of a second. Then Richard remembered where they were and that this was not a gay club in Detroit, but the Cormorant on Longboat Key, Florida.

"Thank you," Daniel said without turning away. "I really appreciate that."

Richard had to break whatever was going on between them. Not that he wasn't excited, but damn, if he wasn't careful, someone was going to come in, and if they joined him behind the bar, there was no damned way they could miss how much Daniel got under his skin.

"Can I get another beer?" Mike asked from a few seats down.

Richard pulled himself away, poured the beer, and put in Daniel's order through the system. At least he could breathe for a few seconds.

Not that this attraction and the innocent flirting he did with Daniel on occasion were ever going to lead anywhere. They couldn't, not in a million years. It didn't matter how many times Richard wondered just what that lithe, compact body looked like under those worn jeans that hugged him like a second skin or the dark blue polo shirt with the tiny hole right at the collar where it sometimes rubbed at Daniel's neck.

Richard, Terrance, and Gerome were only here and stayed alive because they were doing their best to abide by the rules of the Witness Protection Program, and that meant they all needed to stay out of the public eye, not draw attention to themselves, and definitely not tell anyone anything about their past. But more than that, they had had to plead to be allowed to stay together. If they messed up, they wouldn't just be relocated, but separated as well. Sure, Richard could have a fling with Daniel and then they could go on their separate ways, but Richard knew that if he got a single taste of him, he'd want more. Daniel was like potato chips. One would never be enough.

He checked on Daniel's order with the kitchen and refilled glasses, telling himself he was going to ignore Daniel and do his job, keeping himself busy until he left. Daniel had a routine almost as regular as clockwork. Each Wednesday he came in a few minutes after six, had a beer, ordered fish and chips, and nursed his second beer until just before nine o'clock, when he said good night and left the bar. It had been that way since Richard's first week on the job. Richard had tried to talk with him on occasion, and other than his name and a little small talk, he'd learned nothing about him. Richard had cracked some of the hardest men, actually reducing them to tears when he was in charge of the clubs. But hell, Daniel could give lessons on keeping your mouth shut.

When Daniel's order was ready, Richard went to the kitchen to get it, returned, and placed it in front of him. Daniel reached for his cutlery and his hand brushed against Richard's. The gesture was completely innocent and accidental, and yet Richard nearly gasped at the shock that raced through him all the way to his bones.

"Thank you," Daniel said.

Richard nodded and turned away to go back to work, frustration building high enough that he felt it in his temples like the start of a headache, except this held a touch of the delicious and the forbidden, which only made him want it all the more, even though he told himself repeatedly that Daniel—or anyone at all—was off-limits.

Richard made sure all the drinks were filled and that Andi had what she needed before flipping his attention to the baseball game. Detroit was playing Tampa Bay, and Tampa scored a run. The room murmured its approval, and Richard smiled, even though he was pissed inside. One of the hardest things to change had been his allegiance to sports teams. Detroit all the way, even if they sucked. But now he had to root for the local team as part of his cover.

He pulled his attention away from the television and back to his work. The half inning ended, and Detroit came up to bat. Richard noticed that Daniel leaned a little forward, and a few minutes later he grinned when Detroit hit a two-run homer.

"Tampa Bay isn't your team?" he asked, taking away Daniel's empty plate.

Daniel shook his head. "Nope. I always rooted for Detroit. Not that they've done much in years, but it's my team." He finished his beer. "Can I get another?"

"Sure." Richard took his glass and pulled a fresh one out of the cooler, filled it, and passed it over. Detroit hit another homer before the side retired, and Daniel ended up grinning like a cat while the rest of the bar grumbled. At least the guy was smart enough to keep it to himself and revel quietly in his happiness.

The evening went on as most of them did, with Richard keeping the drinks flowing and Andi hopping with drink and food orders. He helped her when he could by delivering some of the food. About the time the game was just getting good, Andi squeaked, wiping her backside. Richard caught the tourist's gaze and fixed him with an icy stare that had him pulling in his arm and mumbling an apology. Yes, he still had it. Over the years, he had perfected his "you do that again and they'll never find the body" stare. It was one of his talents.

"Would you like another beer?" Richard asked Daniel as he checked the time. It was nearing nine o'clock and about the time Daniel usually left… and some of the light went out of the place for Richard. He always asked, though typically Daniel would drain the last of his beer, settle his tab, and say good night.

Daniel finished his beer and passed the glass over. "Maybe one more," he said. Richard almost double-checked that he had heard him correctly. "I want to watch this for a while."

Richard swallowed hard as Daniel turned to him instead of the television. Jesus, the intensity of that gaze was throat-drying. Richard nodded, but damn, he didn't want to turn away, not for a second. He got the beer by feel and placed it in front of Daniel.

The bang of the front door hitting the wall pulled his attention, and a stream of bikers flowed in. Richard had owned a motorcycle before his change in circumstances and he loved a good ride, but he also knew trouble when it came calling, and this group came with a capital T—times about twelve.

Richard remained calm. There was nothing he hadn't or couldn't have handled. He sent a quick message to Terrance, and within five minutes he came in and settled at a table by the door.

Now Terrance, he could intimidate anyone, even a gang of huge biker thugs. No one was going to mess with him… at least not anyone in their right mind. Though Richard was starting to wonder about these guys.

"Could you please bring me my bill?" Daniel asked as the place grew louder.

Richard gave it to him, and he handed over some cash and slipped off his stool before walking toward the door.

"Can I get a beer?" an entitled voice asked from down the bar.

Richard turned to pull it. A glass crashing to the floor yanked his attention to where Daniel stood at the opposite end of the bar, facing a huge tattooed biker, who reached out and grabbed him by the collar.

"Look what you made me do," he snapped, yanking Daniel closer. "You can buy me a new one."

Richard raced around the bar to Daniel's side. "Let him go," he commanded, nodding to Terrance, who stood right behind him. He knew the image they portrayed.

"You sticking up for the little fucking fag?" the biker growled as he released Daniel, who stepped back and right against Richard.

Richard guided Daniel to the side and then behind him. "Hey. There's no need for that kind of talk. How about another beer on the house and you just walk away."

Terrance cracked his knuckles right behind him. Terrance lived for this sort of thing, and he was so much more than just a big man. He knew how to fight and how to make each punch hurt... bad. He was like Picasso, only he worked with intimidation.

"Come on, Howard, we're hungry," one of the other guys said. "Stop being a jerk and sit down." The other bikers all laughed, and Richard watched Howard carefully. At moments like this, men either sat down or lashed out. He was ready for either one.

"Yeah, stop it. You got us kicked out of a place yesterday," another guy said.

Howard huffed and turned to a table, where he sat down with a thud.

"Go on and get the drinks," Terrance whispered from behind him.

Richard nodded, shifting to look at Daniel. "You all right?"

"Yeah," he breathed. "I should get going, but thank you. I just bumped the guy and he dropped his glass." Daniel seemed a little pale, but the color quickly returned to his cheeks.

"Accidents happen, and he was being a real ass," Richard said, loudly enough for Howard to hear. He glared at the man for good measure and then turned back to Daniel.

"I'd better get on home. Thanks for... well, everything," Daniel said and skittered out the door.

Richard swore under his breath, willing to bet that he wasn't going to be seeing Daniel again soon. Shit, one of the highlights of his week just walked out that door. Richard wanted to wring that Howard asshole's neck with his bare hands. In Detroit, he would have made sure Howard got a clear message about that sort of shit. But here there was little he could do.

"Shit," he muttered as he turned away.

"What's gotten into you?" Terrance asked quietly from next to him.

"Nothing." Richard knew as soon as he said it that he had answered too quickly.

Terrance glared and peered out the window near the door before turning back to him. There were times when things skipped right over Terrance's head. This wasn't one of those times, much to Richard's disappointment. "Do you have a thing for the nerdy guy?" He narrowed his gaze. "You do." He grinned. "I can't wait to tell Gerome. He's going to get such a laugh out of that."

"I suggest you button it or the one thing you're going to get is a fat lip and your balls in a sling," Richard threatened.

Terrance, who had heard those threats for years, just laughed and rolled eyes. "You can't begrudge either of us our fun." He turned back to the door and sat down.

There was fuck all Richard could do about the guys or Daniel. Sometimes the life that had turned to shit just dealt up more and more of it for him to wade through.

"Can we get some beers, or do we need to get them ourselves?" one of the guys asked.

Richard hit him with a stare, wanting to rip his head off just to relieve the frustration building up inside from all angles. Maybe a good fight and kicking the ass of some pissant shitheel would make him feel better, but that would only end up getting them noticed and probably moved to yet another location. That had happened once already, and he didn't want it to happen again. Longboat Key was no Detroit, but it was a hell of a lot better than Ottumwa, Iowa, that was for fucking sure.

"Yeah, I'm coming," Richard said. "Don't be in such a hurry. You late to meet your parole officer or something?" He got behind the bar and began filling orders again, the crowd much more subdued and the tension from earlier largely gone. But so was the one thing he looked forward to the whole fucking week. He met Terrance's gaze for a second and then concentrated on mixing some drinks and filling beer glasses. Sometimes life just sucked.

Chapter 2

DANIEL UPTON breathed a soft sigh as he stepped out of the chocolate shop just down the street from the hardware store. When he'd needed a screwdriver to tighten one of the window fasteners in the apartment, he'd seen the huge guy the bartender had been talking to in the bar. Thanks to him, he'd stopped at one of the boutiques and now carried the bag as he walked toward the bar for his regular Wednesday-night outing. Daniel thought Richard was drop-dead sexy. Not that it mattered.

Daniel had caught on last week that Richard was flirting with him, and he'd flirted back because it was fun, and the thought of a guy with those high cheekbones, wide shoulders, and eyes bluer than the Gulf just across the street sent his temperature climbing even higher. He hurried down the road and reached the bar before he got too warm, the air-conditioning hitting him like a wall of cool relief. He breathed deeply and held out his arms a little to cool off and maybe remove some of the damp from his shirt.

Daniel went up to the bar and took his usual seat. Richard was down at the far side, pulling beers and working with the other guys. Daniel set the bag on the counter and got comfortable. He knew the moment Richard saw him because he got that smile. Well, maybe it wasn't an exclusive smile, but it was the one he got every week as soon as he came in. It went almost all the way to Richard's ears. That smile had kept Daniel coming back for weeks. The food was decent enough, but it wasn't the very best, and there were other places he could eat. But none of them had Richard, and at none of the others could he sit, have a beer and dinner, and let his imagination run wild with fantasies about this hunk.

"Can I get you a beer?" Richard was already pouring it, which Daniel liked.

"That would be great," he said and pushed the bag a little closer. "This is a thank-you for helping me out last week." Surprise registered in Richard's expression for a moment. "I saw your friend at the hardware store a little while ago, and when I asked him, and he said you liked chocolate."

"You mean Terrance?" Richard said.

"Yeah. Tall, as wide as a house, and always looks like he's about ready to rip your head off and spit down your neck? He helped me get some tools, and I asked him what your favorite treat was." Daniel pushed the bag closer. "I got them just up the street on my way. I hope they didn't melt."

Richard opened the white paper bag and a look of sheer bliss passed over him. His eyes even glazed a little as he smelled the chocolate. It was sexy and made Daniel happy that he'd pleased him.

Richard thanked him, then put the bag behind the bar.

Daniel picked up the menu and looked it over. He was in the mood for something different, but there wasn't anything that really captured his attention other than the fish. He always got it because at home he never got fish. Sometimes he made salmon, but then he ended up making two meals, and he really didn't have the time for that most nights.

"Fish and chips?" Richard asked.

"Can I get maybe a salad or something instead of the fries? I want the fish, though." He set the menu down.

"Of course," Richard said with a smile and went to put in the order. "What kind of dressing? The ranch is made here."

"Then I'd like that, please." His mother had impressed on him from the age of four that manners mattered, and if he asked for something and didn't say please, he was told no.

The bar was quiet, but Daniel didn't mind. He half watched the baseball game on television and spent the rest of the time watching Richard. It was, after all, the main reason he came in.

"Daniel?"

Daniel turned toward the voice and smiled.

"Can I join you?"

"Sure," he said to Brad, his neighbor with the condo entrance next to his. Brad sat down and ordered a beer and picked up a menu. "Do you eat here often?"

"No. I was out taking an evening walk. The days will only get hotter, so I thought I might as well get out of the house before summer gets here full force. I was walking past and figured I'd come in." He smiled, and Daniel got an unsettled feeling in his belly when Brad held his gaze for longer than he felt comfortable.

Daniel turned away, looking down at his beer. Brad had made numerous attempts at conversation, but they seemed flirty, and Daniel had no interest in him. Brad kept trying, though. Daniel didn't want to be rude, but he didn't appreciate it either.

"What do you get here?"

"The fish. It's fresh and they bread it themselves," Daniel answered as he continued looking at his beer. "I come here once a week just for a quiet night out and to watch a little television without being interrupted." He took a sip and glanced at Brad, finding him looking at him intently. Daniel decided to ignore it even though a little sweat broke out on the back of his neck. Brad wasn't a bad person or mean. It just seemed he had trouble taking a hint, and Daniel didn't want to hurt the guy. He was his neighbor, and Daniel didn't want any more trouble than he already had.

Brad leaned forward, whistling under his breath. "Who is the bartender?"

Daniel swallowed as peak of jealousy rose and then slipped away. He had no right to feel it, but Brad showing interest in Richard rubbed him the wrong way. "Richard?" He tried to sound natural.

"Is that his name?" Brad asked, leering down the bar as Richard turned just enough to show his back.

Brad leaned forward a touch more. "Is he the reason you come here? Not that I blame you in the least." He chuckled and bumped Daniel's shoulder.

Daniel shied away a little, the too-familiar gesture making him nervous. He swallowed and returned his attention to his beer, hoping Brad would move on if he thought he was being ignored. "I like the food, okay?" he said softly.

"Sure. That's cool," Brad said, still watching down the bar. After a minute he sat back. Daniel wished Brad would leave and let him have his quiet evening out in fantasyland. A few hours of peace where he could think and relax were all Daniel wanted. "Do you have something going on with him? I can totally understand if you do. He's spectacular, and I'd certainly love to take him out for a spin and get his motor running." He chuckled at his own comment as though he were trying to lighten things up, but it only added to Daniel's unease.

"No," Daniel said firmly. "I'm not seeing anyone right now." He wanted to tell Brad to back off and go sit somewhere else, preferably in another restaurant or the bar on the bay side of the key. Anywhere but where he was.

Brad sighed, and Richard returned to their end of the bar. He took Brad's order and gave him the beer he requested without any additional comment. Richard did connect with Daniel's gaze for a second, and warmth spread through Daniel. He tried not to show any reaction because he didn't want Brad commenting on it.

"Where the hell did he come from? He talked a little differently and has an accent that I can't quite place." Brad prattled on, and Daniel only half listened. Brad didn't pause for answers to his questions, so Daniel didn't offer any. But his quick comment about where

Richard came from got Daniel thinking. Richard did have a slight accent. He wasn't from Florida, that was for sure, but then, most of the people he saw every day weren't from here.

Richard brought his plate, and Daniel thanked him and offered a quick smile before eating his dinner. At least he had something to do other than sit and not be rude. Brad's plate was delivered as well, and at last, with something else to do with his mouth, he grew quiet.

Finally Daniel relaxed, glancing down the bar to where Richard worked. A few times he noticed Richard looking back at him, and once he even smiled. Daniel smiled in return and then turned away, realizing he'd been caught. This was stupid. He wasn't in high school, and these games couldn't possibly lead anywhere. Richard was stunning, and he wasn't going to be in a place like this for very long. Besides, it was foolish for Daniel to fantasize that Richard would be interested, because guys like Richard didn't go for geeks like him. Richard was just being nice because it meant extra tips.

Not that anything could ever happen between them… or anyone. Daniel had responsibilities, ones that took precedence over everything else, and he wasn't going to mess that up for anything. A relationship with anyone was out of the question.

A voice cut through his thoughts.

"Sorry," Daniel said, trying to hide his annoyance with Brad. He just wanted to be left alone. Daniel wondered why the guy rubbed him the wrong way, and then it hit him as Brad continued talking about some fishing trip, without any clue that Daniel wasn't listening: Brad was a lot like his ex-boyfriend, Cory. He ran full tilt ahead, not listening to or caring much for what Daniel

had to say. Things with Cory had been heady and ex-
tremely energetic, but everything had to be at Cory's
frenetic pace, and Daniel was always just trying to
keep up with him. Things never slowed down enough
for him to enjoy the moment. Important decisions got
made, and Daniel felt like he'd been left out of them because there had never been time for him to think about
anything.

"Can I get you something else?" Richard asked
Brad, cutting off his monologue, which Daniel was
grateful for. There was a sharpness to Richard's voice,
and Daniel sensed the emotional temperature in the
room drop by several degrees. Daniel sipped his beer
and pointedly didn't turn toward him.

"No," Brad said.

"Then I'll get your check," Richard commented
with a touch of ice in his voice.

Daniel lightly bit his lower lip as he finished off his
last bites of salad. Richard hurried away and worked
the register before placing the check in front of Brad.
Daniel used the interruption to shift his attention to the
game on television, watching intently.

"I'll see you around, I'm sure," Brad said as he
slipped off the stool.

Daniel tried not to show too much relief. "Yeah,
definitely." He waved as Brad left the bar and then
breathed an audible sigh and turned his gaze back to
the game.

Someone sat in the empty stool, and Daniel glanced
at them quickly before returning to baseball.

"Hey, Richie, can we get a drink?" a rough voice
asked, followed by laughter. He tipped his head just
enough to see the two men next to him. One was

Terrance from the hardware store, the guy who had stood with Richard last week.

Richard fixed both of them with a glare, placing a beer in front of Terrance and a martini in front of the other man. "I'm working, like both of you are supposed to be," Richard said just loud enough for Daniel to hear.

"I have the evening off," the man with the martini said and sipped elegantly from his glass. "And Terrance's shift ended a half hour ago, so we thought we'd come down here and see how things were with you. Have a drink, look things over." Daniel could almost feel their gazes on him, and he tried not to shiver. It kind of made him uncomfortable, but not in the same way Brad had. More like they were checking him out for their friend, which was a whole different level of discomfort.

"Behave," Richard retorted, his voice quiet but still sharp. "I have work, and I'm sure there are things you could be doing, Gerome, like that pile of laundry that you think is going to clean itself." There was no heat in Richard's words.

Daniel hazarded a glance at the three men, who seemed to know one another.

"Did you get what you needed?" Terrance asked, leaning around Gerome, who sat between them.

"Yes. Thanks, and I appreciate your help last week as well. I'm not sure I'd still have all my teeth if it hadn't been for you guys." He alternated between Terrance and Richard.

"It appears that my friends have no manners. I'm Gerome." He extended his hand, nearly crushing Daniel's hand as they shook. Daniel didn't wince, but the "never mess with me" message of strength was clear.

"Daniel." He took his hand back, wrapping it around the cold beer glass to cool off his fingers.

Richard was still glaring at the other guys, probably in some kind of silent communication. Once again, Brad's question rang in his head, and he wondered where the three guys had come from. They had the same accent and inner confidence. Richard worked as a bartender, but he projected an air like he owned the place. He took care of everything and didn't defer to anyone.

"You guys need to go," Richard said after he'd checked the bar and refilled drinks.

"We're just checking out a few things," Gerome said with hint of sarcasm.

"I know why you're here," Richard growled.

Daniel swallowed hard. That sound went right through him like an electric current. Sexy as hell and so damned strong. Gerome and Terrance were big guys and exuded toughness that was frankly kind of frightening, and Richard was not only unintimidated by them, but they seemed to defer to him. That was fucking hot in a macho sort of way. "You need to finish your drinks and go on out to play or something." He was clearly getting a little pissed. "Just go and leave me alone. You don't need to check out what's happening here," Richard whispered.

"We want to see what the attraction is… with this place," Gerome said, and even Daniel could tell that Gerome had added the last part rather hastily. "Figured we could watch things for a while, but we'll get out of your way." He slipped off the barstool. "We'll have a much better view from one of the tables."

"Bastards…," Richard swore just loudly enough for Daniel to hear. "Andi will make sure you have what you need. Be sure to tip her well."

Daniel watched them go out of the corner of his eye before returning his attention to the television, wondering what was up with them.

"Can I get you another beer?"

"That would be nice, thanks," Daniel said. "Have you tried the chocolates? I've never gotten anything there. I hope they're really good." He was a little nervous about it just because he had never shopped there before.

"I had one a few minutes ago." He glanced behind Daniel and then leaned in a little closer. "It was divine." He licked his lips, and Daniel nearly choked. Damned if Daniel didn't feel himself blushing. "Thank you." He backed away quickly and began wiping down the bar. "I'll get you that beer," he said, much more professionally.

Daniel wondered if his friends were watching now. "Thanks." His heart finally began to slow once Richard had moved away, and he could think again. He checked the time and settled in his seat. He had a little less than an hour before he had to be home—enough time for one more beer, a few more minutes to indulge his fantasy, and then it was back to real life.

When Richard brought his beer this time, there was no flirting, no innuendo, just efficient service. Daniel sighed because he had to admit that he liked it when Richard flirted with him. It made him feel like someone other than a simple computer geek who was just trying to make ends meet. Daniel wasn't sure why, but there was something about him that said that Richard had seen things and was much more worldly than living in just this area of Florida could account for. There was a depth in his eyes, and the lines on his skin told of experiences, maybe even rough, harsh realities.

Daniel watched the TV and drank his beer, enjoying the last few minutes of time to himself. Once he was done, he pulled out his wallet. Richard came down, and Daniel paid his bill, already knowing how much it cost. "Thank you," Daniel said to Richard as he got up.

On his way out, he passed the other two. They were handsome, especially Gerome, but neither of them could hold a candle to Richard, at least as far as Daniel was concerned.

"Good night, Daniel," Gerome said with a smile filled with mirth. The last time Daniel had seen that kind of smile had been high school, and he actually checked that he didn't have toilet paper on his shoes or that someone hadn't put a sign on his back. Daniel knew neither was true, but he got the feeling he was missing something.

Outside, the sun was setting, and the heat of the day had abated slightly. At least there was a breeze off the Gulf, which cooled the air and kept it moving, making the evening much more pleasant. He liked walking this time of day.

He turned toward home, taking his time as he checked his phone. He had fifteen minutes to walk the six long blocks to the condo, though he didn't want to be late. His sister, Renee, came over each Wednesday to give him a night out, and he didn't want to take advantage of her.

Renee was the only member of his family who actually spoke to him other than to tell him everything he had done wrong and what he needed to do in order to get back into the family's good graces. His mother and father hadn't been thrilled when he'd told them he was gay, but they had absolutely hated Cory and had written Daniel off completely while they dated. Daniel figured that after the breakup and their inevitable I-told-yous, they would welcome him back, but that hadn't happened. Renee was his only supporter within the family. She loved him and helped him with what she could. Things were what they were, and the hurt was in the past and best left behind.

He strode faster, swinging his arms, tension gone. He felt happy.

Footsteps sounded behind him, and he walked faster. They kept up. When he stopped, they paused as well.

Daniel turned around but saw only a man a half a block away carrying groceries out of his car. He walked faster and didn't stop again until he turned into the complex and went up to his door. He unlocked it and went inside. The whole thing was probably his imagination, and he was home now.

He sighed and peered out the windows but again saw no one on the street. He must have been imagining it. That was all there was to it. Calming himself, because being all wound up wasn't going to help him or anyone else, he waited a minute and then left the entry area to go farther inside.

Chapter 3

"YOU DID what?" Richard snapped at Terrance and Gerome when they gathered on Saturday after lunch. It was their weekly get-together. Mostly the three of them had their own lives and activities, but Saturday mornings were their time. Terrance would need to be in the store by noon, and Gerome at eleven. Fortunately, Richard didn't work until four. The owner of the bar, Alan, worked Saturday lunch because Richard worked late on Fridays and would do the same on Saturday nights.

"We followed him to see where he lives and to find out a little about him. This Daniel of yours is a bit of a rabbit. He must have heard me behind him. I simply ducked into a gas station shop and he never saw me,"

Gerome said with a satisfied smile. "I'm good at that sort of thing."

Richard huffed. "Normal people do not follow people home. This isn't Detroit, and we need to act like everyone else." He glared daggers at the other two. "Remember, we had to leave Iowa already because Terrance just *had* to make a phone call. I know your mother was dying and I don't blame you, but it upset everything." Granted, it had been worth it in the end. They had gotten out of Iowa, and Terrance had been able to say goodbye to the only blood family any of them had. Terrance's mom had been like a mother to all three of them.

"Fine," Gerome said. "Then you don't want to know what I found out." He drained the last of his orange juice and set the glass on the secondhand, scarred wood coffee table in Richard's living room. Everything in the place had been provided as part of the relocation, from the worn leather recliner to the hideous green sofa, and none of it felt like his. It probably never would.

Richard rolled his eyes. "I really don't."

Gerome waited and then smiled. "I know you do. You've got the hots for this guy, bad. Just like you did for Johnny a couple years ago. Remember him? He came into the club and you drooled all over yourself. He kept you dangling for months, and as soon as you nailed him, you were on to someone else. Well, I'm just trying to help you bang this guy so you can go back to normal instead of acting like some lovesick teenager."

"I do not," Richard countered forcefully.

"Please," Terrance said with a grin. "You flirt with this guy, and he buys you chocolates to say thank you for helping him. The guy is flirting right back. It's cute in a make-me-vomit kind of way." Terrance didn't do relationships that lasted longer than the time it took to meet up, get naked, get off, and get dressed. "But you can't put us at risk either."

"I'm not," Richard said. "It's been months since any of us had any sort of carnal fun."

Gerome shook his head. "That isn't the type of thing you want with rabbit boy. You want the television family, white picket fence, and the 'honey, I'm home' when you get back from work." He laughed, because that was so far from any of their experiences that it was almost a foreign concept.

"Stop being an ass. He's a nice guy. I like him." Richard decided to make as little of it as possible. "Nothing has happened and nothing will happen. He's a customer, and we have to keep our heads down. And that means no fucking guys like that. If we want something, we can go to Tampa and make a night of it somewhere. Pick up the guys we want, blow off some fucking steam, and then come back."

Gerome nodded. "Do you think that's one of the rules?" He rolled his eyes. The marshals had a huge number of rules for anyone who went into Witness Protection, and sometimes they ran afoul of the simplest parts of living. "I'm surprised sometimes that they don't have preferred ways we should take a shit."

"The rules are for our protection," Richard reminded them. He did his best to keep tabs on what was going on in Detroit, but he only did it through national news outlets. "I don't even look at the Detroit paper online in case someone gets hold of my browser history."

"I did, at the library last week. There was still news about the sentencing and the appeals, but they aren't going to get anywhere. Junior is behind bars, and they have him in solitary. The news media is even reporting on his prison digs and access, so he isn't able to communicate with anyone," Gerome explained. "But I'm willing to bet that they are still looking for us, and they will be for quite some time." He cleared his throat. "Now that the shit business is out of the way, let's give Richard crap for a little while longer." He cleared his throat like he was about to make an important pronouncement. "Your rabbit boy lives in a condo just off the main street, about a half a block at most. It's nice, but not hugely extravagant. There was a woman there with him, and I saw him hug her after he got back. It may have been a friend, but she was very affectionate. So maybe your rabbit is bisexual. She left after he got back and didn't return, at least not while I was there."

Richard growled. "You so need to get laid, and maybe find a hobby if you have that kind of time to sit in the bushes and watch someone's house. You're lucky no one called the damned police." That would just thrill their handler within the program. Elizabeth would have a fit and would probably personally come wring Gerome's neck. Not that Richard could blame her after the mess in Iowa.

"So do you," Gerome retorted. "I'm just trying to help. The guy may be flirting, but that doesn't mean he's gay. He could just be secure in himself or some such thing. But I learned nothing from that angle. The lights stayed on for quite a while, and no one moved in the house by the time I left."

"God. Just leave him alone and don't do that again. We're supposed to be acting normal, remember? And stalking people home from a bar is not what normal people do."

"Fuck that," Gerome and Terrance said in unison. "It's what we do," Gerome continued. "What if Junior already found us and this guy has been planted in the bar to check us out and get the lay of the land?"

"You have to be kidding," Richard retorted and then paused. It was true—Daniel was the last type of person he would suspect, which made him more dangerous. He put his hands up. "Okay, fine. You followed him and found out next to nothing. Can you leave it alone, please?" He finished his orange juice. He wanted a stiff drink, but he set his glass in the sink and returned to where the guys lounged in the living room. "We have more important things to worry about. Somehow we have got to see if we can figure out if our enemies are any closer to finding us."

"Okay, we do nothing else, like Elizabeth said," Terrance said, but Richard hated being in the dark about anything. "So leave it alone and let's concentrate on figuring out how to make a life here that isn't going to bore the hell out of us. We only have basic cable, for fuck's sake." He got up and tromped into the kitchen before returning with a can of beer. "What we need is some fucking fun… and we need some money."

"Don't even think about it," Gerome snapped at Terrance. "We cannot touch a cent of that money for quite a while. I put it aside for all of us so we can have a retirement and a chance at something more than this. Besides, it has to sit there for at least seven years because it's stolen and laundered money, and the trail needs to be damned cold. It could also lead back to us. So put the idea out of your head. But I was thinking that if we pool our resources, we could probably charter a boat for a morning and go out on the Gulf for a party or something. We would need to be careful, but it would be fun."

Richard found himself nodding. He knew Gerome was right and he also knew that Terrance had a point—they were all bored. Their lives before had been hectic and full of action. That had been part of the excitement and what kept them going. They were adrenaline junkies at heart, and this workaday life was something none of them had given any thought to prior to all these changes.

"You guys needs to get to work. I'll clean up here and get the dishes done," Richard told the others.

Gerome was the first to head out. He had to be to work in less than half an hour. He went across the hall to his place to change.

"Do you really think we can do this without going out of our minds?" Terrance asked, still seated on the sofa. "I mean, look at this. We had apartments with expensive furniture and nice clothes. We ate well and didn't worry about what shit cost. Now we live in shithole apartments with furniture that came out of some government warehouse. I hate it." He got up and practically growled as he went to the window. "We were important people, and now we're like the crap folks scrape off their shoes." He didn't turn around. "Every day I want to rip some guy's arm off or just break someone's nose for talking to me the way they do." He was so tense his shoulders looked like an airport runway.

"Do you want to be dead?" Richard asked, because that was the bottom line. "We could just chuck it in and say to hell with it." He finished loading the dishes and closed the door on the washer.

"We used to have people who cleaned the fuck up after us. Now I have to do my own fucking laundry, and I'm shit at it." He pulled at his shirt. "My clothes all feel like they're dirty all the time because they scratch. I miss those silk shirts you used to have made for me. Now it's this stuff." He tugged at the material, pulling it away from his skin.

"Do you think it's easy on any of the rest of us? It's not. We all have to do this, and yes, we can do it. But we have to stick together and not go after one another." He poured two mugs of coffee and handed one to Terrance. "It's just the three of us, just like it's always been. Remember?" He put his hand behind Terrance's neck, letting his gaze bore into the big man's eyes.

There was nothing sexual in the touch. This was about something more intimate than sex. This was twenty years of trust and a way to communicate strength and solidarity. To give Terrance what he needed at the moment.

"Maybe I just need to get laid."

Richard stood there for a few seconds and then moved away. "What you need is to feel like a man again, and getting laid isn't going to do it." He knew that pretty clearly, because he felt the exact same way. His own image of himself as a man and a person had taken a beating.

"It might help," Terrance growled.

"No, it won't." Richard had been giving this a lot of thought. "What does being a man mean to you?" They didn't usually talk about this kind of shit, but Richard needed to help the others if he could.

"Well, it meant respect and not taking shit from people. That's for fuck sure. It also meant that I didn't have to take a load of crap from customers looking for a sale on fertilizer." Terrance pulled away, and Richard watched him go. "Being a man is taking things into your own hands and doing what needs to be done, keeping your damned mouth shut, protecting your mama, and doing what you say even if you have to back it up with your body and a gun." He groaned. "These people out here have no idea about respect or doing what they say. There's no honor, no code at all. Just a bunch of wandering sheep."

"Yeah. That's what it meant to all of us. But it has to mean something different now, and fuck if I know what it is, but we'll figure it out." It was all the advice he had to give. Richard was no counselor, and he certainly didn't have the answers. "Go on and get ready to go to work, and try not to punch anyone."

Terrance gave Richard a fist bump and left the apartment, carrying the coffee mug.

"If I had known how fucking hard this was going to be, I probably would have just gone to war with the bastard and let the chips fall where they may," Richard said out loud to the empty room. Still, he'd grown up on the streets of Detroit. He was tough and he could do whatever he set his mind to.

SATURDAY NIGHTS the bar had live music, which meant the place was hopping. All the servers were run off their feet, and Richard moved at top speed just to keep up. Alan even asked Terrance to act as a part-time bouncer to ensure there was no trouble, a role he took on easily, especially after a few incidents including the one with Daniel. The band was pretty good, and they played a mixture of songs. The evening started out with some country music, which pleased part of the crowd, and then switched to dance music, which made the rest of the customers happy. It was a good night, and about nine it got better.

"Hi, Richard," Daniel said with a wide smile as he stood at the bar. "Can I get a couple of drafts?"

"Sure," Richard said at this unexpected treat.

Terrance surveyed the crowd from his position near the bar, and Richard was pretty sure he had seen that Daniel was here. Still, it was hard for Richard not to be happy. "Here you are." He passed them over and started a tab. Daniel thanked him and headed off through the crowd to one of the tables, where a woman waited for him. Richard didn't have much time to think about him... but now that he had seen him, part of his brain was attuned to Daniel.

Richard moved a little to the beat of the music. He liked working when there was music in the bar. It soothed him and gave the place a different atmosphere. As the beat changed, couples got up to dance. Andi and one of the other servers rearranged some of the tables for makeshift floor space, and a few other dancers joined the group, with Daniel and his friend among them.

"Damn, he can move, can't he?" Terrance commented to Richard quietly once he had served a customer at the end of the bar. Richard was three seconds from pulling Terrance's attention away from Daniel when he seemed to notice some trouble and hurried to off to take care of it. Richard checked up and down the bar, making sure all were served before sighing and taking a minute to watch for himself.

The tempo picked up and Daniel went with it, hips and upper body flowing and undulating. The woman who had come along with him moved gracefully but with less abandon. They made a gorgeous sight, and Richard swallowed a groan as his imagination clicked onto images of what Daniel would be like in bed. "Oh my God." He was a firm believer that a guy fucked like he danced, and man, that kind of energy would be scorching hot. He moved closer to the bar to keep the effect Daniel was having on him out of sight. This was a small bar for tourists and locals in Longboat Key, not a gay club in Detroit.

"Too bad we're not at home," Terrance whispered when he returned.

Richard probably would have scolded him for the comment. He had to make do with a stern look, but he couldn't argue. At home Richard would have known exactly what to do with Daniel. But here… everything was different. Not only that, but the things he'd done in Detroit and the way he'd acted then…. Richard was pretty sure Daniel wasn't the kind of guy who went to the back room for a quick fuck and then went on his way.

"This is home now," Richard retorted and shot Terrance another warning for even talking that way, holding his gaze until Terrance nodded and then backed away, returning to the door.

Richard was busy—no-time-to-breathe busy—for the rest of the evening.

"Looks like a good crowd," Alan said as he came behind the bar. "Could you use a little help?" He smiled and started taking care of patrons at the far end of the bar. That gave Richard a break for a few seconds, and he looked over the crowd. Daniel and his friend sat at one of the small tables on the far wall. He wished they'd get up and dance again, but no such luck.

The crowd began to thin a little at eleven, and Alan approached Richard as he finished getting together an order for one of the servers. "It's been a good night," he told Alan.

"Yes. The band is good, and they brought in a lot of their fans." Alan's graying hair was mussed, and it was pretty clear from his rumpled clothes that he had been working a lot of hours. "Can you handle it for now?"

"Certainly," Richard answered. Alan took most of the cash from the till, stuffed it into a green bag, and went through to the back. Richard tried not to pay attention to it and went back to work. Across the bar, he met Terrance's gaze and then looked toward the door.

Terrance got up and walked through the crowd, taking up a position near the door to make sure that anyone else who might have seen didn't get any bright ideas.

A man approached Terrance and knocked on the door to the office. Alan let him in. As soon as the door closed, Terrance turned to Richard, frowning. Richard nodded without giving it much thought and returned to work. If this really was something, they would need to talk about it later. The man exited the door about five minutes later, and Terrance stayed put.

Alan left an hour later as the patrons began to drift out. The band announced their final song of the night, and afterward they began packing up. Terrance kept watch, and Richard used his downtime to get the bar ready for Monday. Thank God they got Sunday off. He turned to the table where Daniel and his companion had been sitting and found it empty.

The rest of the patrons trailed out of the bar, and by two, Richard was exhausted. He and Terrance locked the doors, and the servers cleaned the tables while Richard stocked and finished the last of the bar closing.

"You've been preoccupied all evening," Terrance said after plopping his butt on one of the stools, drinking a soda. "And don't think I didn't see you watching your cutie all night long."

"Oh yeah, Richie is smitten," Andi said as she placed her towel on the bar. "Not that I can blame him. He's a really nice guy." She sat next to Terrance. Richard did his best to ignore them and get his work done, but they seemed intent on giving him shit. "All night long, he told me thank you whenever I brought him a drink, and he kept watching you behind the bar."

"But he was dancing with the woman he was with, and they looked sort of chummy," Terrance said.

Richard nearly dropped the glass he was putting away.

"She was just a friend. That was pretty obvious." Andi patted the counter and slipped off the stool. "We're almost done out here." She looked over her tables and then patted Terrance on the shoulder. "You know, you could help us rather than just sitting there looking mean."

Richard chuckled and turned away, letting Andi deal with Terrance, knowing that Terrance thought tasks like that were beneath him—or at least they had been beneath him.

"Just flip the chairs onto the tables so we can give the floor a scrub, and then all of us can get out of here."

She bustled off, leaving Terrance to do her bidding, and he turned to Richard, baring his teeth, but did what she told him. If Terrance were straight, Richard might have thought he was smitten with her, but as it was, maybe Terrance was a little scared of the energetic server who didn't seem the least bit intimidated by him.

Finally the tasks were done, and Richard called Alan to let him know they were closing and locking up. He put the remaining take into the safe and closed it, marveling at how trusting Alan was. Not that Richard would touch a cent of his money. In Detroit, the take from the club was expected to be divided up. The staff had to be paid, the additional payroll handled, he and his guys got their cut, and Harold got his piece. It was all so civilized, but there was an agreement and a pecking order. It was how business was done. That wasn't how things were done here.

"Let's go," he said. "It's late, and thankfully we're closed tomorrow." Richard locked up the outside door, and he and Terrance headed for his car.

"I don't want to go home," Terrance said after they got inside.

"Yeah, I get it. But this isn't Detroit. There's nothing open for miles. We could try to get a pizza, but that's about it." He pulled out of the parking lot and made the left down the main road toward the south.

"You know, I didn't think it would be this hard," Terrance said as the air-conditioning cooled the interior. "Losing Mama was hard, but losing everything else and then not being able to tell anyone about it, that sucked."

Richard nodded. "Yeah, but whining about it and wishing shit was different isn't going to help any of us. We made our choice and took the deal. You know what that means."

In the organization, your word was your bond and that was it. You always did what you said you were going to do, and if that meant ripping some guy's nose off because he didn't pay up, so be it. "This was the deal we took, so pissing and moaning about it is just too damned bad." He made the turn and continued the couple of blocks to the building before pulling into his parking spot. "Things will get easier," he said, wondering if it was for Terrance's benefit for his own. Maybe it was for both of them.

Chapter 4

IT WAS hot. Not just humid hot, but the sun felt like it was broiling him alive, and yet Daniel had no choice. He was careful to walk on the shadier side of the road, but that was the only relief he had. The grocery bags weighed down his arms until his shoulders were sore. He couldn't buy anything frozen or that needed refrigeration because he had no way to get it home. It would be cooked by the time he got it there.

He paused when his phone vibrated in his pocket and set down the grocery bags before he pulled it out, sighing when he saw the number. "Hello."

"Daniel, it's Clare at Consolidated Physicians. I'm so sorry about the mix-up. The payment was sent to the wrong address. We stopped payment on that check and are sending out another to the correct place. You should have it in a few days." She sounded almost as upset as Daniel felt. He had been counting on that check and had literally just spent the last money he had on food. The car had broken down, and he had no money to pay for repairs. This payment delay meant he was going to have to eat as little as possible for a few days.

"Thank you." He breathed with relief even as he tried to figure out what he was going to do to get through the next few days.

"We did add something for the inconvenience as well," Clare told him. "And there is some additional work that we're thinking about in the next few months. We'll definitely call you." She seemed happy. Daniel was relieved that he was going to have some cash coming in. It had been a lean couple of months, and even though he had been working very hard, the payments hadn't come in yet. "Please call me when you get the check so I know you got paid."

Daniel said that he would and hung up, slipping his phone back into his pocket and continuing down the road.

Most of the time Daniel loved living on Longboat Key. He had his condo, and the neighbors were nice. With the bay on one side and the Gulf on the other, there was almost always a breeze, so even when the humidity was through the roof, the air moved and made it easier to breathe. But not today. It was just sultry hot, and he still had four blocks to go. His shirt had long ago plastered itself to his back, and he was starting to feel lightheaded.

"Do you need a ride?" a voice called from behind him. Daniel looked back and saw that Richard had pulled his car off to the side of the road. "It's hot as hell and you look about ready to wilt."

"Thanks." Daniel schlepped to the passenger door and opened it, the air-conditioning calling to him like a siren song. He put his bags inside, got in, and closed the door.

Richard reached behind him, and some ice rustled before he handed Daniel a dripping, ice-cold bottle of water.

"Drink. It will make you feel better." He didn't pull back onto the road, waiting as Daniel opened the bottle and downed half of it. The water and the AC combined to revive him.

"Thanks. My car broke down, and it's going to take some time to fix it. I was out of so much at the house. The walk to the store wasn't so bad, but I guess I didn't take into account carrying everything back." He took a deep breath and drank some more water. "I've lived here almost my entire life. I know how to deal with the heat, though I guess I forgot how debilitating it can be."

"It's okay. I'm glad I could help." Richard seemed different from how he was at the club—more relaxed. Daniel finished the water and sat back, half closing his eyes to try to pick up a little of the energy the heat had drained away. "How much farther do you have to go?"

"About four blocks." It wasn't that far, it just seemed that the more he walked, the farther home seemed to get. "Can I ask where you're from? You have a slight accent, and I can't place it."

Richard hesitated a few seconds. "The Midwest. I came down here in December. It was really nice then, and the weather was perfect. But this heat sure takes some getting used to."

"It does. I guess I'm one of the few people who isn't from somewhere else. I grew up in Sarasota and went to school there. I like it out here a lot more than I did in town. It's nicer, and I can breathe." Plus, if you continued south along this road and went through a couple other keys, you would eventually be right in the city. "Out here it's like another world."

"Yeah, I suppose it is. We found the places in town and that was it." Richard seemed to measure his words. "What do you like to do for fun around here? My friends and I were looking for things to do."

"There's always the beach. If there isn't a red tide, it's pretty awesome. You can walk right out. Sometimes there are waves, and other times it's almost as calm as glass… all in the same day even. I love the water. I grew up near it with boats and Jet Skis… all the toys." He told himself he wasn't going to let sadness creep in. Those were only things. He had something so much more important in his life.

"That must have been fun."

"It was, but it came with a price. Everything does, and sometimes it's just too high to pay." He shifted in the seat as Richard pulled onto the road after a huge spate of traffic. He shrugged.

"Is it okay if I make a stop before I drop you off?" Richard asked and pulled into a shopping center. "It will only be a minute."

Daniel nodded—like he was going to do anything else—and waited in the car while Richard hurried into the hardware store. He took a bag with him. Daniel figured that Terrance had needed something. Richard returned quickly and hopped back in the car.

"You know, you could go boating if you wanted. It's great out on the water. Just get one that has a cover so you can have some relief from the sun. You can probably rent one for the day if you have a boating license. Otherwise, they charter them by the half or full day." He couldn't suppress a sigh. His father had a beautiful boat—still did. It was a fully restored and lovingly cared-for vintage Chris-Craft. "I got my license a number of years ago and love boating with a passion." But it was something he could no longer afford. He turned to Richard and pointed out the turn coming up. "Make a left here."

Richard nodded. "The guys and I were talking about getting a boat sometime soon. Maybe you'd like to join us? A half day on the water would be fun."

Daniel was floored but found himself nodding. "That *would* be fun," he admitted, even though he figured nothing would come of it. "The condo is another block down on the left."

"Great," Richard said. "Give me your number and I'll call you when we decide what we're going to do and make some plans."

Daniel wrote down his number and handed it to Richard, who called his phone as soon as they stopped at a light.

A new excitement filled the car, and Daniel was so tempted to give in to it. Richard turned in and parked, leaving the engine running. Daniel faced him, and damned if those intense blue eyes didn't draw him in. The longing he found in them combined with loneliness in the lines around them echoed what he saw in the mirror most mornings. Daniel wondered where the loss came from, but it wasn't his place to ask.

Richard licked his lips and touched his hand to Daniel's fingers, sliding over them with the lightest touch. Daniel knew he should pull away—it was the smart thing to do for his heart—but it had been so long since anyone had touched him as more than a friend or family. Daniel closed his eyes, and for a second he could be happy again and have the dream he'd thought he'd come close to four years ago. But those dreams hadn't been meant to be then, and Daniel was sure as hell they weren't on the horizon now.

The door to his condo opened and Coby ran out. Daniel opened the car door. "Thank you for the ride. I really appreciate it."

"Daddy!" Coby jumped up and down like he'd been gone for hours. Daniel got out, and Coby practically leaped into his arms. "I'm playing blocks with Mrs. C." He grinned and rested his head on Daniel's shoulder. "She doesn't do it right. Not like you."

"Okay. I need to get the groceries. Go on inside and don't let the cool out. I'll be there in a minute." He set Coby down and the boy ran back inside. The door closed with a thud. Daniel leaned into the car. "Thank you again for the ride."

"Is that your son?" Richard asked, his tone a little shell-shocked.

"Yeah. It's a long story." He smiled and grabbed the bags of groceries off the floor. "I'll see you later, and thank you again."

Daniel closed the car door and headed to the condo, knowing there would be no call to go boating… or anything else. Hot-as-hell guys like Richard didn't date guys like him, let alone guys with kids. That was just too much baggage. Still, the fantasy and flirting had been fun while they lasted.

IN THE condo, he greeted Mrs. Cunningham, who was sitting on the sofa, watching the Game Show

Network and talking to the television while Coby played with his Legos on the living room floor. "Thank you for looking after him for me."

"It's no problem," she said gently. "He's so good and played by himself most of the time." She turned off the television and picked up her purse. "I like sitting with him. He reminds me of my own grandchildren at that age." Mrs. C. put a brave face on it, but Daniel knew her grandchildren lived outside Chicago and that she only got to see them twice a year. They came down in the winter, and she went there in the fall, but that was it.

She headed toward the door. "Thank you again."

He saw her out and made sure she got inside her unit before he closed the door and returned to the kitchen to put things away and figure out what he and Coby were going to have for dinner.

"Who was the man?" Coby asked while Daniel worked.

"A friend of Daddy's." There was no need for him to explain that Richard had become his fantasy man. "He was nice enough to give me a ride so I didn't have to walk all the way home."

"Because the car is sick?" Coby asked. "I left my doggie in the car, and I hope the car is better soon so I can get him. He's lonely." Coby's lower lip poked out. Daniel did his best not to react to the cuteness, or Coby would fall back on that look all the time.

"It won't be long now and we'll have the car back." Especially if the check came. With the last of the groceries put away, he got the mail and ripped open one of the envelopes, smiling at another check for work he'd done last month. He immediately picked up the phone and called the garage to authorize the repairs to the car.

"Then can we go to the zoo? Billy Taranto got to go to the zoo, and he saw lions and tigers and big mana-bees. I wanna see the manabees. Can we go?"

Daniel smiled and nodded. "I promise that once I get the car fixed, we can go see the manatees over by the power plant in the winter when it's colder. Why don't you put your blocks back in their bag and I'll make some dinner. What do you want?"

He was so tired already, and he still had hours of work to do once Coby was in bed. "Nuggets," Coby said as he started picking up the blocks, playing as he did.

Daniel knew that in about five minutes, he would lose interest and just start playing again. "Okay. As long as you get all the blocks picked up."

"With yellow sauce?" Coby asked. "Not white sauce. But yellow."

"Okay. Yellow sauce," Daniel agreed. For whatever reason, Coby liked mustard sauce on his chicken. He was probably the only kid in the world who did, but that was fine because Daniel liked it too. "Then you can have a bath and get in your jammies, and I'll read you a story before bed." It was always a production to get him to rest. Coby had boundless energy and never wanted to go to bed because he was afraid he'd miss something. Mostly what he missed was his daddy sitting at a computer working and wishing he could go to bed too.

"Okay." He put the blocks in the bag, and Daniel pulled out a bag of chicken nuggets from the freezer and cooked up the last of them. He also made a salad for both of them on the slim hope he could get Coby to eat something green and not frozen. Yeah, he knew it was fighting a losing battle, but hope sprang eternal. Maybe if he put the mustard sauce on it….

Soon he and Coby sat at their little table with their plates and a glass and sippy cup of the last milk in the house. The place was starting to seem like Mother Hubbard's cupboard, but that would change tomorrow, though he was dreading another walking trip to the store. Maybe his sister would be willing to come and help him out for an hour. Renee was the only member of his family who cared about the two of them. Well, at least cared enough not to put herself and her own desires before what was best for Coby.

"Is good," Coby said between bites, lapping up the sauce of mustard with a little mayonnaise and a touch of honey with his fingers.

"I'm glad." Coby was the most important thing in his life, and Daniel would fight anyone he had to in order to make sure he was happy and healthy—even his own parents. He and Coby might not have all the things Daniel had grown up with, but Coby knew that he was loved and would never have cause to doubt that. Daniel had been right when he'd told Richard that some things came with too big a price, and his family had been one of those costs he'd had to pay to be accepted.

COBY WAS finally asleep after three stories and singing *The Wheels on the Bus*... twice. By the end, Daniel's singing had become more of a hum as Coby's eyes finally drifted closed.

Daniel checked the time and got a soda and a bowl of white cheddar cheesy crackers, placing both next to his computer. Then he grabbed the rest of the mail and sat down to get to work.

First he pulled up his banking app, took a picture of the check he'd received, and loaded it through the app to make his direct deposit. With one less errand he needed to run in the morning, Daniel went through the rest of the mail, pulling out a blank, sealed envelope, wondering where that had come from. He turned it over, pondering it, actually looking more closely at it for some indication of where it came from, and then opened it. Inside was a printed sheet of paper with a picture of Coby playing in the yard of the condo, Mrs. Cunningham's body partially in the frame. What the fuck? The temperature in the room dropped in an instant.

We need your skills and we'll be in touch was all the note said, but it sent a chill running through him. Holy hell, someone had been in the back area of the condo just feet from Coby. They'd been able to take a picture of him, and Mrs. Cunningham had said nothing. Daniel's head throbbed. He shoved the note back into the envelope, wondering what in the hell he was going to do.

His phone chimed with a message, and he jumped halfway to the ceiling. *Are you working?* It was from Kerry. Daniel picked up the phone and texted back. His phone rang a few seconds later.

"Hey," Daniel said and plugged in the earpiece so he could work and talk.

"You sound awful."

Daniel gathered his thoughts and took a deep breath. He thought of telling him about the note, but he was too frightened. If someone was watching Coby, then what if they were watching him too… or worse? "I'm just getting started with work. Coby is asleep, and I have hours of things to do before I can go to bed myself." With a few exceptions, Daniel had determined he was going to do his very best to be a stay-at-home parent to Coby. So he worked a little less, but Coby wasn't in day care and spent his time at home. "What's up?"

"I haven't talked to you and thought I'd see how you were doing. I've been traveling like crazy with your father." Daniel could see Kerry rolling his eyes. His father was not an easy man to work for, and his and Kerry's friendship was a strange one. Kerry was one of his father's two assistants at the bank. Kerry never talked about any work details, and Daniel never asked. They kept that separate from their friendship. "But I'm back for a while and I wanted to see how you were."

"I'm good. Coby has been asking about Uncle Kerry." He opened the files in progress and got them situated across multiple screens so he could easily see the various things he needed to do. This client wanted a great deal of audio and video content, so he was working to cut and edit so that the best pieces were available instead of dumping in all the content and weighing down the site. Part of his job was to balance cost and performance.

"I got him a few things when I was in New York on business. They had a great Lego Store, and I couldn't resist." Daniel could hear Kerry's smile.

"How is my dad?" Daniel asked. They never went into details, but every now and then he couldn't help wondering if the old goat was okay.

"The usual. I'm working with him and your mother on a big charity event they're holding next month. Other than that, things are the same as they've always been." He sounded tired, and Daniel found himself getting depressed. He really didn't need to talk about them. It was a road to nowhere and he knew it. "On a happier note, how are things with the flirting bartender?"

Daniel smiled and then let it fade. "Well, I don't know. I was walking home today from the store because the car got sick, as Coby says, and he gave me a ride. He and his friends are new here, and he asked about things to do. It was nice. I told him he could charter a boat or rent one if they had a license." Excitement built a little at the memory. "He said he and his friends were arranging an outing and invited me. We even exchanged phone numbers. It was nice and he seemed interested. That I could tell. It felt nice to have someone look at me that way." He sighed.

"Okay, what happened? Do I need to pay this guy a visit?" Kerry had a huge personality, but he was no bigger than Daniel.

"What are you going to do, approach him and have a hissy fit? Richard is huge and he knows things. The guy doesn't take shit from anyone. He stood up to this huge biker like it was nothing. And… no, you don't need to do anything. When he took me home, Coby ran out to greet me, and you should have seen the expression on his face, like he couldn't get out of here fast enough." Daniel shrugged. "It was bound to happen sooner or later. Guys like that don't go for geeky gay dads like me. He was a fantasy, someone to flirt with, and it made me feel like I'm more than just… well, me." He managed to complete a few tasks and then sat back while he talked because what he needed to do yet would require concentration he couldn't give it at the moment.

"There is nothing wrong with you. And dammit, Daniel, you need to stop with that crap. It doesn't matter what he looks like or you look like. It's what's inside that counts, and if either of you isn't willing to see that, then it isn't worth your time. So don't worry about it."

Daniel sighed. "Yeah, but you didn't see his face. It was like the concept was completely foreign to him, like his CD had flown out of the player and crashed against the wall."

"So what? If that's true, then he isn't someone you want around Coby. You live for that little boy, and if he isn't going to accept both of you, then you aren't going to want him in your life or your head. So write the jerk off and let that be the end of it." Sometimes Kerry was too practical for words. Daniel knew he was right, and his head echoed with the idea, but his heart wasn't quite ready to give it up.

"I better get back to work. I have plenty of things I have to do before I can go to bed. I'll talk to you soon."

"Okay. Give Coby a hug for me and tell him that Uncle Kerry will see him soon."

Daniel paused. "Before you go, I have to ask. Does my dad know that you and I are friends?" Kerry had never been a back-channel conduit to his dad, and Daniel would never ask him to act that way.

Kerry paused a second. "To tell you the truth, he and I don't talk about it, and I don't volunteer the information. It's none of his business who I spend my time with. You and I don't talk about things at the bank, and I don't talk with him about the people in my personal life. Your dad and I have a professional relationship, I'm fantastic at my job, and the confidential information that I may know goes in one ear and out the other and I don't speak of it. Not with you or anyone."

That almost seemed rehearsed, like Kerry had been keeping that little speech in some corner of his brain for just such an occasion.

"Go on back to work and I'll see you soon." He ended the call, and Daniel took a few seconds to clear the swirling thoughts in his head, forced his mind onto the task at hand, and got to work. Right now it didn't matter what his heart wanted—he had to get the job done for Coby's sake.

Chapter 5

"YOU HAVE to be shitting me. This Daniel guy has a kid?" Gerome said almost too loudly as Richard tried to wrap his head around it. He had come right home, pulled out a bottle of Jack, sat on the sofa, and started drinking.

"That's what I told you," Richard growled.

Gerome sat down in the old throw-covered chair across from him. Richard hated this fucking furniture and shifted to try to get comfortable. Where in the hell had the government found this stuff? All he could think was that they must have had a warehouse of boring, ugly beige furniture somewhere and they hauled pieces out of it as needed.

"And you invited this guy to go out on the boat with us. What the hell were you thinking?" Gerome leaned forward.

"I didn't know he had a kid then, and now I have his number and told him I'd call." Richard set the bottle on the coffee table. Drinking wasn't going to help him, and he didn't need to get plastered. Thank God he didn't have to go in to the bar early today, because getting his ass off this couch was going to require a crane.

"So just don't call him," Gerome said as though the answer was obvious.

Richard leaned forward and was grateful the room stayed still… for now. "When was the last time you told someone you were going to do something and then didn't do it?" He cocked his eyebrows, or at least thought he did. "When I asked him, I was thinking he was cute, and Daniel said that he had a boating license, so if he went with us to rent a boat, he could captain it." Richard held his head. "God, I am so wrong for this guy," he muttered softly.

"What the hell are you talking about? You can't get involved with *anyone*, not right now. None of us can. This stint here in Florida is about lying low and keeping our asses down so Junior's people don't take our heads off. This is not the time for you to decide you want true love or some fucking shit."

Richard sighed. "Give it a rest. I'm saying I agree with you. But it's also pretty obvious that if I did like the guy and wanted something to happen, it wouldn't matter. I would be so wrong for him, especially if he has a kid. That would suck. I mean, I'm a former gangster, living in fucking Florida, who knows nothing more about kids other than how to use them as leverage to get what the hell I want." He shook his head. "I'd be really bad for them."

Richard wasn't ready to admit to anyone, least of all Gerome, that he was disappointed—that he had allowed himself to hope just a little bit. Their lives here were mostly shades of gray surrounded by a technicolor world, and Daniel had been a bolt of color, even if it was mostly just him wanting a little more than what he had.

Gerome levered himself out of the chair. "Just don't do something stupid." He took his glass to the kitchen and left Richard alone with his thoughts.

"I THINK we have a boat for Sunday," Terrance told him one evening when Richard had a minute to take a break. "Gerome found one that's available, and it comes with a captain." He kept his attention on the bar while he was talking. "So you aren't going to need to…." Terrance nudged him. "Look who just came in."

"I see," Richard said, turning away to return to work.

Terrance stood with his hands on the end of the bar. He seemed to be doing his job of watching and making his presence known to try to stop trouble before it started. Richard washed glasses and glanced up at Daniel, who had his hands folded on the table.

Richard did his best not to keep lifting his gaze to check on him. Having anything to do with Daniel was a bad idea. He didn't need to draw attention to himself or the guys in any way. And yet turning away from him seemed impossible, and the thought of never seeing Daniel again made his insides itchy.

"I need a beer for your boyfriend," Andi said, placing her order. "Why is he sitting over there and not at the bar?" she asked with a wink.

Richard shrugged and pulled the beer. She took it over to Daniel, and he sat cradling the glass in his hands without drinking or looking up.

Richard told himself for the millionth time in the past five minutes that this was for the best. No matter what, Daniel deserved more than him and anything he could offer.

So why did he find himself walking across the floor, with Daniel's table growing nearer, having no idea what to say? But there he was, standing at the end of Daniel's table. "Is the beer okay?"

Daniel lifted his gaze. "Y-yeah," he stammered. He seemed to remember that the glass was there and took a drink. "I wanted to thank you for the ride. You really saved my life, and I appreciate it." His hand shook a little, and he held the glass, presumably to stop it. "I just came in here to say that and…." He began to slide out of the booth.

Richard felt a near panic that tried to take over. The sensation was very foreign. He never panicked. Even when it became apparent that their lives would end up in tatters around their feet back in Detroit, he never panicked. He kept his head about him. But at this moment, he knew deep down that as soon as Daniel walked out that door, he was never going to see him again.

"I told you that we were looking to go boating. One of my friends has made a reservation for Sunday. Do you want to come with us?" The words were out of his mouth before he could think about them, which never happened, but he had to say something.

"You have to be kidding me," Daniel said. "Look, I have a kid, you saw him, and I couldn't help seeing that the thought of a kid made you want to run for cover. I can understand that, I really can, and there are no hard feelings, but Coby is the most important part of my life and I can't...." He appeared to falter. "I'm not going to hold you to anything."

"I'm a man of my word, and I invited you to come with us. Bring Coby. It will be fun." Richard smiled when some of the rigidity leached out of Daniel and he chuckled.

"Like I said, it's okay. There's no need for you and your friends to include us. You asked me, and you've fulfilled your obligation." Daniel drank what remained of his beer, pulled out his wallet, and put a few bills on the table.

"Then you don't want to go?" Richard pressed.

Daniel shrugged. "Boating sounds like fun, and Coby loves being on the water. A friend runs a dolphin tour, and he loves to go out with her. But you can't understand what being with a four-year-old is like, and...."

"So you'll come, then." Richard was used to getting his way, and somehow this had morphed into one of those situations where he wasn't going to give up. Daniel had presented a challenge, and Richard never backed away from one. "I have your number. I'll text you with the time and where to meet the boat."

Daniel turned, his deep eyes meeting Richard's, and he hesitated. Richard expected a negative answer, but Daniel's shoulders slumped slightly. "Are you really sure about this? What are your friends going to think?"

"It will be fun," he countered.

Daniel nodded. "Okay. If you're serious, Coby and I would love to go boating for a couple of hours." He actually smiled—at him!—and Richard stepped back to let him go, watching Daniel head out of the bar.

"Why in the heck do I get the feeling that we are going to have company on this boating trip?" Terrance half growled from behind him. "I thought you were going to stay away from him and let the whole invitation drop, but instead he practically skipped out the door with a smile plastered on his cute-as-a-bunny face." His words might have sounded funny, but there was no humor in his voice. "Gerome is going to have a fucking cow."

Richard was about to argue, but he turned back to the bar instead. He had thirsty customers, and he wasn't going to stand here and argue with Terrance about it now. The guys could give him all the shit they wanted later.

He was busy for the next few hours. Alan came out to check on things before returning to his office. Richard continued working, half thinking about Daniel. Why the man could turn his head and occupy his mind like this was a mystery to him. Richard had had some of the prettiest boys and hottest men after his attention for years—it came with what he did—but he never paid much attention to them other than for a quick fuck or maybe a few hours of fun. Then they were out the door and he went back to his life with barely a second thought. So what was special about Daniel?

Richard pulled another couple of beers for Andi and filled the rest of her order.

He could remember the way Daniel smelled: a hint of spice, maybe from a touch of aftershave. But under that was a mix of soap and then the sweetest scent that had ever tickled his nose. Speaking of noses, Daniel's was almost perfect, with a little bump, probably from an injury. He sighed, and when Daniel turned and smiled at him, he did the same back.

"Where's Alan?" a man he'd seen before asked.

"In the back," Richard answered, pausing in mixing a tequila sunrise to look the man over. He was well dressed, with eyes as hard as granite. Richard knew that look well. "I'll call him for you." He picked up the bar phone. "Alan, there's a man here to see you."

The pause on the other end could have delivered twins. "Go ahead and send him back."

"Okay. Will do."

He pretended not to have heard the fear in Alan's voice. That was something he knew well too. He hung up the phone and motioned Terrance over. "Can you take him back to see Alan?" He pointedly caught Terrance's gaze and then went back to work.

Terrance returned a few minutes later. "You know what's happening?"

Richard nodded. "The bastard." How dare anyone shake down the man who had given him a job and a chance at a life, even if it was in Longboat Key. "Say nothing, ignore him, and we'll talk about it tonight." He returned to his work and let Terrance keep an eye on things. Between seething about the asshole shaking down the bar and Daniel's flirting, his emotions were on a roller coaster.

"DO YOU really think he's going to come?" Gerome asked as they unloaded their gear at the dock on Sunday morning. "You know, I think this is the stupidest thing you've ever done."

Richard was past angry about his friends being a pain in the ass. "You're just jealous." He smacked Gerome on the shoulder. "Relax. This will be a nice day, and we're going to have some fun in the sun." He hefted the cooler and carried it toward the boat as Terrance got the rest of the gear.

"There's your boyfriend," Terrance teased. He was more at ease with the idea of them having company than Gerome was.

Gerome muttered as he got the last of their gear and kicked the truck door closed. "I just wanted a day where I wasn't going to have to worry about what I said and I could let go. I can't do that with a kid around."

"Can't do that in front of the captain either," Richard told him and then smiled as Daniel approached the boat, holding Coby's hand. The little one already had his life jacket on, and he half skipped next to his dad, grinning.

"Is that our boat?" He looked up at Daniel.

"I think so." They approached, and Daniel set down a huge bag. "This is Mr. Richard. Can you say hi?"

"Hi, Mr. Richard. Will we see dolphins and birdies? Daddy said we will."

"Then Daddy is probably right." He shared a smile with the four-year-old.

"Goody!" Coby bounced.

"Are you ready to get on the boat?"

Coby nodded and then his face grew serious. "Are you a giant?" he asked, looking up at Terrance. "Daddy?" He suddenly seemed really timid.

Richard turned to Terrance, who actually smiled. "No. He's just tall. Mr. Terrance is nice. Most of the time." Richard shot him a "you'd better be nice" look.

"Yup. I'm nice, I promise. Do you want to get on the boat? The captain is just about ready, and we can take our places." Terrance hefted the last of the gear, and they followed him, with Daniel helping Coby to board and then find a seat in the shade.

"Who's he?" Coby asked.

"That's Captain Tommy, and he's Mr. Gerome." Richard leaned closer. "He's grumpy today."

"I am not," Gerome protested, proving Richard's point.

"Don't be grumpy, Mr. Gerome. I'll share my apple juice with you." He smiled and rocked back and forth on his feet, and danged if even grumpy Gerome didn't actually crack a smile. Maybe what they needed was a four-year-old.

"We're ready to cast off," the captain said.

Once they all sat down to let him do his work, they were off across the bay. "I thought we would head to the more open area up this way. We usually see pods of dolphins, and there are osprey nests around the bend."

"Sounds great. We were just interested in a leisurely few hours," Richard clarified and opened the cooler to hand out drinks. He sat back down next to Daniel, and they shared a smile.

"Thank you for inviting Coby and me. He's been asking to go boating for a while."

"That's Grampy's house," Coby said, pointing to a huge mansion and what looked like a compound of buildings at the top of a great lawn sloping to the water. "I like it there, but Grampy is grumpy like Mr. Gerome."

Daniel handed him some crackers and a juice box, probably to give him something else to do besides talk. "We don't talk about Grampy."

Coby grew quiet and nodded. "I know. He doesn't like us." Coby sat still, some of his energy abating. Richard shared a look with Terrance, who seemed as curious as he was. Coby snuggled against his dad. Gerome joined them in the seating area, and Coby cradled his unopened box of juice as though he was afraid Gerome was going to take it.

Gerome grumped big-time, and Coby giggled, offering the juice box and then pulling it back before breaking out into a laugh. It was cute, and some of Gerome's reticence slipped away.

"Dolphins!" Coby said, standing on the seat so he could see better. Daniel held on to him, and Richard found himself smiling as he followed where Coby was pointing.

"They like to play, and one of them might run along with us," Tommy said. "And over there, those big birds are cormorants."

"Look, Mr. Gerome, Mr. Terrance," Coby said as he jumped down from the seat and climbed between them.

"Careful, little dude," Terrance said. "You don't wanna go swimming." He held him, and Richard shook his head in wonderment.

"Coby is pretty much fearless, which can be worrying for me. He'll run everywhere," Daniel said. The guys watched Coby, and Richard slid closer to Daniel.

"Look, Daddy." Coby pointed. Richard had no idea what was so fascinating to him, but Daniel nodded and smiled, and Coby turned back to the slowly changing scenery.

"Was that really your parents' place?" Richard asked. The estate was a pile if he'd ever seen one.

"Yeah. Dad and Mom don't agree with what they see as my choices in life." He turned to Coby, who bounced as a pod of dolphins swam alongside them. It looked like he wanted to pet one, but Gerome held on to him, and danged if the big grump wasn't smiling. If Daniel only knew that the man protecting his son had done things that would curl his hair. They all had.

A thought occurred to Richard as he watched Terrance and Gerome with Coby. They were loyal to each other and would do anything to protect themselves. It was part of how they lived. Do whatever was necessary to protect what was yours. Richard never thought about the families of the guys he'd had to have taken care of, or their parents. If they stood in his way or the way of the family, they had to be eliminated. It was just business. At least that was what he had told himself. But it wasn't just business—not to the families of the people he'd hurt. It was…. Shit, what in the hell was he thinking about? Where was this shit coming from? He did what he had to in order to survive, and he and the guys would continue to do that. This second-guessing and hashing over the fucking past was not going to help anyone. He needed to stay strong and not go down that road.

He pulled his thoughts to the present. "What sort of choices?" Daniel looked at Coby, and Richard felt his eyebrows furrowing. "Your son?"

Daniel shrugged. "Coby came out of an unfortunate drunken experiment that didn't go very well. His mother is a friend, and we got together once. That was enough for nature to take its course. She wasn't ready to be a mother and… well, she sees him a couple times a year, but she travels and has a career of her own. Maureen is going places, and this wasn't part of the plan. We had talked about adoption, but as soon as I saw him, there was no way. I brought him home, and Maureen signed over her parental rights. My parents thought that since I'd been 'straight' once, I could live my life that way forever and that I should get married in order to fit their idea of social convention. When I explained reality to them, they decided that they could live without us in their lives. Then they tried to take Coby from me." Daniel fidgeted, and Coby sat down and then slid off the seat before climbing into Daniel's lap.

"Don't make sad face," Coby said, patting his dad's cheek. It was so cute.

"I'm not sad, I promise," Daniel said with a smile and held Coby in his arms. "You always make me happy." Coby let himself be held for a moment and then squirmed until Daniel placed him on the seat. "Sit still and watch the water. Maybe there will be more dolphins."

Coby handed Daniel his juice box, and Daniel got the straw in it for him and had him drink some before leaving him alone.

"Your parents did that?" Richard asked.

"Yeah. Now they don't have much to do with us. Though my mom does ask to spend time with Coby. Apparently my father is less than thrilled—hence the whole 'Grampy is grumpy' thing." He sighed.

"And they have that kind of money," he asked as they passed the house.

Daniel shrugged. "I was raised to have everything money could buy and nothing it couldn't. Dad worked all the time, and Mom has her charities and events in order to boost their social standing so she can help my father and his business. It's a vicious circle. I have a sister."

"Aunt Renee," Coby supplied and drank more juice before handing off the box to Daniel so he could visit Terrance and pepper him with questions about how he got to be so big. It was adorable.

"Yes. She comes each Wednesday and spends the evening with Coby. They have some time together, and that gives me an evening out." That explained his weekly visits to the bar. "What about your family?"

Richard swallowed. Damn it all, he hadn't thought that by asking Daniel, he was going to open himself to questions as well. But he had always been good at getting people to talk to him without actually giving away any information about himself. "I pretty much grew up in foster care."

Daniel's eyes widened and then softened. "Do you remember your parents?"

"I remember my mother, but not fondly. She was more interested in her own issues than she was in me." He shrugged and leaned back. "I love it out here. This is the first time I've been out on the water like this since I moved here." He looked around.

Coby climbed onto his dad's lap, curling up to him, and promptly fell to sleep.

"He goes like crazy for hours and then goes to sleep. He won't be out long, and then the energy will be back." Daniel held his son closely, lightly stroking his hair.

"Does anyone want a beer?" Gerome asked and went to the cooler.

Richard shook his head. It was a little early for one as far as he was concerned, but Gerome popped one open and took a swig, sitting back down. Richard could tell there were things he wanted to talk about, and his gaze kept shifting from Daniel to Tommy.

Coby woke ten minutes later needing the bathroom, and Captain Tommy pulled into the slip at a waterside restaurant. Daniel and Coby got off and hurried up the dock.

"They aren't so bad, and the kid is cute," Terrance said. "He had your number, Mr. Grumpy."

Gerome humphed and leaned closer. "What are we going to do about Alan and the situation? It could get ugly fast."

Richard nodded. "I think we call Elizabeth. Let her know what's going on."

"And let them handle it?" he whispered. "This is…."

"I know what it is," Richard hissed. "This isn't our turf, and we can't take action ourselves." He glanced at Terrance. "What do you think?"

"I want to rip the asshole apart. But that wouldn't be good." He grew quiet. "Tell her, and then we sit back and watch the fireworks. No one needs to know we're involved."

Gerome's expression hardened. "I say we do nothing and stay out of it. Unless we want to get moved again." He turned to where Coby skipped down the dock holding Daniel's hand, shaking his head. "If you want to do it, then go ahead. You will anyway."

"If I have no job…," Richard warned. "And Alan doesn't deserve this kind of shit."

Gerome clenched his fist. "I wish we could take care of this ourselves." He sat back, and Richard did the same as Daniel and Coby joined them.

Tommy shoved off, and they were on their way once again. He explained the various boats on the pier and what they were used for, and then began heading up the key. More dolphins frolicked around them, to Coby's delight. He seemed to relish trying to make Gerome not grumpy.

"What do you do?" Daniel asked Gerome. "I know he works at the hardware store and the bar."

"I help in one of the tourist boutiques," Gerome answered. "I like it for the most part. The customers are nice enough. What about you?"

"Computer design and web integration. I have a number of clients, and I offer some pretty specialized integration so systems can talk to one another more easily through the web. Companies are finding that they have all these systems that don't really communicate with one another except in ways that take a lot of time, conversion, and effort. I make that process easier for them, and I design some pretty robust websites and formats to help them cope." Daniel sighed. "Okay, it's a lot more exciting to me than it sounds." He flashed a smile, and Richard hated that it was at Gerome.

"You must have a lot of experience," Gerome said.

"In college and just afterwards, I used to… let's just say that I used to be a lot more fun. I could get into any system at almost any time. It was like a game. But then a bunch of shit went down with hacking and stuff, and I backed away from it and went in a different direction. I never stole anything, but I did leave markers just to say I'd been there."

Gerome nodded. "You signed your hacks, didn't you?" He leaned forward. Richard wondered where Gerome was going and why this was so interesting to him.

"Daddy, I'm hungry," Coby said.

Richard opened the cooler, hoping the subject would drop. He got out a bag of grapes, and Coby dug into them like he was starving. Richard also opened a tub of store-bought hummus and set out some crackers.

There wasn't very far to go on the boat, and Richard mused on how he could get a few minutes with Daniel alone, but it wasn't going to happen. Still, the day was relaxing, and he found himself wondering less and less about bars and his past, and sank into the moment instead. Daniel slid closer when Coby spread out on the seat next to him, playing with a few toys that Daniel had brought. "Don't run them up there. If they fall in, we can't get them again. Play down here on the seat."

The rocking of the boat was soothing, and Daniel leaned slightly against him. It was nice. He glanced at the other two, who pointedly looked elsewhere.

"I thought we would head out into the Gulf a little. The water is calm enough today, and we have time," Captain Tommy explained and guided the boat under the bridge to the bay. The water was so blue. Richard leaned back against Daniel as they went along.

The boat rocked back and forth slightly, lulling him into a half doze of contentment. It was enough that he could forget about his life for a while and enjoy being with Daniel and his friends.

Terrance and Gerome moved toward the bow, leaving him and Daniel alone with Coby, who bounded up after a few minutes and joined the guys up front. Gerome and Terrance were intimidating men, yet Coby didn't seem the least bit unsure around them.

"Be careful and don't stand on the seat," Daniel called, and Coby sat right between Terrance and Gerome, grinning up at each of them before pointing and unleashing a barrage of questions.

"Like I said, he has no fear. I mean, to look at them, they're scary as heck, but he doesn't see that at all." Daniel lightly tugged at his collar and cleared his throat. "Look, there's something I have to ask you, and… well, it's probably kind of dumb, but I have to know." He shifted on the seat a little. "I have Coby, and I can't get involved with just anyone." God, he seemed nervous, and it was rather cute. Richard sat calmly, at least on the outside. Inside, his belly fluttered and he wondered what could have Daniel so flustered.

"Just say what you want to say," he told him softly.

"Well, do you go after every gay guy who comes in the bar? I mean, you flirted with me for weeks, right? Is that something you do with the guys who come in the bar to, like, get better tips and stuff?" His cheeks flamed bright red. "Sorry, that sounded really bad. I didn't mean to suggest that you sold yourself for tips or anything, but…." He sighed dramatically. "I have to watch out for Coby. He's the most important person in my life. My sister helps, but basically it's all me, and he has to come first."

Richard leaned close and inhaled gently, pulling in Daniel's sweet scent, which went right to his groin. He shifted slightly to make things more comfortable. "No, I don't flirt to make better tips, and I've only flirted with you."

Daniel shook a little, and Richard could almost scent his arousal in the salty air. It was probably his imagination, but the temperature of the air around him definitely seemed to have climbed a good five degrees.

"Did you date a lot of guys before you came here?" Daniel seemed nervous. "I'm sorry, I shouldn't have asked that. It's really none of my business." He turned, and their gazes met, increasing the heat a little more. "I should shut up now."

Richard paused as he thought out his answer. It would be so much easier if he could tell the truth about his past, but that was out of the question. "I didn't date guys… before I came here. I had sex sometimes, but I didn't date. It wasn't my thing then." He wondered how that would seem to Daniel, and damned if he had to wonder what was getting into him. Richard had run a huge operation and he had been proud of it. He'd done everything he had been tasked with and had returned a lot of money to his bosses. But he couldn't talk about any of it, and he was even reluctant to mention where he'd lived in case someone made a connection. "I never flirted with anyone else the way I did with you." And that was the truth. He had fucked hundreds of guys. He was attractive, used to have money and power, and that meant he had had his choice of sex partners any time he'd wanted them.

"So I'm different?" Daniel asked.

Richard nodded, glancing at the others, whose attention was forward. He leaned closer, wondering at the taste of Daniel's full lips. He licked his, and when Daniel leaned toward him, Richard drew closer, inhaling his intense scent. Fuck, he was going to do this. Part of him felt like a fucking teenager.

Daniel's breath hitched and he stilled, anticipation building between them. Richard touched the soft cotton T-shirt covering Daniel's sleek arm muscles. This was what he'd been waiting for ever since Daniel had first stepped into the bar on a Wednesday night a few months ago.

He parted his lips, wetting them, watching as Daniel's pink tongue did the same. Once again, he glanced to where Terrance and Gerome sat with Coby, watching intently forward. Relieved to have a few seconds without being scrutinized, he leaned forward to close the gap between them.

"Look, Daddy," Coby called, pointing to a ball of smoke rising above the water. Daniel straightened up, and Richard humphed. "Smoke."

"Maybe there's a boat on fire."

Coby hurried over, and Daniel tugged him onto his lap. It was damned clear that the moment was gone. Richard stifled a groan.

"I'm calling it in," Captain Tommy said as he picked up speed. "Everyone sit down back here. We're close enough that we might be able to help." He pointed the bow toward the smoke, and the others all came to sit under the cabin roof. As they drew closer, flames became apparent on the small craft ahead. "The Coast Guard is responding."

"There are people in the water," Richard said as Tommy slowed. He pointed, and Tommy grabbed the life rings and tossed them to the first person before pulling her in. She climbed onto the boat, and Tommy threw the ring again. It missed. He threw again, but the kid was foundering. Richard took off his shoes and shirt and dove over the side. The water was warm and it surrounded him, buoying him upward. Richard surfaced near his target, a young teenager tiring in the water.

"It's okay, I have you." He put an arm around him and rolled him onto his back before swimming him toward the boat. "Stop fighting me and relax. I have you," Richard snapped, and it must have gotten through, because he stopped flailing as Richard made progress back to the boat.

"Oh God, Kevin, are you okay?" the woman asked, cradling him in her arms as soon as he was on board, with the third person joining them.

"Was there anyone else on the boat?" Tommy asked as he backed the boat away from the still-burning vessel.

"No. It was just the three of us. I rented it out of Key West, and we were heading north." The man seemed winded, and it took a few breaths for him to speak again. "I think there was a leak in one of the propane lines that caught fire."

Richard got a good look at the man and backed away from the bow area, letting them have their reunion. He recognized the man as a patron of the club in Detroit, and he hoped the guy hadn't gotten too good a look at him. In the water he'd had cover, and Richard figured he had gone in before they pulled the man onto the boat. All he had to do was keep his distance long enough for the Coast Guard to arrive and he'd be okay.

A horn sounded and grew closer. The captain maneuvered the boat so the cutter could come alongside. There was only so far Richard could go on the relatively small boat, but fortunately the family seemed so concerned with their rescue and what caused the fire that they weren't paying much attention to Richard and his friends.

"Are you shy?" Daniel asked, sitting down next to him, placing Coby on his lap while the activity went on maybe ten feet away. The burning boat was going down, but Richard didn't join the others in witnessing its death throes. Fortunately, Daniel sat between him and the others. "You were a hero. You saved that kid's life. He wasn't going to stay afloat much longer."

"I guess." He sat back and closed his eyes, trying to hide behind Daniel as much as possible.

Questions continued, and finally the family members were taken off their boat and onto the cutter.

Captain Tommy pulled away, and Richard's heart began beating once again now that there was some distance between him and the man who might have identified him. Jesus, that had been a close call.

"Can we go back into the bay now?" Daniel asked.

Richard squeezed his hand without really thinking about it.

"Of course," the captain answered. "Do you need a towel?" Tommy handed him one from a locker, and Richard dried his hair and body and then the seat.

"Thank you," Richard said. He placed the towel on the seat under him to soak up any additional water from his pants.

Captain Tommy set course back the way they'd come, and soon enough the boat glided under the bridge.

It seemed the entire experience had pulled most of the fun out of the day. "Could those people have drowned?" Coby asked after a while.

"Yes. But we saved them. Richard dove in to help the boy."

"Is he a hero?" Coby asked, his eyes wide.

"Yes," Gerome said. "He's definitely a hero." He and Terrance sat across from Richard and Daniel. Coby slid down and scooted between the two of them. It seemed his friends had won the heart of a four-year-old. The guys back home would never believe it. Not that Richard would ever be able to tell them.

It was funny how many times a day he had to push away thoughts like that. He was never going to see any of those people again, and if he did, it would be because they had been sent to kill him—all of them. Shit, if they did find him and Daniel was anywhere nearby, he and Coby would be used to get to him, and they wouldn't care what happened to either of them as long as they got what they wanted.

Richard raised his gaze, and both Terrance and Gerome met it. He knew they were thinking the same thing he was, and shit, Richard knew he had to back away. His life was toxic to Daniel and Coby. As much as he liked the guy and the kid—oh my God—he was so bad for them.

Captain Tommy crossed the bay and then motored down to his dock. "I don't think things turned out the way any of us expected today."

"It's okay," Gerome said. "You did good, and we'll all have a great story to tell." He pressed some cash into Tommy's hand. "Thank you."

"Did you have fun?" Richard asked Coby, who nodded. It seemed at least that he wasn't going to let the rescue ruin his boat ride.

"I liked the dolphins." He turned to Daniel. "Can we go out on the boat again tomorrow?"

Daniel chuckled. "Not tomorrow, but we can go on a boat again. Now thank Mr. Richard for inviting us."

"Thank you," he said and then put his arms partway around Richard's waist to hug him. He did the same for each of the other guys, and it was like ice cubes in the Florida sun. Three former gangsters damn near melted at the hug of a four-year-old.

"Yes, thank you," Daniel said, and to Richard's surprise, he hugged him.

Richard closed his arms around Daniel, and damn it all if the smaller man didn't feel just right against him. It would be so easy to hold on like this forever. In his fantasies it was possible, but in real life, well, that was a completely different matter.

When Richard released Daniel, he missed that touch immediately. It was so tempting to grab him and hold him again. Hell, if the boat had had a cabin down below, he'd have been tempted to drag Daniel down there and see if the sounds he made in real life matched the ones Richard's imagination conjured up at night.

Captain Tommy tied off the boat, and Richard and the guys gathered all their stuff and hauled it up to the truck. Daniel and Coby followed and went on to the car, with Coby waving. "I made Mr. Gerome not grumpy," Coby told his dad, and Richard smirked as Gerome humphed next to him.

"Don't worry. You'll always be grumpy," Terrance teased as they slammed the tailgate shut and climbed inside. It was a tight fit to get Gerome in back, but they did, and soon enough they were headed home.

"That kid was something else," Terrance said. "He sure had Gerome's number."

Richard swallowed. He hated to kill the mood, but he didn't have a choice. "The guy we rescued—I recognized him from the Ostrich in Detroit. He was a patron a few times. Not a regular or anything, but he was there."

Gerome patted his shoulder. "Is that why you hid like a virgin at a tea dance?"

"It's not funny. If he fingered me, we'd be dead. You know that. Did he recognize you?" Richard asked Terrance and then turned back to the road.

"I doubt it. The guy was too busy making sure he and his nephew didn't drown when that cheap POS boat they were using caught fire." He sat back. "They didn't recognize any of us. We aren't where they expect us to be and we don't look the same."

"Okay. We should tell Elizabeth when we call her, though." He hated the idea but knew it was the right thing to do. Richard couldn't help feeling as though a cloud had passed over him, blocking out some of the sun's light.

"He's right," Gerome said. "If he remembers us at all, it will be as the people who helped rescue them, not the guys who ran a nightclub in another area of the country." Gerome patted his shoulder. "But the bigger question is, what are you going to do about Coby and the daddy you spent the entire time making cow eyes at?"

"I did not," Richard retorted, and both Terrance and Gerome laughed.

"You so did. And don't think we didn't see you trying to kiss Daddy when you thought it was safe. I have eyes in the back of my head. How do you think I kept you both out of trouble all these years?" Gerome was such a smartass sometimes. "You like the guy, but you know that's a recipe for disaster, unless you're just trying to get in his pants or something."

Richard pressed the brake more forcefully than he intended to. "That's enough." He released the brake and continued forward, gripping the wheel. "When you guys meet someone you like, I'm going to give you just as much shit."

"Never going to happen," they said in near unison.

"Yeah, sure. You two horndogs are going to keep to yourselves with your right hands as company for the next forty years." He'd believe that when he saw it. "I like him." Richard expected the teasing to commence big-time, but instead the other two were quiet.

"For real?" Terrance asked, and Richard nodded. "Then you're fucking screwed."

"Thanks for that, asshole," Richard retorted without heat.

"What are you planning to do? Tell him about all of us and what we used to do? Why we're here… oh, and that there are people who want us all dead and that if he's part of your life it will put a target on him and his four-year-old son, who is as precious as can be? Yeah, that's going to fucking happen. WITSEC will have a fit." Terrance's voice grew louder and more forceful. "Wake up out of dreamland, Richard, and get your head on straight." He grew quiet, and Richard expected Gerome to chime in, but no one said anything more until they reached their apartments. Richard got out, slammed the truck door, and stalked to his place, where he went right to the refrigerator. He popped a beer and chugged the damned thing before having another.

"Just leave me alone."

The others ignored him as they carried in the cooler and the rest of the gear.

"Bullshit. We've been through hell and back together, and you don't get to shut us out because you're having a temper tantrum. Little Richie can't have the guy he wants, so he's going to throw himself on the floor and kick and cry until the world bends to his will." Damn, Gerome could be a sarcastic ass when he wanted.

Richard knew he was right, but it still hurt. "Is it so bad that I might want to have someone in my life?"

"Fuck no," Terrance agreed. "But is it fair to pull Daniel and Coby into our mess? You know it isn't. He's a nice man trying to make a living and raise his son. We used to call them workaday schmucks, and now we are them, except we're not. We don't fit here, and we don't fit in Detroit either, so we can't have the benefits of either one." Terrance slumped on the sofa and put his feet up on the coffee table.

Richard gaped at Terrance. "That was quite insightful." And unusual for Terrance.

"Yeah? Cool. I heard it in some movie last week." He grinned, and Richard rolled his eyes. He should have known Terrance wasn't going to come up with that all on his own. Still, what he'd said was spot-on.

"So what are you going to do?" Gerome asked.

"I don't know," Richard answered honestly. "I like him like I haven't liked anyone before." That was the best he could come up with. God, he felt like he was in awful high school again, except without the ability to have any kid who crossed him beaten up. "But I suppose that's a moot point. I can't put you guys in danger if he turns us in, and I can't put him in danger if we get found out." There was no good solution. He just had to accept that it was best for him to walk away… and it really sucked.

Terrance thumped his leg once, and Gerome nodded, his lips straight. These guys were his oldest friends in the world, and they understood. Talking about their feelings wasn't something they did. So they sat without saying a word to let the air around them change and shift a little, each finishing their beer and setting the bottles on the table.

"We need to call Elizabeth," Terrance said and stared at Richard, who nodded. He knew the task would fall to him. It was pretty much inevitable.

Richard picked up his phone and dialed the number he had memorized.

"How can we help you?" There was no other greeting or indication that he had the right number.

"This is Richard Marsden. I need to leave a message for Elizabeth Lowell. Have her call me back. It is not a dire emergency, but I need to speak with her," Richard said.

"All right. The message will be passed on." The call ended, and Richard deleted the number from the call history. Then he placed his phone on the coffee table and got up to retrieve another beer, but pulled the bottle of tequila out of the cupboard instead. He might as well get good and stinking drunk to dull the disappointment of the reality of his life. He flopped onto the sofa, opened the bottle, and tipped it to his lips.

"How in the hell did we end up here?" he asked out loud. Richard of course already knew the path they had taken, and he didn't need a fucking answer from anyone. He swigged the powerful liquor, relishing the burn on its way down as warmth spread through his belly.

Gerome held out his hand, and Richard passed him the bottle. The asshole put the lid back on it, and fuck if he didn't put it back in the cupboard. "You are not going to sit here and get drunk. Elizabeth is going to call, and we need to keep our heads. We all talked about this shit. You don't get to feel sorry for yourself. This isn't just about you, but all of us." He sat back down and handed Richard a soda.

"I don't want this," Richard said as he placed the can on the table.

"Then I'm going to my own apartment, and you can get shitfaced on your own. Wallow in your own crapulence if you want, but I'm not doing this shit." He turned to Terrance, who hefted himself out of the chair.

"I'm out of here too," Terrance said. He turned to follow Gerome but paused. "You're always telling us we need to keep it together. Well, you need to do the same thing now."

Richard knew there was no way to win this argument, though part of him wanted to dig in and just be stubborn and get roaring drunk and pissed off at the world. "Go if you want." There was nothing he could do to stop them.

Gerome patted his shoulder from behind. "Don't do anything stupid, and message when she calls. Terrance and I will leave you alone."

There was so much meaning in those words and that touch. Richard placed his hand on top of Gerome's for just a second, and then he backed away. They understood; Richard knew that. The hurt from their situation could happen to any of them, and probably would at some point. Richard was just the first to feel the confines. The three of them had taken relocation and Witness Protection in exchange for their help rather than going to prison and probably ending up in coffins. But he hadn't understood that Witness Protection was its own kind of prison, and right now Richard was paying the price.

ELIZABETH CALLED a few hours later, and Richard messaged Gerome and Terrance to come over. He'd mostly sat in the quiet room thinking and, yeah, wallowing a little. But he was allowed.

"What's the problem?" Elizabeth asked.

"A couple of things. First, we want you to be aware that this afternoon we were out on an excursion boat in the Gulf. Another boat was on fire. The passengers were rescued, but I recognized one of them from the Ostrich in Detroit. I believe that he didn't recognize any of us, and he said nothing. I stayed out of his line of sight as best I could." Richard sat and waited for her response while the guys sat as well. He put the phone on speaker but kept the volume low.

"Did you have direct contact with him in Detroit?" Elizabeth asked.

"No. He was just a patron." Richard didn't go into why he remembered him, but it had nothing to do with the two of them having direct contact. "He might have seen either Terrance or me, but I remembered him."

"I see." She grew quiet. "I don't see any cause to be alarmed at this point. He was under stress today."

Terrance leaned forward. "He didn't recognize either of us. I saw nothing at all from him."

"We'll monitor the situation," Elizabeth said. "What else do you have for me?"

Terrance and Gerome both waited. "I need you to get in touch with local law enforcement. The bar where I'm working is being shaken down."

"How do you know?" She sounded worried.

"Because I used to do it years ago. I know what it looks like. The man is in his forties, brown hair, an older Don Johnson wannabe. He comes in on Saturday about nine when the place is busy, probably so he can blend in with the crowd."

"I saw him putting the money in his coat pocket this last week," Terrance chimed in. "It's definitely a shakedown, likely protection money of some kind."

"If they lean on this guy, he'll lead them wherever they want to go. I know his type. The guy is nervous the entire time he's in the bar. We know we can't be directly involved, but if I lose my job, it's going to be hard to find another. And Alan has been good to Terrance and me, and he doesn't deserve this kind of shit," Richard added strongly.

"Have any of you approached him?" Elizabeth asked. "You haven't tried to intimidate him or warn him away?" She seemed wary.

Richard was about to go ballistic. "No!" he responded more loudly than necessary. "We agreed when we came into this program to be law-abiding citizens, and that's what we're doing. Contrary to what you seem to think, when we make a deal, we stick to it. We always have. So like law-abiding citizens, we came to you." He huffed and realized his temper hung by a thread.

"Old habits die hard," Elizabeth told them calmly.

Gerome cleared his throat. "Look, lady, if this were Detroit, we would have hit this asshole so hard his grandkids would have black eyes. That is if you flatfoots ever managed to find his body." He snorted. "If Richard and Terrance told you what's going on, believe them. Coming to you wasn't easy, and we're trusting you to help." Menace rang in his voice. "We can take care of this, but then you'll be moving us again. And while this place isn't known for its fun and happening night life, it beats the hell out of the fucking snow and cold."

"Okay. If you give me the description again and the time he comes in, I'll see what I can do." Elizabeth sounded about as excited as for a gift of two-day-old fish, but they repeated the information and indicated the time.

"We can't help you further or it will blow our cover, but I hope you get this guy," Richard said. They answered the last of her questions and hung up.

"Do you think she'll help?" Terrance asked.

Richard smiled. "Yes. She's a Goody Two-Shoes and she hates people who break the rules. It's part of how she's wired, so she'll turn what she has over to someone." He met the gazes of the other two. "This is our turf, and one way or another, we'll keep it clean." He could hardly believe he was saying that, but it was true. To protect themselves, they needed to help the people who helped them. It was that simple.

"You know it's more than just protection," Terrance said. "That's just the tip of the iceberg. If they have a protection racket, then they have other things too."

"Yeah, but this guy seems like easy pickings, and they can go on up from him. I'd never let a guy like that idiot work for me. He looks scared to death half the time, even if he tries to cover it up." Richard had learned how to read people long ago, and this guy was a scared rabbit in a suit of armor. "We'll watch and see what happens. If they don't do anything, then we'll see what we can do." They could give Elizabeth a chance.

"What do we do now?"

"Nothing but watch and see what happens," Richard said. Absolutely nothing, which was the hardest thing for all of them. Richard was used to taking action. When there was a problem, he fixed it. But there was nothing he could do about Alan's shakedown, and the same went for Daniel. He could do nothing. He just had to walk away, for all of their sakes.

Chapter 6

"DANNY," RENEE called as she came inside.

"Aunty Renee," Coby called as soon as he heard her voice, racing away from where Daniel had been trying to change him out of the pants he'd managed to get caked with sand and mud.

"Stop," he snapped, and Coby skidded in his socks. "Let's get your pants on, and then you can see Aunty Renee."

"Daddy," Coby complained. Daniel helped Coby into his pants before letting him go.

Coby raced out to greet her, and Daniel cleaned up the rest of the mess, putting the pants in the washer with the rest of the things and getting it started.

"This is a surprise," Daniel said as he came into the living room where Coby was explaining what he'd built with his Legos.

"Mom and Dad are driving me crazy," Renee said. "Mom has decided that I should marry Geoffrey Mantel. His folks go to their club, and she keeps gushing about how dashing he is." She rolled her eyes.

"He is handsome," Daniel agreed.

"And he knows it and can't understand why every woman within a hundred miles isn't throwing herself at him. No, thank you. I want a nice guy who likes me and thinks I'm special. I want someone I don't have to beat the women off with a stick. Someone I can trust. Besides, the guy is a jerk." She ruffled Coby's hair. "It's too bad this one is too young."

Coby flashed his aunt an adoring smile and then settled on the floor to play with his cars and blocks.

"So, how's the guy you've been seeing?" Renee asked. "I'm tempted to go down to the bar and see this hunk for myself." She had this naughty gleam in her eyes, and Daniel shrugged.

"We had a good time on the boat on Sunday. Well, except for saving people from the fire and all." He lowered his voice. "And he almost kissed me, but I haven't heard a thing from him since, so I guess I'm not what he was looking for." He flipped through the mail that Renee had brought in and nearly dropped it when he saw the blank envelope in with the rest.

"What's wrong?" Renee asked.

Daniel did his best to school his expression and slid the envelope back in with the rest of the mail.

"Nothing. What are you here for?"

"Just as refuge. I thought I'd take the Cobester out for something to eat and then we can have ice cream afterwards. You can have a chance to go out if you want." She waggled her eyebrows.

"Thanks, but I don't need to go out, and it's been a while since you and I spent some time together." He was prevaricating and she knew it. "Things are best left alone. I doubt Richard is the kid type of person. Coby got along with the guys when we were on the boat, but it takes a pretty special kind of man to want to date someone with a kid." He shrugged.

"Did you call him? What if he's just been busy this week? Did you go in and see him on Wednesday like you usually do?" she pressed, and Daniel shook his head. "So you don't know what's been happening, and you've been hiding out waiting by the phone. You know, he could have been waiting to see you on Wednesday, but you chickened out and didn't show." She gave him that "I know best" look. "Go on in, have a drink, a bite of dinner, and see what he says. The worst thing that happens is you come home and have to watch cartoons with me and Coby. I'll even bring you some ice cream so you can drown your sorrows in Rocky Road if you need to." She shooed him out of the room. "And find something hot to wear."

"How can you wear hot?" Coby asked, looking up from his blocks.

Daniel rolled his eyes. "Ask your Aunt Renee. She'll be happy to explain it to you." He left the room with a smirk on his face. She had opened that can of worms, so she could do some explaining. He chuckled as he went to his room and rummaged in his closet. This was ridiculous. He was just going to the bar, not to a fancy restaurant. Still, he found a nice pair of jeans and a light blue T-shirt that was a little tight. That was going to have to do in the hotness category. He got some shoes and checked that his hair wasn't all over the place before rejoining Renee and Coby in the living room. "Good enough?" he asked.

"You look hot, Daddy," Coby said. Daniel knew he never should have let his sister explain anything.

"Thank you," Daniel said and gathered his things. "I won't be late and should be home in time to put Coby to bed."

"You have fun. I can read Coby stories and make sure he gets tucked in, can't I?" She turned to Coby, who shook his head.

"Daddy says night-night." He made it a pronouncement and then went back to his blocks like his word was law.

"I'll be home in time for you to go to bed. You can watch all the cartoons with Aunt Renee that you want." He kissed Coby on the forehead. "Be a good boy. I love you." He hugged him and Renee before heading out to his car. If this evening went the way he expected it to, he'd be home in plenty of time to put Coby to bed.

THE BAR was just as he had expected, only maybe a little worse. Daniel had sat at the bar in the hope that he might have a chance to speak with Richard, but he was busy all the time, and after a quick exchange, he spent his time at the other end of the bar. Maybe it was best if he just gave up and went home.

Daniel finished eating his dinner and drank the last of his beer. He had to drive, so that was all he intended to drink. After placing his money on the bar and getting Richard's attention, he slid off the stool and headed for the door. He didn't need an anvil to fall on him.

"Going already?" Terrance asked as he got close to the door.

"Yeah. There's nothing for me here." He couldn't help looking back at Richard. "He was nice… you all were on the boat, and now he doesn't want to give me the time of day." There was nothing else to say. "Tell him I hope he has a nice life and I won't bother him again."

He pushed through the door and out into the parking lot. It was time to go home. He reached his car and pulled open the door.

"Daniel," Richard called.

He turned. "What do you want?" he asked. "You made your feelings pretty clear in there, and don't try to tell me you were busy. You made work and stayed away from my end of the bar. You couldn't even tell me that you weren't interested. You just ignored me. Well"— he shrugged—"I would have thought you'd have had the guts to tell me you weren't interested, but I got the message."

Richard glanced around and then pulled him into his arms, kissing him hard right there in the parking lot.

Daniel's knees felt weak, even though this was a terrible idea. He pushed away and gasped for breath in the humid night air.

"I wanted to do that all night, but…." Richard sighed. "Look, I like you. I think you're special, but I'm…."

A car pulled into the lot, and Richard backed away.

"I have to get back to work. But I'll call you—I promise. I was an ass. I know that. Please come back inside for a little while."

Daniel wasn't sure if that was a good idea. "Why did you act that way?" He crossed his arms over his chest.

"It's a long story, and I have to get back inside. But… we need to talk. We can't out here, and not right now." He turned back toward the front door of the bar. "Alan is covering for me, and I have to get back."

Daniel nodded and followed Richard inside. There was one seat available at the far end of the bar. It was the least desirable place because it was closest to the office. Still, it was where Richard tended to work because the dish sink was nearby. They shared a smile as he scrubbed glasses and set them beside the sink to drain.

Daniel still wasn't convinced that this was a good idea.

"You came back," Terrance said when he stood next to him, looking down the bar.

Daniel turned slightly and found Terrance glaring at Richard, who stared back. It was like they were having a silent argument.

Richard stepped closer. "Watch the door," he said flatly without breaking the gaze.

Daniel got the feeling that this was about him for some reason, and his gaze bounced between them like he was at a tennis match. Finally Terrance turned away and headed back between the tables to the front door, people stepping out of the way.

"He's not very happy," Daniel observed.

Richard shrugged. "He'll get over it." He pulled a beer and slid it in front of him. Daniel smiled and sipped from the glass. "How's Coby?"

"He wants to go back on the boat and asks about Grumpy Gerome all the time. I think he took Gerome as a challenge, and every time he got him to smile was some sort of victory for him. And it's hard to stay unhappy with Coby around." Daniel knew that well enough. His son was the light of his life.

Richard returned to work, and Daniel couldn't help following him with his gaze, especially with the way his jeans tightened around his thighs whenever he bent down. Damn, that was some view.

"Where's Alan?" a man demanded from behind him.

Richard approached from behind the bar. "In the back. Just knock and he should open the door for you." The tension in Richard's voice made Daniel turn as the Miami Vice wannabe knocked firmly on the door. It opened and he went inside, closing the door behind him.

Daniel turned to Richard, following his gaze to Terrance. The tension between the two of them seemed to skyrocket, and Daniel had no idea why.

When the man came out of the office and strode toward the front door, Daniel followed him with his eyes, because… well, those clothes. Jesus. Who dressed like that nowadays?

"What's going on?" Daniel asked when he found Richard staring after the man as well. He whirled away immediately and began washing more glasses, even though they were already clean, and he still kept half watching the man.

"Nothing."

Two men stopped the man as he was about halfway to the door. "What is this?" the Miami Vice guy asked.

"We need you to come with us," one of the others said, and suddenly all hell broke loose.

The man in pastel pulled a gun from the back of his pants. Before he could use it, the other men drew their own weapons.

"Freeze! Get down on the floor!"

Daniel slipped off the stool and lay on the floor. He had no idea what was happening and was prepared to give these people whatever they wanted. They could have his money and anything else as long as he got to stay in one piece and go home to see Coby again. He could barely move as he wondered what was going on. Cold fear slid through him, leaving his legs quivering as he wondered what was happening.

"It will be okay," Richard said from the other side of the bar, which didn't go all the way to the floor. He reached under the wood, and Daniel took his hand to try to keep himself from shaking like a leaf.

"Lie down and don't make a move," a gruff voice called. "It's okay. We need each of you to stay where you are."

Daniel chanced a look as two men escorted the man who'd come from talking to Alan out the front door. He tried not to let his fear take over, but it was nearly impossible and he squeezed Richard's hand for reassurance. The patrons began talking as soon as they were allowed up, and slowly people got to their feet as question after question built one on top of the other.

"It's all right," a policeman in uniform said. "Is anyone hurt?"

Daniel stood and looked around, with everyone doing the same. It seemed they were all right. The police cordoned everyone off and began speaking to people before letting them pay their tabs and leave.

Daniel checked the time and called Renee. "I'm running late," he told her.

She snickered. "I see."

"Not like that. There was a robbery or something and I'm waiting for the police to finish with us. I'm fine, but I have to talk to them before I can leave. Is Coby still up?"

"He's asleep on the sofa. He was determined to see you before going to bed. I left him there. You can carry him in when you get home."

"Thanks. I think I'm next." He hung up and spent a few minutes with the police. He hadn't seen anything much, and after giving his name and details, he was free to go.

"Sir, you should have a ride home if you've been drinking," one of the officers said. Even though he hadn't gotten to drink much of the second beer, he wondered if he should call Renee back.

"I'll take him home. We're closing just as soon as the police are done," Richard explained and went to answer police questions. The owner was still there. He seemed shaken up, but he sent Richard home. Daniel followed him out to the parking lot.

"What was all that about?" Daniel asked at the truck. "I didn't see him do anything."

Richard hesitated. "The police asked me about money and if I had ever been approached by him."

Daniel paused and got inside the now-familiar vehicle. Richard did the same and started the engine, letting the air conditioner run. "Do you mean like a payoff or something?" He pulled the door closed. "Or was it protection money?" He grew quiet. His father used to talk about certain types of people in town. "Dad said there were people in town who did that sort of thing."

"I'm not sure. They didn't tell me, and Alan hasn't told me what they were doing either. I hope he will eventually, but they got the guy, whatever he was doing. And maybe he'll lead them to other people if there are any. I hope that Alan is going to be okay." Richard put the truck into reverse and pulled out of the parking lot. It wasn't long before Richard parked in front of Daniel's condo.

"Do you want to come in? I can make some coffee or something. My sister is here, and I'm willing to bet that she's peeking out the windows trying to get a glimpse of you." He grinned as the curtains near the doorway fell back into place. "Are you brave enough to run the gauntlet? If not, I understand."

Richard laughed, and Daniel had no idea why. He turned to him and opened his mouth as though he were about to say something and then snapped it shut again. "Let's see." He turned off the engine and opened the truck door.

Daniel had expected him to decline, but he got out as well before leading Richard inside his apartment.

"Richard, this is my nosy sister, Renee, who has this bad habit of peeking out through the curtains." He smiled as they greeted each other and went into the living room. Coby lay on the sofa, and Daniel lifted him gently into his arms. "It's me, sweetheart. Let's get you into bed."

"Daddy," Coby said, winding his arms around Daniel's neck and settling his head on Daniel's shoulder. Daniel rubbed his back and took him to his room, changed him into his pajamas, and got him under the covers. Coby was sound asleep before Daniel kissed him on the forehead and left the room, Renee's soft laughter trailing down the hall and causing him to wonder what was going on.

"Apparently the family is fine, and the kid I rescued told me was going to learn to swim better so if they were ever on a boat that caught fire again, he could swim to shore or save his mom if she needed it." Richard sat on the sofa near Renee with a smile on his face and eyes that seemed as bright and alive as any Daniel had ever seen. They hadn't seemed to realize he was there, and Daniel took the opportunity to study Richard for a few seconds, just to commit the happy image to his mind.

"There you are," Renee said when she noticed him. "Is he asleep?"

Daniel nodded. "He barely woke up."

Renee got to her feet. "I should get home." She shook Richard's hand. "It was nice to meet you." Renee hugged Daniel and then she was gone.

"Your sister is something else," Richard said, lifting one of the mugs of coffee from the table.

"Yeah. She's the reason I have Wednesdays for dinner. She comes to spend time with Coby. Renee thinks I need to get out of the house more. Her mission in life is to make sure I don't become a hermit." He sipped the coffee that was clearly meant for him. No one else he knew took his with that much cream.

"I like her," Richard said and drank a little more.

"I think she likes you too." He wasn't there long enough to judge, but most people didn't make his sister laugh like that. Daniel drank some more of his coffee, intensely aware of how close Richard was to him.

Daniel was drawn to Richard like a moth to flame. He set down his mug, meeting Richard's gaze. He swallowed as Richard drew nearer, knowing, hoping what was to come.

The air around him grew warmer, and Richard's heady scent hung in the air. The old leather of the sofa crunched under them as they moved, and Richard's blue eyes intensified in the lamplight.

Daniel licked his lips, the taste of the coffee and cream mixing with the excitement that built from inside him. He held his breath as Richard came so close he could feel the heat of his breath on his skin. It was Daniel who closed the final distance, drawn by Richard's magnetic force, until their lips met.

Richard's lips were hot, and energy seared through him. He cupped the back of Daniel's head, carding his fingers through his hair, and then the kiss intensified, becoming deeper and more electric, threatening to overwhelm him. It had been too long since anyone had held him like this. As Richard drew nearer, pressing him back onto the cushions, Daniel went willingly.

He groaned softly against Richard's lips as his hand slid under his shirt, warmth spreading over his belly as Richard's fingers moved upward. Daniel arched his back, kissing more deeply, willing Richard to go farther. God, being touched and held felt so good. Most of the time he had to be the strong one, the person making the decisions and the one to do the comforting. It felt good to have someone taking care of him, if only for a few minutes.

"Daddy, are you playing house?" Coby held his stuffed dinosaur, Rex, under his arm.

He stilled, and Richard backed away almost instantly. Daniel scrambled to his feet. "What is it, Coby?" Daniel pulled his shirt down and went to Coby, lifting him into his arms.

"I'm firsty," he said.

Daniel took him into the kitchen, got him a drink of water, and carried him down the hall. "Do you have to potty?"

Coby nodded.

Daniel took him in the bathroom, let him use the toilet, and then carried him back to bed.

"Read to me," Coby said softly.

"How about I read to you in the morning? You go back to sleep, and tomorrow we'll go to the library and get some new books. How about that?" He smiled, and Coby nodded, already dropping off.

Daniel sighed and left the room, cracking the door open so he'd hear him if he woke up again.

"I should be going," Richard said.

"I know that Coby was a mood-killer and that a guy with a kid isn't the sexiest thing…."

Richard strode across the room and cupped Daniel's cheeks in his hot hands. "You're sexy just as you are." Then he kissed him again, pressing Daniel back against the wall. The energy in the room skyrocketed. Daniel reached for Richard to steady himself and press against his hard body.

"Richard," Daniel whimpered when he pulled back.

"I like you and I like your son. There is nothing about you that frightens me. So stop worrying about it."

"Then why didn't you call me all week?" Daniel pressed, because he was an idiot and needed to have the answer to his questions… even if it was a bad idea. He needed to learn to think before he engaged his mouth.

Richard took a deep breath. "It's complicated. God, it's so complicated, and a pain in the ass. But at the moment it isn't important. You and I can see where things go if you'd like." He leaned forward. "And I really hope that's what you want to do."

Daniel found himself nodding. "Okay." Maybe it was the stupidest decision he had ever made. He didn't know much about this man, but he was curious, and his body sure as hell wanted him. Richard was smoking hot, and he seemed nice and was willing to admit that he was wrong. That alone was a rare attribute in a guy, at least in Daniel's experience.

"I have to go." Richard breathed heavily. "It's either that or I'm going to take you down that hallway and into your bedroom, and I have a feeling that if that happens, well… I'm not going to be able to stop." He turned back to the table, picked up his mug, and accidentally knocked the stack of mail onto the floor.

Richard picked it up, and Daniel almost gasped when the initial note he'd received with Coby's picture on it fluttered separate from the others. Richard gathered up the papers and set them back on the table. "Good night," Richard said as he stacked the mail neatly and patted the stack once.

Daniel walked him to the door, looking for some sort of indication he'd seen the contents of the note. "Night."

"I'll call you tomorrow," Richard said and kissed him at the door.

Daniel opened it, and Richard stepped out into the night. Daniel watched him go before closing the door once again. Then he returned to see what the latest little missive had to say.

Chapter 7

"WHAT IN the hell do you think you're doing?" Terrance asked as soon as Richard entered his apartment. Gerome stood right behind him, glaring at him.

"I decided I was going to live my own fucking life. That's what I'm doing." He closed the door and locked it. "I get to make my own life decisions, just like you do." He stepped forward. "Remember calling your mother? You made that decision, and we all got moved and we were lucky to stay together." His heart raced. He shook with frustration. He wanted to hit something but restrained himself. That behavior needed to stay in his past if he wanted his future to be different. "Whether I like this guy or if he makes me happy isn't a majority-rules decision. It's something I get to decide for myself. And I like him. He makes me happy just being in the same room with him."

"Told you," Terrance said as he turned to Gerome.

"I don't care," Gerome pressed. "Well, I do care, because you're my brother and I want you happy. But this is going to end badly."

Richard grabbed a beer out of the refrigerator. "Probably. But it's my decision about whether I want to risk my shit on this. Not you two. I'm not telling him anything about us." He huffed. "Now, this discussion is over. I'm going to see him again, and I'm going to call him."

They hadn't seen the heartbreak in Daniel's eyes. Part of Richard wondered where this piece of him had been all these years and what the hell had happened to him ever since Daniel had walked into the bar and given him that first tentative smile.

"What about all that talk about being bad for him?" Gerome asked. "What if things fall apart and get really bad? You know that can happen. What if today we're here and tomorrow we're gone? What do you think he's going to feel? Or that little boy when you become part of his life and then all of a sudden you're gone?"

Gerome actually seemed concerned for him—for Daniel and Coby. But damn it all, Richard wanted Daniel. Maybe it was selfish, but didn't he deserve some happiness? Didn't all of them? "Does that mean that we have to shut ourselves off from everything?" Richard downed his beer. "Just back off, guys. I'm not going to put us in danger." He sat on the sofa and put his feet up on the coffee table.

"How in the hell do you know that? This isn't some kind of game. It's our lives." Gerome was being a sanctimonious pain in the ass, and Richard was pretty sure he was aware of it.

"I fucking know that. It's my life too." God, the pull of Daniel and Coby and the need to stay safe and stick to the way they had always done things warred with what he wanted, what his heart yearned for. He couldn't talk to these guys—or anyone—about the fact that he was sick and tired of being alone. Sleeping alone every night sucked. He was caught in the middle, and Terrance and Gerome weren't making it any easier. He wondered how they would feel if they had met someone who caught their interest. Richard would bet that they would be more than willing to leave the others behind to see what happened. "What about that kid who makes regular deliveries at the store?"

"Ronald?" Gerome asked.

Richard smiled a little, because he hadn't had to say anything more and Gerome knew exactly who he was talking about. "Yeah. Him. If he was interested, you're telling me that you wouldn't follow that guy around like a puppy dog? With his brown eyes and hair that flops into his face? I've seen the way you look at him, and you're saying I should stay away?"

"I have. He comes in every few days and specifically asks for me, and I'm professional and polite. Sure, the kid is hot as sin, but I haven't gone and invited him boating and tried to take him out on a date or had dinner to meet the family. He's just some guy, and the three of us are more important." He sipped his beer. "It's all a matter of priorities."

"And maybe yours are completely fucked-up. Have you thought of that?" Richard set his bottle on the coffee table. "Or maybe the three of us should just get naked and fuck each other until Terrance can't move and his ass can't stand it anymore."

Richard grinned at the way Terrance puffed. All three of them were most definitely tops, and neither of them would ever submit to any of the other three. Richard knew that instinctively. They all needed to be the one in charge in the bedroom. It came with the territory and the personality it took to do what they'd done.

"Fucker," Terrance said.

"So I take it that's a no?" Richard teased, glaring at each of them.

"It's a fucking no way in hell and you know it," Terrance growled.

Richard tuned to Gerome. "See? It isn't going to work. So you want us to be monks and shit for the rest of our lives? Are you willing to go along with that?" He knew damned well that Gerome was in no way willing to spend the rest of this life with his own hand for company. "So give it up and let me have a little peace." He knew he had won the argument. The others might bluster, but he had made his point. "Can we move on from discussing my love life to something more important?"

"Like that asshole. The cops got him. Do you think he'll talk?" Terrance asked.

"Probably. But he's small-time. There's something bigger going on." Richard leaned forward. "Someone is trying to pressure Daniel." He made sure he had the others' attention.

"Yeah? Did he tell you that?" Gerome asked, being a smartass. "Now he wants something from you."

"No, shithead. I was at his place after taking him home and a bunch of mail dropped on the floor. I saw a note with Coby's picture on it. Classic pressure for a parent. 'We want something and we'll be in touch.'

I don't know how long ago he got the note, but if you want something from someone and don't think you're going to get it, you threaten their weak spot."

Gerome and Terrance nodded. It was how the three of them had gotten what they wanted part of the time. They were damned good at eliminating anyone who might be a threat.

"There was also a blank envelope that he hadn't opened. I bet it's another note."

"So what do you want us to do?" Terrance asked. "We should stay away and not get the hell involved."

"Right. And that kid who had you both wrapped around his little finger last Sunday goes into foster care the way Gerome and I did because his dad gets pressured into doing something and gets caught, while the people behind it walk away." It was probably a low blow, but he knew his shot had hit home. As much as they might bluster, both of these guys had hearts under their rough exteriors. Richard was probably the only one who had actually seen them.

"Richard," Gerome said, "what the hell are you trying to do, turn us into a bunch of Goody Two-Shoes? This has nothing at all to do with us. We turned in the guys who were shaking Alan down because they were a threat to us. It was self-preservation, but this is more than we should do."

"So Daniel should get hung out to dry? Is that it?" Richard had had enough.

"No. He needs to handle his shit on his own, and we need to stay out of it and keep our heads down. The stuff at the bar worked out well, but we don't have a clue what's going on here. Daniel hasn't asked for our help, and you could be jumping to conclusions." Gerome retrieved a few more beers.

"Bullshit. I know what I saw, and I know what it means. The picture was of Coby, and it was probably taken right in his own backyard. That was meant to scare the shit out of Daniel."

Terrance opened his beer. "What are you going to do?"

"I don't know. But this is our territory, and we have to protect it from guys… like us." The notion hit him strongly. "We can't allow anyone to get a foothold here. If they grow powerful enough, there's the chance that connections will be made and all of us will be in danger again."

"But we don't know that this has anything to do with any of the family businesses. This note could have been sent by anyone." Gerome's eyes drifted half closed. "This could be the work of a lone criminal who sees an opportunity. Not everything is the result of the families. You know that." He tipped his beer to his lips. "But I understand, even if I don't agree with any of it. You want to help this guy because you want a piece of his ass."

Richard was out of his seat and had his hand on Gerome's chest before he could even think about it. "Don't talk about Daniel that way." He pulled back as Gerome's eyes widened, calming himself. "If you have to talk that sort of shit, then you can go back to your place and drink yourself into a stupor alone." He heaved for breath as his entire world had gone red. Slowly the color returned to normal, but it took a great deal of self-control to get that to happen. He needed to get hold of himself. Violence was part of his past, and he needed to leave it behind so he could have a better future. All of them did.

Gerome didn't turn away to rub his chest. "I see. So that's how you feel." He actually smiled. "I had to know what you felt for this person." Leave it to Gerome to play devil's advocate.

"This was some sort of test?" Richard shook his head.

Gerome shifted his gaze to Terrance. "We're all in deep trouble." He sighed. "Okay. You have to ask Daniel what's going on, and if he tells you, then we'll try to figure out a way to help him." Terrance and Gerome both nodded. "I think this is a foolish errand, but I also know that you're right about one thing. If we allow anyone associated with the families to get a foothold here, then our chances of being discovered go up dramatically. And for some reason, someone has their eye on this small section of the world. Maybe this stupid man from the club is going out on his own, but we can't take that chance."

"Okay." It was as good an answer and as much agreement as he was ever going to get. "I'll have to speak with Daniel and find out what's going on." His mind was already rolling with ways he could get Daniel to talk to him.

Terrance patted his shoulder.

"You're probably overthinking this. If you care for Daniel the way you say you do, just ask him. If he's as scared and alone as I think he probably is, then he'll be looking for someone to help him. If he feels the way you do about him, then he'll probably just tell you."

Gerome had a point, but Richard was used to finding things out on his own. In his world, information was usually a lot harder to come by than just asking a question. It took observation, logic, and intuition to figure out other people's motives and then counter them before they had a chance to act. It was one of the things Richard had become very good at. Terrance was the muscle and intimidation personified, and Gerome developed the business ideas, but Richard made things happen and had gotten the way cleared for what the three of them—and the family—wanted to do.

Richard nodded and finished the last of his drink. It had been one hell of a night and his head was swimming from the beer, the action, and what he'd found out about Daniel. There was a lot he needed to get his head around. He gathered the bottles and dropped them in the recycle bin. "I'll see you guys tomorrow." Fortunately tomorrow was Sunday and he didn't have to work, though he'd probably call Alan late in the morning to find out the latest news and see if he needed help at the bar.

The guys got up and left the apartment, and Richard sat back down, closing his eyes, taking a few minutes to try to get his head around all the changes. He was just starting to get used to the physical ones. He liked where they lived now, though it was hot, unrelentingly so, but there was no snow. And he was still with his friends… and brothers. Richard could get through anything as long as Gerome and Terrance were with him. But the idea that rocked the ground under his feet even more was Daniel. The fact that he was choosing to put him and his own love life, or the chance at one, ahead of Gerome and Terrance—that was an earthquake of epic proportions.

A knock sounded, and he went to the door. Gerome stepped inside as soon as he opened it. "None of us has ever let a guy come between us before. The three of us are brothers, and we stay together. We have to. We're all we have, all we've ever had."

"I know, and a guy isn't going to come between us. But I think we all need to have a chance at happiness, and maybe this is my chance." Richard sure as hell didn't know, but he wanted to find out. "If the positions were reversed, you'd want Terrance and me to support you." He held Gerome's gaze. "Because that's what brothers do. We support one another."

"And keep each other from making a damn fool of themselves," Gerome added sagely.

Richard shook his head. "No. Everyone makes a fool of themselves at some point or another. What brothers do is help put the pieces back together when things fall apart." And it was probably inevitable that they would.

RICHARD USUALLY loved Sunday mornings. He got to sleep in, and he didn't have to worry about work.

When he got up, he messaged Alan to see if he was up and received a response that everything was okay and that the bar was stocked and ready. He messaged Daniel and received a response that he and Coby were going to Durante Park so Coby could play. *You're welcome to come if you want.*

What time? Richard could hardly believe that his heart beat a little faster at the idea of going to a playground park.

Half hour. Meet you there? Daniel sent, and Richard agreed, figuring it was time to get dressed. The park was close enough that he could walk, and he decided that was probably best as opposed to him taking the truck the way he usually did.

Richard dressed and shaved, meeting Gerome in the hall on his way out. "Not staying in?"

"I'm meeting Daniel and Coby at the park," he told him, and Gerome smirked. "What?"

"Going to play on the monkey bars?" He laughed for a second and then grew serious. "Are you going to talk to him?"

Richard nodded. "I don't know how, though."

Gerome blew out his breath, and they stepped back into the apartment. "You're on your own with this one. I don't have any answers for you. Be as honest as you can, but stay within the cover story that was developed for us and don't deviate. From there it's up to you."

"Yeah, great. Be honest, but not too honest."

Gerome chuckled again. "Like, the life we had before moving to Iowa doesn't exist. It's like nothing happened before then. The marshals gave us backgrounds that they laid down for us, so we stick to them. And as far as any of us are concerned, those are the lives we lead. Period!"

"Act your ass off," Richard said, and Gerome nodded. He had a point. They had been acting out their own lives for months, and he needed to continue or else…. Well, he didn't want to think about that right now. Richard followed Gerome into the hallway again, heading right out and down the road toward the park.

"Mr. Richard, watch!" Coby called almost as soon as Richard was in sight of the playground. Then Coby did an almost-headstand and jumped back up with a grin on his face.

"That's great," he said with a smile and gave Coby a thumbs-up.

"He's been trying to stand on his head for a while now," Daniel said from a table in the shade. Richard joined him under the shelter. It was still warm, but much more comfortable out of the sun. "He loves the playground, and I think this is the only one on the key. His friends come here too, so sometimes he'll stay here all day if I let him." Daniel smiled, but the tension behind his eyes didn't dissipate the way Richard would have expected at a time like this.

"I bet." Richard leaned across the scarred picnic table. "What do you do for fun?" He grinned. "What sort of adult things does Daddy like to do when Coby isn't around or when he's with your sister? I know you come to the bar, but what else do you like?"

Daniel sighed. "In college I was in this computer club. We used to play games and have so much fun back then. Now I spend my computer time on much more productive things."

"What sort of games?" Richard asked. Not that he would know what any of them were. His time had been spent trying to survive, and while Daniel was in school, he had been either fighting on the streets or trying to work his way up in the family and become invaluable to them.

"Well…." He hesitated and looked down at the table. "We used to develop them ourselves." Daniel picked up a cooler and placed it on the table. "Coby, do you want a juice box?" he called, and Coby ran over.

"Grape?" he asked. Daniel gave him a box with the straw in it, partially holding it until Coby had drunk some.

"Finish it up and then you can go back and play." Daniel made sure Coby drank everything and then sprayed his arms, legs, and neck with sunscreen before letting him go.

"You were saying," Richard said as Coby raced back toward the other kids in the play area.

"Yeah...." He groaned. "We used to challenge each other. It was all a game of sorts. We had to see who could break into the most secure computer system. I never did anything bad when I got in other than leave a marker to prove to the guys that I was there. A few times the systems were so easy that I left messages to tell them that they needed to beef up their security."

"I see." Richard couldn't help smiling. It seemed Daniel had a bit of a shady past. In a roundabout way, that made him feel a little better. "Who won?"

Daniel blushed. "I did. Once I was able to get into one of the DOD systems. I left them a message and said that I didn't touch anything but that they needed to close a particular hole in their systems. I won the game, but that one made the news a few months later once it was fixed." He grinned. "It was just a game to me, nothing more, and we all stopped after the news broke. I was able to cover my trail pretty well, but if we had kept it up, we would have been traced." He twisted a napkin that he'd gotten out when he'd grabbed Coby's drink box, little shreds of it falling on the tabletop. "That was something I left behind a long time ago." He swallowed hard.

"All right...," Richard said gently, his mind already rushing ahead. "Did anyone besides the guys in school know about this little game you all played?"

Daniel shrugged. "I don't think so. It was some time... a whole lifetime ago. I have Coby and a career now. I do really good work, and people trust me with sensitive information. I'm always careful, and I haven't broken into a system in years." He scratched the back of his head lightly and rubbed his hand behind his neck.

"I don't do that anymore." His hand shook a little. "I think Coby and I should go home now." He hurriedly put his things in the cooler, shaking as he closed it, and got up, stumbling a little toward where Coby was playing.

"Daniel…," Richard said without raising his voice.

"I have to go home." He looked around as though he expected someone to jump out of the bushes at any second. "What is it you want?" Daniel asked. "I just want to be left alone and to live my life." He hurried away and got Coby, lifting the fussing four-year-old into his arms and hurrying toward the car. Richard slowly followed him. "Just leave me alone and tell whoever you're working with to leave me the hell alone."

"I don't know what you're talking about," Richard said. Then he realized Daniel thought that he was involved in whatever had him so spooked. "I'm honestly not sure what's been happening and why you're upset." He touched Daniel's shoulder as he leaned over to put Coby in his car seat. "Whatever is happening, I promise you that I'm not part of it."

Daniel straightened up and looked all around again. "I'm sorry, but I can't be sure of anything." The fear in his eyes went right to Richard's core. "And the two of us need to get home."

Richard stepped closer, and Daniel put his arms in front of his chest as if protecting himself. Richard stopped. "I'm not going to hurt you, and I have no idea what's going on, but something has you scared half to death." He continued speaking as gently as he could. "Do you want to tell me about it?"

Daniel shook his head. "I want this to go away and to be left alone." He closed the door and stayed in front of it. "I have to keep Coby safe. That's all that matters."

He sighed. "Maybe I should just leave and go somewhere else. If I get out of town and try to hide, maybe they won't be able to find us." He shook like a palm frond in a gale.

"Okay. Let's get you home, and you can get Coby playing and then tell me what's going on. You're terrified, and I can't help if I don't know what's happening."

Daniel paused. "I don't think you can help me. No one can. They… I don't even know who they are, and I'm so scared that I try to keep Coby inside the house all the time. He's climbing the walls because he needs to run and get some exercise, and instead I'm trying to turn the condo into a fortress." He stepped back and motioned to the door. "You may as well get in." He went around to the other side, and Richard got into the passenger side for the quick ride back to Daniel's condo.

Daniel got out and looked all around before helping Coby out of his seat. He took his hand, led him to the door, and unlocked it. Daniel was so tentative, and he checked inside before actually going in. Richard knew the signs of terror. He'd inflicted that terror on others often enough. He followed them inside, and Daniel checked the mailbox and locked the door after.

"I know I'm being watched sometimes. They always leave the notes for me when I can't see them." He pulled out three envelopes and handed them over.

The first one was the note Richard had already seen. The second was another picture of Coby with Daniel in the park they had just left. *We'll be in touch soon. Tell no one. We can get to you and your kid any time*, it read.

"Jesus." Richard swore under his breath. "Is this the last one?"

"Yeah. It came yesterday." Daniel clutched Coby to him until he squirmed to get down on the floor. Daniel let him as Richard unfolded the paper.

The picture was Daniel and Coby in the backyard with a bullseye drawn around Coby. Richard turned to the glass doors. Holy hell, these people were fucking close. That was the point—make the mark as frightened as possible so that he would do whatever they wanted. Wear him down so he would think of nothing else, including who might be behind this. The implication was crystal clear.

Just so you understand what we can do at any time. He turned the sheet over, but that was all there was.

"Do you have any idea who might be behind this or what they want?" Richard asked.

"All I can think of is that someone somehow found out about my hacking skills and they want me to do something for them. I don't know what. This is all I've gotten, and I'm scared half to death. I thought of taking Coby to my parents'. They have security around the house. But then if they did get him, I...." He gasped and went into the kitchen to get a drink. "I don't know what the hell to do."

The truth was that Richard didn't either. In Detroit he'd have had the resources to find out what was going on and put an end to it. The family had their ears to the ground, and he would talk to a few people who would talk to others. A picture of what they wanted would emerge, and Richard and the guys would put a stop to it.

"Neither do I," Richard admitted. He found it a terrible position to be in. He was used to knowing how to handle most situations, but this left him stumped. "Why don't we sit down?"

Daniel nodded and they went into the living room. Richard carried the notes along with him and sat down to examine them. They were rather crude and the printed images grainy, as if they were done on an older printer. Still, they got their meaning across. "I wish I knew what it was that they wanted. That would give us a clue as to their motives." He swallowed.

"Let's try to start at the beginning. I know your family lives here, so you grew up in this area," Richard said, and Daniel nodded. "I'm going to rule out that your family is behind this because that would be too sick for words. Where did you go to college?"

"University of Florida. I had wanted to go there ever since I was a little kid, and my dad was so proud of me. He wanted me to follow in his footsteps, and he saw that as my first step. Dad was interested in finance and banking, and he started out after college with a small local bank, First Florida. At least that's their name now. He rose quickly and was promoted to the head of the bank ten years ago."

"They're huge," Richard said, remembering seeing their signs everywhere.

"That's because of Dad. He had a vision and made it come true. They're one of the biggest banks in the state. I think Dad has national aspirations." He paused. "Anyway, I guess the disappointments started when I went into computer science instead of what he wanted. And of course I turned out to be gay, and Dad wasn't too thrilled with either of those things." Daniel spoke softly as Coby ran his cars up and down the hallway. He seemed out of earshot, but Richard figured Daniel wasn't going to let him out of his sight.

"So this group of hackers you knew, would they have told someone about you?" Richard asked.

Daniel shrugged. "It was five years ago. I have no idea."

"What about any neighbors? Friends? It's sometimes the people closest to us who can have an ulterior motive," Richard asked, and a cold chill crept up his spine.

"There's Brad. He lives in the complex, and we're friends, but not super close. Though I can't really see him as the kind of guy to do this." Though he sure as hell wasn't an expert. "I hate the idea that someone I know could be behind this."

"What would Brad want you to hack?"

"His car. He's always locking his keys in it." There was no way Brad could be part of this. At least he hoped to hell not. His hands still shook. "They haven't asked for anything yet."

Richard stood and pulled a cold water out of the cooler and handed it to Daniel. "True. But judging from the note, it's a pretty good bet they aren't asking you to design a website. I suspect they might want you to break into a system somewhere." He turned to Daniel, thinking. "Could you develop one of those computer viruses? Maybe they want something to infect computers." He was thinking out loud, but Daniel only seemed to grow more nervous.

"I never tried. I did build certain programs to help me break into the various systems and exploit their weaknesses." Richard had no idea how that sort of thing worked, and he leaned forward, slightly intrigued. "Okay. Let's say you want to break into a retailer's systems. They have a number of connections that they maintain and probably an internal network, so if you can get into the network, then you can get access to things from the inside. One of the ways to do that might be by picking a small local store and gaining access through them. Now if they're smart, they have their networks partitioned off, so access to one section doesn't gain access to all. But there has to be a gateway where the pieces talk to one another, or they can't retrieve their own information. Basically, you work your way through the network somehow, or just walk away."

"But then you lose the game," Richard supplied.

Daniel nodded. "The point is that I had software that helped me map things once I got inside so I could get the lay of the land, so to speak, as well as other utilities that I developed." He drank from the water and hung his head. "I never thought I would be doing this sort of thing again. I gave it up years ago and left it behind. I have a life now and a son; that's more important than any game."

Richard narrowed his gaze. "It was a game to you, but it wasn't to anyone else. I know you didn't do any harm." He held Daniel's gaze. "You don't have that in you."

Daniel shook his head. "I like to think I helped more than anything else. I never damaged anything or took information, though I could have."

"Did someone rat you out, do you think?" Richard asked.

Daniel shrugged. "I don't know. I mean, it was years ago. Maybe someone who knew of what we were doing talked to someone else. I have no idea." He finished his water and stood to pace the room. "I never thought that after all this time what I did would come back to haunt me. I stopped before I graduated and hung up my hacker hat. I threw all my energy into my studies and never looked back." He sat back down.

"Okay." Richard took Daniel's hand. "I think the first step is to make sure that you and Coby are safe. Then we probably need to wait to see what it is they want." He tried to think of what he could do to help. Judging by the tone of the notes and the way the threats had intensified, they were probably getting ready to break the news. At that point Daniel would be scared enough to do whatever they wanted.

"I've been trying. But they keep sending me those notes, and I watch everyone around us. They got close enough to take the pictures in my own yard and at the playground. What if they decide they want to take him? I might not see it coming, and how can I protect him from that?" Daniel grew more agitated.

Richard could easily see the aims of the people behind this. He had been there more than once in his nefarious career. But he was hesitant to say anything in case he gave away too much. "If they want you to do something for them, then taking Coby would probably be a step too far. You see it on television, but what parent isn't going to call the police if their child is taken? That's the last thing they want, I would think." He wanted to tread lightly. "My guess is that they want you scared so you will do what they ask."

"Great. So I should just wait and see what they want? It could be days. I can't think of anything else. I tried to work, but I can't concentrate. Coby wanted to go to the park, and all I wanted to do was keep him inside. What if they did something to him while he was playing?"

"Too many other people," Richard said. "There were plenty of parents there, and some of them knew you and Coby, correct?"

"Yeah. I see the same parents and kids when we go there. That's part of why Coby likes it so much. He gets to play with his friends."

"So they are going to notice someone who tries to take Coby, and there would be plenty of witnesses." He paused, and Daniel seemed to understand what he was driving at.

"What do I do?" Daniel asked.

Richard slid closer to Daniel and put an arm around his shoulder. "It seems to me the best thing is to keep your head, think, and watch around you. They'll let you know what they want, and then we can figure out what to do about it."

"We?" Daniel asked. "You'll help me? I don't know the first thing about what I should do. I thought of calling the police, but at first it seemed ridiculous. I thought that maybe someone was playing a joke on me, but with the last note, I…."

"Yeah. Try to relax and keep your head about you. You could go to the police, but who knows how they'll react?" Richard had to think about that. Maybe telling the police was the proper course of action. It went against his instincts because in his old life, no matter what, you didn't go to the police to solve your problems. You took care of things yourself. But things were different now. *This* was different. They weren't in Detroit, where he had the resources of the family to draw on.

"I know. They could hurt Coby just to get back at me, and then what?" Daniel asked.

"Daddy, I want a drink," Coby said, hurrying over and practically bouncing off the sofa before climbing up. "Apple juice."

"Okay." Daniel got up and went to the kitchen before returning with a sippy cup. He handed it to Coby and sat back down. Coby drank his juice like he was desert thirsty, handed Daniel the cup, and bounded away. Richard tugged Daniel to him once again.

"We'll figure this out," Richard said.

Daniel shook his head, blinking up at him. "I can't believe all of this. First I expected you to run for the hills when you found out about Coby, and now you know the mess I've got myself in and you aren't running for the hills. What the heck is wrong with you?" He smirked. "Any sane person would be out that door and never look back. Either that or they'd tell me to call the police and all I would see would be taillights."

Richard had thought about that, but.... "I don't have an answer for you. Maybe I am crazy." He used a single finger to turn Daniel toward him, then captured his lips in a soft kiss. "Or maybe I like you and I don't want to see you hurt." Richard smiled to himself when he realized the answer was just that simple.

"You kissed Daddy," Coby said, standing in front of him. Richard wondered what he should say.

"Yes, he did," Daniel agreed.

Coby watched both of them for a few seconds. "Okay." He turned and went back to playing with his blocks.

Richard tugged Daniel to him once again, holding him tightly. He needed to figure out what was going on if he was to protect both of them. But he also had to do things so no one paid attention to him or suspected he was involved. It might be best if he and the guys stayed away from Daniel. God, this could quickly turn into a huge mess. If Daniel was being watched, then someone was going to notice the time he and Richard spent together, and they were going to wonder who he was. Things could go downhill fast. Not that there was a fucking thing he could do about it now. The only good thing was that they were a thousand miles from Detroit, and whatever was going down probably had nothing to do with anyone connected with the families. At least that was Richard's hope.

"You seem a million miles away," Daniel commented.

Richard smiled and decided to distract him, kissing Daniel until they were both breathless. It had the effect he wanted, as well as the additional result that if he didn't stop right away, he wasn't going to be able to. Richard wanted Daniel in the worst way. His heart beat in his ears, and his entire body felt as tight as a bowstring. Daniel's scent and the way his big eyes silently pleaded nearly snapped Richard's control, but he sat back up and pulled away.

"Do you and Coby want to come over to my place for a while? Terrance and Grumpy Gerome will be there part of the day too." Richard knew their presence would intimidate just about anyone, even if they were only seen coming and going. "Coby can bring his blocks if he wants."

"Are you sure?" Daniel asked.

"You can't stay in here all the time. We can get some lunch."

"But if I'm being watched?" Daniel asked.

Richard nodded. "I hope so. Let them know that you aren't alone. Maybe they'll think twice before they take the next step." He didn't think that was likely, but it would send a message. Richard only hoped that it didn't raise a million red flags for him and the guys. "Get your things and we'll go."

Daniel got up and gathered a bag. He also checked the cooler and refilled it with drinks. Then he and Coby got in the car, and Daniel followed Richard's directions to his place.

"This is nice," Daniel said when he stepped inside.

Richard laughed and had to swallow the joke about the furniture coming from the government warehouse of dull and uninteresting. "It was furnished. I'm hoping to find a better place eventually, but for now this serves my needs." He closed the door and turned on the television, finding a channel with cartoons. Coby sat on the floor, enraptured, and Richard started on a light lunch. He wasn't sure what Coby would eat, but he figured crackers, some fruit, and maybe a little cheese would be good.

"This whole thing has me so on edge all the time," Daniel admitted as he stood at the snack bar that separated the kitchen from the rest of the place.

Richard worked on the other side, putting the finger food on the counter. This seemed so domestic, which was both strange and comforting. Richard was never domestic in Detroit. He went out to eat and never had anyone to his place except the guys. His world there had been very controlled. This was a big step for him.

"I understand. But if you want to unravel who is doing this and figure out a way to stop them eventually, then you need to keep your head and try to think one step ahead." He set down the plate of cheese and some strawberries.

"How do you know all this?" Daniel asked. "Are you a cop or something?" He stepped back. "Have I confessed and now you're going to take me away? I should have kept my mouth shut." The nervousness was back big-time.

"No. I'm not a cop, and you're fine." Richard need-ed to play off the way he knew what to do. He didn't want Daniel suspicious. "I just understand people and things, I guess." He finished getting things together and called over to Terrance's and Gerome's. Terrance ap-parently had to work, but Gerome came over. Coby hid behind the curtains as soon as he arrived.

"Go find him," Daniel said, and Gerome made monster noises while Coby giggled. It was so cute to see a former gangster playing like that. Once Coby had been "found," Gerome brought him back to the table while Coby pretended to be an airplane.

"Terrance is working today," Gerome said. "He said he gets off at five or so. He'll come over then." He took a seat, and Coby climbed up next to him, grinning at Gerome.

"You not grumpy today," Coby said with addition-al giggles as he reached for the cheese. He popped a tiny piece into his mouth, still giggling.

"Do you laugh all the time?" Gerome asked.

Coby nodded as he continued chewing. He ate just a little before returning to the television.

Daniel picked at his food and excused himself to use the bathroom.

"Did he tell you what was going on?" Gerome asked as soon as Daniel left.

Richard nodded. "Yeah. Someone is threatening him through Coby, and he's about to freak out com-pletely. I didn't bring the notes, but they don't tell us anything about who's sending them."

"Do you know what they want?" Gerome asked.

"Not yet. They haven't told him, but I have my suspicions." He raised his eyebrows. "Let's just say that Daniel has a bit of a past and though he's sweet, he has more in common with us than I ever thought."

Gerome's eyebrows rose almost to his hairline.

Daniel returned and sat back down to eat a few bits of cheese. "Did Richard tell you what's going on?"

Gerome nodded. "A little. And I take it you guys came here so that if he's being watched, he'll be seen with us?" he said, and Richard nodded. "A little reverse intimidation. I like it."

"But what do I do next?" Daniel asked.

"Nothing. You wait for them to come to you and find out what they want. Don't give them any reason to doubt that you're scared as hell and will do whatever they want. From there, we can figure out what our next move will be."

Daniel sighed. "Why are you both doing this?"

Gerome answered before Richard could chime in. "Because Richard cares for you, and I want him to be happy." Gerome's gaze held so much more meaning than just what he was saying. He might be telling Daniel the right thing, but Richard knew there was a lot more than simply words. "We aren't brothers by the same mother, but we will do whatever we can for each other."

Daniel sniffed. "What in the hell did I do to deserve this kind of support? My mom and dad don't help me like this, and here you guys are, watching my back, and I barely know you—any of you."

Richard and Gerome shared a moment, and then Gerome stood. "Coby, do you want to see my apartment? We can play hide and seek there."

Coby jumped to his feet and followed Gerome out the door.

"They're just across the hall," Richard said to make sure Daniel knew where his son was and to try to keep him calm.

Daniel nodded as though he were in a daze. "I don't understand anything right now. I've worked so hard to build a life for Coby and me, and now it seems like it's all falling to pieces."

Richard certainly understood that. "I don't have any advice for you other than to be strong and see where this is leading. We can determine a way out once we know a little more."

"But why are you even getting involved?"

Richard slid his hand around the back of Daniel's neck, pulling him close until their lips came together once again. And this time Richard deepened the kiss, reveling in the taste of the cheese mixed with the sweetness of Daniel's firm but soft lips.

"I want you, Daniel," Richard whispered when they broke apart. "And I think you're special." The more he learned about him, the more Daniel intrigued him.

"Is this about a roll in the hay?" Daniel asked. "Is that all you're interested in? I can't do that. My life is more than just my own. I have Coby to think about, and he already likes you and the guys. I can't have some fling. When you and the guys disappear, Coby will get hurt."

Richard was so close to Daniel he could count each delicate eyelash. "I don't want a fling. I've had plenty of those." He wanted something more, something special. Richard slipped off the stool, bringing Daniel slowly along with him. He didn't touch him, but let his gaze draw Daniel. It was amazingly simple and attractive that he needed nothing more than a look to communicate what he wanted. He sat on the sofa, and as soon as Daniel did the same, he brought him into his arms and held him close. "I know what it feels like to have the life you know fall to pieces." As soon as the words crossed his lips, he knew he should have said nothing.

"But...."

"I've wanted this since the first night you walked into the bar." Richard slid his hands under Daniel's shirt, sliding them up along his side and then over his chest. Without thinking, he lifted Daniel's shirt, baring his golden skin to his eyes. Richard leaned forward, bringing his lips in contact with the expanse of perfection.

"Richard.... Richie... I...." Daniel's stammering was gorgeous. Richard was well aware that he didn't have time to do more than a little tasting and touching, but he would take whatever he could get of this incredible man who made his heart race with just a single look. When Richard lifted his gaze, Daniel's eyes smoldered with banked passion. Richard swirled his tongue around a small pert nipple, and Daniel gasped.

Richard backed away. He had to get his head about him. Coby and Gerome were across the hall, but he had no idea how long they were going to be gone, and Richard wasn't going to allow their first time to be on the damned ugly sofa in his living room. Still, Daniel's excitement was obvious, and he stroked the tips of his fingers down Daniel's belly to a soft moan that wound around Richard's own desire like moth to flame. It would be so easy to slip off his clothes and feast his eyes, tongue, and lips on that skin. He wanted to taste Daniel in every way, feel him inside and out.

He closed his eyes, willing some control over the desire that pounded through him. Daniel drew him like no one else he had ever met, and fuck it all, he wanted him, to hold, to protect… to love.

The last word entered his mind with a bang, and it took Richard by complete surprise. He backed away as the full implications of what he felt washed over him. Richard let his fingers trail off Daniel's skin. He sat up and helped Daniel to do the same. His head spun, and he wasn't sure what he was going to do.

"What happened? You were… and then you stopped." Daniel blinked at him.

Richard leaned in to kiss him. The same energy coursed through Richard as before. Just looking at Daniel made him hard as a rock. He wanted him. There was no doubt of that. But falling in love with Daniel—or anyone—would come with a price that could be way too high, because not only was it his to pay, but potentially Terrance's and Gerome's as well. The path he found himself on was fraught with danger, and yet he didn't want to change or alter that path. Richard wanted it badly.

"Because we can't do this now," Richard whispered. "And I won't have our first time be fumbling on the sofa." He leaned closer, pressing Daniel back onto the cushions. "I want to spend all night getting to know you, every inch of you." He kissed him gently. "In a bed with soft sheets, plush pillows, and a closed and locked door to keep out everyone and everything." He smiled and received one in return, wiping Daniel's hair out of his eyes. "You deserve that, and I want it as well. Not rushing, no interruptions—" As if on cue, a voice and giggles drifted in from the hall. Richard groaned softly as he sat back up and helped Daniel, letting him adjust his clothes. They finished as Coby raced into the apartment.

"I finded him! I'm a good finder." Coby raced over to Daniel and jumped up next to him on the sofa. He settled right away, returning his attention to the television, which Richard had forgotten was on. Eventually Coby slid onto the floor, his attention glued to the screen.

Richard asked if anyone wanted anything to drink, and Gerome grabbed a beer before settling in one of the chairs. "I never thought I'd spend an afternoon watching cartoons." Richard wasn't sure if he was complaining.

"Neither did I, originally," Daniel said with a chuckle.

"If you don't mind my asking, how did you end up with Coby?" Gerome asked. "I know you didn't get pregnant."

"No. That was Maureen." Daniel leaned against Richard and relaxed a little. "It was an experiment, mixing alcohol and a girl, neither of which worked out. But I was lucky. She gave me Coby." He sighed. "I was so young back then. At least it felt that way. We had Coby when I was twenty-three. I was just out of college and trying to figure out what I was going to do with my life. Where did you go to school?"

"College?" Gerome asked. "Richard and I never went. After high school, he and I went to work. It was how things were for us." There was a sadness there that Richard had never seen before. "But we've done okay."

"Yeah, we have," Richard echoed.

"Daddy is very smart. He says that I'm gonna be smart just like him." Coby climbed back on the sofa, sitting next to Daniel to watch his show. For a second, if Richard let his mind go, he could picture them as a family. Not that he knew much of what regular families were like or how they acted. He'd never had one.

"I hope so," Richard said and slowly stood. He needed some distance. He went to the kitchen to clean up from their lunch and take care of the dishes.

"What's going on?" Gerome asked quietly when he joined him. "You were out of there like a shot."

Richard didn't want to talk about it. "I just need to clean up. It's Florida, and I don't want bugs." He put everything away and made sure all the food was sealed. Then he wiped down the counter as though it were the bar at work. Daniel watched him, a puzzled expression coloring his features.

"What you need is to get your head on straight. You're acting like you're playing volleyball and can't figure out which team you're on. Get your head where it belongs and make up your mind," Gerome hissed. "Terrance and I are behind you no matter what. We always have been, and we're not going to be dicks about whatever you choose. Not really."

Richard paused midwipe. "Why?"

"Because you were fucking right. Don't make me say it again or I'll punch you in the gut." His stony glare grew warmer. "Whatever you decide, just don't fuck it up." Gerome winked and tossed his empty into the recycling.

"Thanks for the help," Richard smartassed. He knew better than to make a big deal of the fact that Gerome had said he was right. That was something he would probably never hear again as long as he lived.

"I need to go to the store and get some things. It's my one day off, and then I have to work most of the week. I'll see you later." Gerome said goodbye and left the apartment after ruffling Coby's hair.

After Gerome left, Richard wasn't sure what to do. It seemed strange to just sit and watch television all day, but Coby appeared content, nestling right next to him and falling asleep. "He goes and goes until… boom," Daniel said. "I can take him home if you like."

"No. He's fine." Richard was surprised at how much he liked the fact that Coby trusted him enough to just fall to sleep next to him. "Should we be talking?"

"It's fine as long as we're quiet." Daniel took his hand. "And he must think quite a bit of you for him to do that."

"He's a great little boy." Richard tried to remember other interactions he'd had with kids and couldn't—not since he was one. "I…." He swallowed. He wasn't convinced that he was good for this little family, but it seemed that for now they needed him, and he wasn't going to turn his back on Daniel. If someone was pressuring him into something, Richard would do his best to stop it and keep Daniel and Coby safe.

At least that instinct he understood. Richard had stood in the line of fire for Terrance and Gerome on multiple occasions… and they had for him as well.

"This has to be very strange for you. I somehow don't see you as the parental type," Daniel said. "Not that you aren't great with Coby. It's just that guys like you… hot, well, smoking hot…" Daniel blushed. "… don't usually go for guys like me with a kid."

"What kind of guys have you dated?" Richard was curious. Daniel wasn't wrong. Richard had never seen himself as a parent, yet here he was with a four-year-old sleeping peacefully against him, and he wasn't running for the hills.

"Mostly self-absorbed losers. Let me see." Daniel leaned against him. "Cory was my first and the reason for the falling-out with my parents. What a mistake he was. There was James, maybe a year ago. I had exactly three days with him. The first two were very nice, and the third was really special. He looked at me like I was the center of the world, and then when I brought him home and he saw Coby, he looked almost exactly the same way you did that first time. But he never returned my calls, and I didn't talk to him again. The only communication was a text. I still have it in my phone somewhere. And basically he said he wasn't ready for a family." Daniel shrugged. "I wouldn't give up Coby for anything."

"And you shouldn't." Richard said the words without thinking. All those years in foster care, basically on the outside looking in, had left him wondering what it would be like to have a family of his own. He had Terrance and Gerome, and he was certain he always would. Their bonds and experiences had long ago melded them together closer than any blood could possibly be. "Not for this James guy… not for anyone." Richard found himself putting an arm around Coby as if to shield him from some imagined threat.

"That never entered my mind." Daniel smiled. "I remember being in the delivery room with Maureen. She wasn't sure she wanted me there at first, but as soon as labor started, I was there for her. I'll never forget the first time I got to hold him. Coby was wrapped in a receiving blanket, and I took off my shirt, holding him to my skin." Daniel sniffed. "I never in my life thought I could feel like that. He was my son. Maureen told me that in that moment, she knew that I would never give him up. And I didn't." He wiped his eyes. "It was a spur-of-the-moment thing. After that I had about two days to get everything ready for him to come home with me. I bought a crib and stuff. Renee and one of her friends who had a three-year-old helped me out. We got all the things he was going to need and made up the second room in the condo for him." Daniel sighed, still smiling. "It was the busiest and happiest time of my life. If I wasn't at the hospital with Coby, I was getting things for him to come home and helping Renee, who took charge of things for me. After that, my life changed forever. My grandfather left me a trust fund. It isn't huge, but it's enough to cover the mortgage and car payments." Daniel's smile faded and darkness filled his brown eyes until they were almost black. "I can't let anything happen to him. I just can't." He buried his face against Richard's shoulder. "I need him as much as I need to breathe. He's my world, and I will do anything to keep him safe."

"I know," Richard said automatically. He really didn't know that kind of love. He had never experienced it for himself, and yet he craved it. He was a little jealous of Coby, because he had it already and it was something Richard had never known. "Well, I can understand how you feel."

"You never had a family," Daniel said.

"Just the guys. They're all I've ever had." He tried not to think too much about his feelings on this. Richard had long ago figured things out, and there was no use dwelling on what he didn't have and probably never would. This was an interlude, and he needed to face it. Sooner or later reality would rear its ugly head and he'd be back to what he'd always had and nothing more.

Chapter 8

COBY'S NAP ended almost as quickly as it had started, and then he was off again. Daniel worried that it was going to be too much for Richard, but the big guy spent part of the afternoon on the floor with Coby, playing with cars and blocks.

Daniel was still trying to figure Richard out, and so far he was having one hell of a time getting a read on him. Richard seemed to understand about the notes and was nice enough when Daniel had freaked and thought that Richard might have sent them. That had been the stupidest conclusion he'd ever jumped to. And now he was playing with Coby, which was fucking adorable, especially after Coby knocked down Richard's tower for the tenth time, giggling like an idiot.

"Maybe we should go on home and leave you alone," Daniel offered.

Coby looked up, his lower lip already quivering, and damned if Richard didn't have a touch of that puppy-dog look too.

"We can order some pizza or something. Terrance and Gerome will probably be over, and we can make a night of it." He was already up, grabbing a couple of takeout menus and handing them to him. Daniel took them. "We can order from wherever you like."

"Or we could cook," Daniel offered. He and Coby didn't eat out much. It was a luxury they couldn't often afford, and he wanted Coby to eat better than fried food.

"If you want to," Richard agreed and motioned to the kitchen. "I'm not sure what I have for a serious dinner. Mostly I have stuff for snacking and things. I eat at the bar a lot."

Daniel went to see what he had and pulled out some pasta. He found some canned tomatoes and garlic and spices in a prepackaged rack in one of the cupboards. Richard also had some frozen hamburger that he pulled out to thaw. "What do you think of spaghetti? Coby loves it, and I can make something simple for him and a really good sauce for us." Daniel even managed to find an onion and got chopping.

"Daddy, I crying," Coby said.

Daniel got a tissue and wiped Coby's eyes. "I know. It's the onions. They make me cry too, but that will go away pretty soon." He got them in a pan with some butter and started cooking. Coby and Richard continued running cars around the floor as Gerome and Terrance joined them. Daniel greeted both of them, and they peered over his shoulder.

"Dang, you can cook? Do you want to be my boyfriend?" Terrance asked after inhaling the scent, and then turned to Richard. "Do you want us to stay?"

"Of course," Daniel answered. "I'm making enough for an army." He loved to cook. There was something rewarding and kind of soothing about putting ingredients together and having them come out just right. Of course, the opposite was also true, and when things didn't turn out, he usually got upset for a couple of reasons, the biggest being that he didn't have the resources to remake whatever he had screwed up.

Once the onions and garlic were set, Daniel started browning off the ground beef and added the tomatoes and other spices to the pan, turning down the heat to let it simmer and flavor through.

"Oh wow," Terrance hummed as he hung around the kitchen. "That smells so good."

Richard came up right behind him, sliding his arms around Daniel's waist. "Now that's something incredible."

"I usually add just a pinch of pepper flakes to the sauce to give it a slight hint of heat, but that's too much for Coby, so I didn't this time." Actually, he half expected Coby to just want his "sketti" with butter.

Terrance left the room, and Richard tugged Daniel closer. "This was very nice of you to do. The guys and I don't get much home cooking, so it's kind of special."

Daniel turned in Richard's arms, only to be drawn even closer.

"Get a room," Gerome teased from the living area, and damned if Richard didn't flash him a stone-cold look before returning his gaze to Daniel. That look softened and warmed immediately. God, Daniel loved that

Richard actually looked at him like he was the center of the world, even if it was only for a few seconds.

Daniel knew there was some conflict behind those eyes—he saw it and thought it had to do with Gerome and Terrance. That was part of the reason he was cooking for them. Daniel wanted Richard's friends, the guys he called brothers, to like him. Maybe then some of that worry would dissipate. Not that he didn't have his own worries. There were plenty of those. The damned letters weighed on his mind almost constantly, and he feared what the people who sent them thought he could do. Richard himself was a source of wonder and worry as well. Daniel knew almost nothing about him, and what he did know was vague. Richard was so reluctant to talk about himself, and Daniel was worried about how Coby—and himself—would feel when whatever was going on between them ended. Daniel had little doubt that it would. Hell, his own parents didn't want him in their lives, so what the hell, why would someone like Richard? Still, Richard hadn't run for the hills when he met Coby, and he'd offered to help with the notes. There were times when—

"The sauce is spattering," Richard said softly, pulling Daniel's thoughts back to the present. He stirred and turned it down even further. The last thing he wanted was to burn it.

"Sorry, I was a little distracted." He covered his preoccupation and gave Richard a gentle kiss before slipping out of his arms and returning his attention to the food. He drained the meat and added it to the sauce, letting the entire mixture cook some more while he threw together a salad from what Richard had on hand and what Terrance brought over from his place.

The water for the pasta was already on and hot, so he turned up the flame, got the water boiling, and added the entire box of spaghetti, hoping it would be enough for these guys. Daniel suspected that they ate quite a bit, but it was all there was, so it was going to have to do.

"Do you need us to set the table?" Gerome asked, and he bustled past where Daniel and Richard stood and got things out to set up the table. It seemed they were hungry.

By the time Terrance and Gerome were done, Daniel tested the pasta, then turned off the heat, drained it, and returned the cooked pasta to the pot.

"Coby, do you want butter or sauce?" Daniel asked.

Coby came in, and Daniel lifted him so he could see. "Sauce," Coby pronounced, and Daniel groaned a little. He wasn't going to tell him no, but there was going to be a mess.

"Don't worry," Richard said and pulled open one of the drawers. "Coby, how about some special spaghetti-eating clothes?" Richard got an old T-shirt out of one of the drawers and put it on Coby. Then he tied a knot behind his waist to bring it higher. It looked like Coby was wrapped in a white cylinder. "You're the chef today. Okay?"

"I the chef," Coby said, and Richard zoomed him into the other room to giggles as Daniel finished putting the dinner together.

"Yes, you are. You're your daddy's little chef, and someday you're going to learn to cook just like he does." Richard got him into a seat, and Daniel brought over his bowl of cut-up spaghetti with a little sauce on it. Coby dug in.

"Is it good?"

"Yummy, Daddy," Coby said and continued eating as though he were starved.

Daniel smiled and brought the big bowl of sauced pasta to the table.

Terrance brought the salad, and they all sat down. At first there wasn't much conversation as the guys inhaled their food. Daniel chuckled to himself. They must have been hungry, and they sure seemed to like his cooking.

"I guess it's okay," Daniel said.

Terrance lifted his gaze, and there were tears at the edge of the huge man's eyes. Daniel wondered what the hell he had done wrong.

"This is as good as my mama's." He lowered his gaze once again and returned to his dinner.

"She was the only real 'mother' any of us had. Gerome and I had foster parents for a while, but Josie was our mom, and she could cook like nobody's business." Richard grew quiet, and Daniel realized that once more, Richard had reached the limit of what he would talk about. There was no way Daniel could press him in front of his friends, who all seemed to understand that limit as well. It was like being left out in the cold once again.

"I love Italian food. I have my version of a carbonara, pesto, Amatriciana, Bolognese, and a few others. I don't really care for Alfredo sauce, though. It's too heavy and Coby doesn't like it, but I make incredible lasagna, and Coby loves that."

"Big noodles," Coby said as he spooned in some more of his pasta. Daniel was grateful that Richard had the T-shirt; otherwise the sauce would have been all over Coby's clothes. As it was, the shirt was covered in a tomatoey mess.

It didn't take long before the pasta and salad were completely gone. Terrance and Gerome cleared the table, and Richard, bless his heart, took Coby into the bathroom to wash up. When he came out, there hadn't been any screaming, which was a miracle. Daniel wanted to ask how that had been accomplished, but he didn't have to. "I washed my own face," Coby said with a smile. There were still touches of sauce around his lips, but he was mostly clean, and that was what mattered—spaghetti sauce wouldn't end up all over everything.

"Thank you for dinner," Terrance said as he and Gerome left the kitchen. "It was very good." He actually shook Daniel's hand. "And it tasted a lot like my mom's." He left the apartment without another word, and Daniel swallowed hard and turned to Richard for guidance. Clearly there was still some residual grief there.

"Yes, thank you," Gerome said, and then he turned to Richard and spoke softly before he left as well.

Coby played on the floor, and Daniel finished up in the kitchen while Richard used the bathroom. When Daniel finished, he looked in on Coby as music began to play from the television. It was slow and soft. Richard set the remote aside and moved close, holding out his hand. He didn't say anything but took Daniel in his arms and slowly danced with him in the living room. Daniel rested his head on Richard's shoulder, loving the sensation of just being held.

"Where did you learn to dance?" Daniel asked.

"Terrance's mom. She taught all of us," Richard answered and spun him once.

Daniel laughed and held tighter, closing his eyes. "Renee taught me. That was before… well, before I told her… but she said that girls like a guy who could dance, and she was going to make sure I didn't move like some chicken in heat." Daniel smiled as Richard chuckled.

"I've seen plenty of guys like that," Richard said.

Daniel hummed, not asking about it as he stored away the detail. Not that it meant anything really, but it was something he didn't know before. Richard held him closer. The song ended and another began. Richard didn't stop moving, swaying him gently to the lyric tones.

Daniel looked down when Coby tugged on his pant leg. "You wanna dance too?" Daniel asked, and Richard stepped back, lifting Coby into his arms. Coby put his head on Richard's shoulder, and Daniel took the other one. Richard continued dancing, and for a while Daniel could imagine they were happy and that his little family was more than just Coby and him.

"COBY NEEDS to go to bed or else he's going to get cranky as anything," Daniel said a few hours later. Coby had crawled onto his lap as they watched television. "I should get him home."

"I want to check your place over before you go inside," Richard said, and Daniel agreed. He got Coby into the car and buckled into his car seat. Richard followed him home and got out of his truck. He got Daniel's keys and checked out the front before unlocking the door. He went inside and came back out a few minutes later, motioning for him to come in. "I don't see anything, and there's no sign of another note."

He held the door, and Daniel brought Coby inside. "If you want something to drink, help yourself. I'll get him to bed and be right out."

Daniel took Coby to his room and got him into his pajamas. Then he helped him wash up and brush his teeth. He figured Coby could have a bath in the morning.

Coby went right to sleep, and Daniel kissed him good night, closing the door most of the way on his way out. He joined Richard in the living room, where he stood and tugged Daniel into his arms, kissing him hard.

Instantly Daniel was carried away on a crest of heat and passion that brushed aside all his caution and reasoning. He had wanted Richard for a long time. His hands worked at the hem of Richard's shirt, tugging it up and off in a matter of seconds.

God, Richard was stunning, with all that muscle and power, and under Daniel's hands, it only became hotter. He drew nearer, running his hands over Richard's belly and then his sides before clinging to him while Richard kissed him within an inch of his life.

Daniel's senses went nuts. In the quiet of the room, their kisses felt so loud, the blood rushing in Daniel's ears. He held on to Richard because at any second he wondered if his knees were going to give out on him.

It wouldn't have mattered. Richard nearly lifted him off his feet, guiding him down the hallway to Daniel's bedroom. "I want you to be mine," Richard said.

Daniel nodded as he lay back on the bed, arms stretching over his head. Richard could have whatever he wanted. The possessiveness in Richard's voice intrigued him. No, it did more than that—it turned him on. Daniel had always felt like the guy nobody wanted. He wasn't popular in school. Even though his father had money and Daniel had been able to afford the trappings of popularity, they hadn't worked for him. In college he had taken refuge among the super nerds, and he had fit in there. Heck, to most people, he wasn't even a good gay guy, with Coby and all. So to have Richard's gaze burning into him, the scent of desire filling the room, musky and rich, followed by the growl from deep in Richard's throat, sent Daniel's control racing for refuge in some faraway corner as he let himself surrender.

"I want that too," he managed to say, but it took a huge amount of energy because his voice didn't want to work.

Only one thing did at this point. The blood had all rushed away from his head and had pooled in his groin, which throbbed and ached until he could barely stand it. Richard tugged at Daniel's clothes, stripping him physically as well as spiritually, baring Daniel to him. It was so intimate, so close, it was nearly frightening. He reflexively wanted to cover himself, just for a moment's respite from the intensity. But Richard didn't let him, taking Daniel's hands in his, drawing nearer.

"It's not fair." Daniel was naked and completely vulnerable under Richard's gaze.

Richard must have agreed, because he slipped off the bed. Richard's shoes thunked to the floor, and he unfastened his pants. They dropped as well. Then the last of his clothes followed and Richard stood naked next to Daniel's bed. Jesus, the man was a sight—narrow hips, broad shoulders, a dusting of light red across his pecs. Richard raised a leg and climbed on the bed. Daniel smiled and then snorted.

"Do you have a thing for socks?" Daniel asked when he noticed that Richard was still wearing his.

"They're my lucky socks," Richard told him, and Daniel rolled his eyes. "We're about to get lucky, and damned if I'm not going to wear the same pair every time I see you."

"So, they're new lucky socks," Daniel teased.

"Yup. New today," Richard said softly and covered Daniel's body with his, skin to skin, warmth and warmth. Their lips met, and Daniel forgot all about socks, lucky or otherwise. "I've wondered what you would feel like under me for weeks now," he whispered. "Sometimes at the bar, I'd forget what I was supposed to be doing just because you were sitting close to me." Richard took his lips, kissing him hard, his tongue pressing for entrance. Daniel parted his lips and Richard feasted on him, carrying Daniel away on wings of passion. The energy only built on itself, filling Daniel nearly to the point of bursting. To be wanted this way with such intensity and impatience was almost too much.

"And I used to wonder if this could ever be possible," Daniel whispered. He hugged Richard closer, their bodies melding together in a quivering mass of heat. Outside, the temperature grew by the day, but that was nothing compared to the volcanic heat in this room at this moment.

"What do you like?" Richard asked, and it took Daniel a second to understand what he wanted.

Daniel shrugged and turned away.

"How can you not know?"

Daniel cleared his throat. "Because…." He shrugged again. It was hard to put into words. "I guess they were selfish. None of them ever asked, and…."

"They did what they liked?" Richard drew even closer. "Well, that stops. Sex, passion, and tenderness are a two-way street. They're about both of us, not just me or you." He backed away and then gently raised Daniel's hands over his head, holding them in one of his. "I need you to stay just like that. Can you? Whatever happens, just keep your hands right there."

Daniel nodded, and Richard kissed him again, then backed away.

Richard's hands slipped away, and Daniel kept his where Richard instructed. He met his gaze, wondering what was on his mind behind those blue eyes with flecks of purple. When Richard came closer, Daniel closed his eyes, ready to be kissed, but instead he arched upward as Richard kissed down the base of his neck and along his shoulder. He moaned softly, and Richard teased the skin some more. "Sensitive?" he crooned, and Daniel whimpered an affirmative.

It was so tempting to reach for Richard. Daniel had to stop himself more than once as Richard explored his body. Nothing seemed off-limits, and Daniel's eyes damned near permanently crossed. Every fiber in his being wanted Richard to go further, to just take him. But Richard didn't even touch his cock. He touched everything else, gently, erotically, driving Daniel out of his mind as every cell in his body willed him to lunge forward and take what he wanted. "Richard, what are you doing to me?"

"Making you want," Richard answered. "Making you understand just what it is that you like. You said you didn't know before. Do you now?"

"I think I'm getting there." One of the things he knew he liked was Richard's touch. When his hands roved across his skin, Daniel loved it, and when they stopped, he felt the loss as an ache. Richard was like the best drug on the planet, and Daniel was already addicted. He didn't want a cure, just more and more until he was up to his neck. Daniel groaned softly and finally broke, pulled Richard down to him, taking charge of his own pleasure and what he wanted.

"That's it. Take what you want."

"Is that what you were doing?" Daniel asked, and Richard nodded. "You wanted me to take charge?"

"I wanted you to decide what it was that you needed. Did you want me to be in charge, or were you going to take charge?" Why Daniel thought he might have passed some sort of test, he wasn't sure, but Richard's smile lit the room.

"But what is it you want?" Daniel asked, throwing Richard's words back at him.

Richard kissed him lightly. "I want someone who is going to give as good as he gets. I've had guys who wanted me to be in charge all the time, and that was fine, but I think what I really want is an equal." He flashed a smile.

"Good." Daniel rolled them on the bed until Richard ended up beneath him. "Because I don't intend to lie still and just let things happen." He held Richard's shoulders. "I did that for a very long time, and it got me nowhere. My family mostly turned their back on me, and I ended up alone." He took a deep breath. "I don't want to be that person anymore."

Richard humphed. "Then don't." It seemed like such an easy answer, but maybe Richard was right. Maybe you became the person you wanted to be just by deciding to. And Daniel wanted to be someone Richard would find interesting—someone who would hold his attention. The only problem was, he wasn't sure what that was going to be. "Be the person you want to be, not the one to make me or anyone else happy."

It was like Richard was reading his mind. Daniel wanted to ask how he did that, but there wasn't an easy answer, not to that, or, it seemed, anything else in his life.

Daniel nodded and then leaned forward, sucking at the base of Richard's neck just like Richard had done to him, tasting the light saltiness of his skin. Richard tasted good, and Daniel let his hands roam in the low light, feeling his way over the planes of muscle. Richard was sexy as hell, and even if Daniel couldn't see much, what passed under his hands told him plenty and only whetted his appetite. "It's been a long time."

"Then we'll take things slow," Richard whispered, and a quiver ran through him. Daniel loved that he could make Richard react that way.

Richard slid his hands down Daniel's back and then over his butt, gripping his cheeks and holding them closer as their hips met. Energy and intensity built, adding friction. Richard was the hottest guy Daniel had ever met, and everything seemed bigger, better, more important at this moment. It was like everything they did mattered to each other, but maybe even on a more important scale. Daniel didn't understand it, and he didn't have the energy or the brain power to right now. All he knew was that he wanted Richard, and for the time being at least, he had him right in his bed.

Daniel slowly rocked back and forth until Richard's breathing changed, becoming more ragged and shallower until neither of them could hold back any longer. Daniel tried to be as quiet as he could, but even then, the joy was too much. He held Richard through his release, which seemed to send Richard into his own.

The walls might have fallen down around them and Daniel would not have noticed for hours. He was happy and content with Richard's arms around him. Once his heart slowed to normal and his body decided it would work again, he slipped off the bed and went to the bathroom. He cleaned himself up and brought a towel back for Richard. "Do you want to stay?"

Richard handed him back the towel and tugged Daniel back onto the bed. The terry cloth fell to the floor, and Daniel left it there. "I'd love to." Daniel yawned, and Richard rolled over, tugging Daniel back until his butt and back rested against Richard.

It took him a while to fall to sleep. There were so many things on his mind that it didn't seem to want to turn off. Daniel sighed and wished he could let himself believe that things could truly work out this well. But he had lived enough and knew enough about his own luck to be well aware of how quickly things could change.

Chapter 9

RICHARD BLINKED as he tried to get his mind off Daniel and the night they'd spent together, but it was nearly impossible. He was supposed to keep his attention on the patrons and the bar.

Just as he forced his attention where it belonged, his phone vibrated in his pocket. Richard pulled it out and answered the blocked number. "This is Richard," he said gently, looking up and down the bar before excusing himself and heading toward the restroom.

"Just listen," Elizabeth said. "The man was apprehended on Saturday; I'm sure you know that. He was part of a small group who had decided the area was ripe for picking. They don't seem to be aligned with anyone, and the police force there is working the other agencies to ensure this issue is mopped up properly." She cleared her throat. "Thank you, and don't make a habit of it."

"You're welcome… and you never know." He thought of telling her about what was going on with Daniel, but he didn't want to have to explain their relationship to her.

"For now we have no concerns, but be careful and remember the rules." She ended the call, and Richard deleted the call history on his phone before returning to the bar. That was one bit of good news, but a worse one followed right behind in the form of a text from Daniel. It seemed he had gotten another note. Daniel sent him an image, and Richard called to say that he would be over as soon as he was done with his shift. Fortunately they closed at eleven on Mondays, so he wouldn't be too late.

"Keep everything, including the windows, locked and Coby inside. I can see if Gerome or Terrance can come over if you like," he offered and checked the time once again.

"I have the house all closed up, and I'm not going to let anyone in." He seemed very shaken up. "This message is more detailed. They don't tell me exactly what the target is, but I know what they want." He breathed deeply. "I'll see you tonight."

"I'll call Terrance. He's working at the hardware store, but I can ask him to stop on his way home."

Daniel sighed. "No. It's fine. I'll call if anything happens, but for now I think we're okay. Coby is watching cartoons, and I'll give him a bath and put him to bed."

Richard pulled a beer as he talked with a Bluetooth headpiece. "Call if you hear anything."

Daniel promised. Richard had to go back to work. He said goodbye and placed his phone in his pocket, then spent the next few hours trying not to worry his head off.

"What's wrong with you?" Terrance asked when he came in, leaning over the bar. "You look like you're a million miles away. Get your head in the game. It's times like this when shit happens."

"Tell me about it," Richard told him and passed Terrance a beer since he wasn't on the clock. "I'll be just fine. Daniel is having an issue, and I need to see him after work."

Terrance nodded and half chugged the beer before wiping his lips on the back of his hand. "Of course you do."

"What does that mean?" Richard hissed softly.

"Just be careful. I don't know about you, but I don't want to move again and end up separated from you, my family. With my luck they'd put me someplace cold again, like Helena or Boise, and I don't want to be cold. I'm just getting used to the heat." He glared. "I'm with you, but you gotta be careful because this is about all of us." He pulled away from the bar and half stomped out the door.

Richard wanted to go after him and give him a piece of his mind. He was allowed to have a life of his own, dammit. Still, it was hard to argue with Terrance's point, and Richard didn't have an answer to his question, not right now. But he probably needed to figure his shit out.

Alan patted him on the shoulder, and Richard moved forward to let the older man pass behind him. "You seem happy," Richard said, noticing that some of the wrinkles from around his eyes had disappeared.

"It's a good day," Alan said as he waited on a patron.

For the rest of the evening, the two of them worked together in companionship until it was time to close. Richard handed Alan the cash drawers and finished closing and stocking the bar area. He couldn't do it fast enough. Once he was done, Richard bade Alan good night and they left together, locking up.

"Next month I have to take a trip north for my great-nephew's baptism. Would you be able to manage the bar while I'm gone?" Alan asked. He seemed a little tentative as they spoke in the parking lot. "I'll make sure you have enough help. I haven't seen them in a while, and I'd really like to go."

Richard nodded. "Alan, I've got your back. When you want to go, have fun and don't worry about a thing." He'd make damn sure everything ran as smooth as clockwork. Alan deserved a vacation, and Richard owed Alan for his trust, which he had every intention of holding on to tightly.

"Thanks."

"I won't betray your faith in me," Richard told him.

Alan patted his shoulder. "I know." Then he turned toward his car. Richard watched him leave, smiling as he got into his truck and headed for Daniel's.

He parked next to Daniel's car, got out, and knocked on the door. "It's me," he said when he heard footsteps on the other side of the door. The lock clicked and Daniel opened the door. Richard went inside, and Daniel locked the door behind him. "Has it been quiet?"

"Yes. No one has tried to contact me further." He went to the counter and handed Richard the note.

We have a job for you, and your college skills will be put to good use. It would be a shame if any harm were to come to you or your son if you were to contact the police or refuse to help us. We will be in contact soon with the details of what we require, and we will make your work well worth your while. And you may even find it very satisfying. There were more pictures of Coby, and Richard's gut twisted.

"They want you to hack into something?"

Daniel nodded. "That makes sense to me, but I think I know what it is they want me to do." He was pale.

Richard set the page down and hugged him.

"I think they want me to hack into my father's bank. They say that I will find it satisfying. I think they think that I would like to get even with my dad for something." Daniel shook in his arms. Richard hoped to hell that he was wrong, but it made sense. Daniel could hack a system; Richard had no reason to doubt him. It also made sense, especially if they thought Daniel might have some sort of inside information on the systems at his father's bank.

"God," Richard groaned, wondering what he could do to help. "Do you really think you can do that? I would think that banking systems would be hard as hell to hack."

"They are. Most banks have people like me on staff, hackers protecting their systems. People who think like me to help stop other people like me. I can probably hack their system, but I don't want to do that any longer. But I can't put Coby in danger for anything. He's my son, and I can't let anything happen to him." Daniel buried his face in Richard's shirt. "I don't know what to do."

Richard didn't either, but that didn't mean that ideas weren't already spinning through his head. "First thing, they are trying to keep you off-balance until they're ready for you. They obviously have some sort of plan." Richard gently stroked Daniel's soft hair. He understood what fear could do. Richard had used it more than once in his previous life, and he had seen how he could wield it to get people to do what he wanted. But in some ways, he could have taken lessons from these people. They knew exactly what Daniel's weaknesses were, and they exploited them to the point that this wonderful, strong, and kind man in his arms was reduced to tears and shaking with abject fear.

That really pissed him off. "Do you really think you could hack into those banking systems?" Daniel sniffed and stiffened. "Not that I want you to. But could you, without getting caught?" The last thing he wanted was for Daniel to get pressured into something and then be the one dangling at the end of the rope. That was most likely these people's game. If things went right, they'd get away with their ill-gotten gains, and if things blew up, everything would lead to Daniel and he'd be the one in jail… and Coby would find himself without a father. Richard's hands clenched into fists at that thought.

"Yeah, I could probably do it. I'd have to study the systems they want me to hack." He lifted his gaze. "But there have been a lot of advances in technological security in the past five years, so I'd need to get myself up to speed on all of them." He sniffed. "The thing no one understands is that hackers are on the cutting edge. We attack first, and then security professionals react to us. They make advances, and we out-advance them. So most of my skills are outdated, and the things I used to do won't work any longer." He sighed.

"Okay. But the basic skills are the same," Richard said, even as Daniel shook his head.

"They're not. We used to develop password gen-
erators that would try every combination to find the
right one. Now systems lock after so many unsuccess-
ful tries and you have to reset through a process. That
was in response to us and those programs. It's been five
years… so in reality, I don't know if I can do it. And
this isn't one of those *Oceans* movies where realities
are ignored because they're inconvenient to the plot."
He groaned. "I don't fucking know what I'm going to
do." He buried his face once again, and Richard hugged
him, getting angrier by the second at these people for
the anguish they were inflicting on Daniel.

He was also mad at himself. There should be a
way he could protect Daniel. Back in Detroit, he would
have put the word out and made sure that one or two
people felt the physical pain of his displeasure. That
would have sent a message to everyone that Daniel was
not to be messed with. Here, he had no such authority.
Sure, he could have Terrance hurt someone, if he fucking knew who was behind this, but that would expose
all of them, and then they'd be whisked the fuck away
one more time.

"You should go to bed and try to get some sleep,"
Richard whispered. There was nothing they could do
tonight, and he needed a chance to think. Feeling this
damned helpless really sucked, and he itched to take
some sort of action. It felt like he had his legs cut out
from under him. He wanted to help—that was one of
the hallmarks of the family and the way business was
done. He helped others, and then they owed him a fa-
vor—one that he would collect when it was advanta-
geous to him. But this situation stank, and he wanted
the whole thing to go away just as badly as Daniel did.

"I don't think I can," Daniel said. "I keep jumping at every sound. And what if someone tries to get in here to send another message?"

"It's okay. I'm not going anywhere. You go get ready for bed, and I'll make a check around the condo in case someone is out there." He didn't think that was the case, but if it made Daniel feel better….

He went out the back and checked around. There was no one about, and the sea breeze rustled the foliage. He checked for shadows that didn't move and then checked out front. There was no one in the bushes or lingering out by the street. Not that he expected anything. These guys thought they had Daniel where they wanted him. Maybe that wasn't such a bad thing.

He went back inside and relocked the doors. He found Daniel in his room, half burrowed under the covers and shaking. Richard pulled off his clothes and got in bed along with him, holding Daniel tight. He wished he could provide real relief from the threat, but he would have to settle for comfort.

He gently rubbed Daniel's back as his mind raced. He was beginning to understand how hard it was to do nothing.

"How am I going to come out of this in one piece?" Daniel asked.

Richard wished he had an answer. "With these assholes, this isn't about you at all. It's all about them and what they want. They don't really care what happens to you." Protecting Daniel was becoming his job, and Richard would happily do it for the rest of his life. He tugged Daniel closer. "Just try to go to sleep, and we'll figure it out. Nothing is going to happen until they approach you with the specifics of what they want. This is all just the warm-up to make sure you'll be so relieved when they actually talk to you that you'll do what they want."

Daniel rolled over. "How do you know all that? I mean, you talk about this stuff like you're some kind of expert. You seem so damned confident."

Richard pursed his lips. "It's just common sense," he answered while silently berating himself. He needed to be more careful, but he wasn't going to let Daniel suffer either, if he could help it. "I think I used to watch too much television or something." He needed to pass it off, but the more time he spent with Daniel, the more wrong it felt to keep his real past from him. Not that he had much choice. If he told Daniel his history, he'd be putting all of them in danger.

In the past he would have had no problem lying to protect himself or the family. He always did what he said he was going to do. But to outsiders or marks, manipulation and obfuscation were facts of life. Surprisingly, he hated not telling Daniel the truth. Daniel deserved to know the person in his life… in Coby's life. But what if he didn't want someone like Richard in their lives once he found out about his past?

Richard sighed. When in the hell had he developed a fucking conscience? "Just try to rest. You won't be able to think clearly if you're tired." He rubbed Daniel's belly and wondered if there was a way he and the guys could intimidate these people once they knew who they were. He wished he had the contacts here that he'd had in Detroit. Nothing would have been able to escape them there. This stank big-time.

DANIEL EVENTUALLY fell asleep in his arms, though Richard stayed awake for much of the rest of the night, listening and running things through his mind. But for all that effort, he came up with nothing. He only wanted to beat the shit out of these guys.

Eventually he fell asleep, only waking when he felt Daniel getting out of bed. "You rest if you want. I can hear Coby, and I need to get him up and dressed." Daniel kissed him on the cheek, and Richard burrowed under the covers in the cool, air-conditioned room and went back to sleep.

A ringing phone woke him later, and he got out of bed, dressed, and followed the sound to where Daniel sat on the sofa, with Coby playing on the floor. He smiled and lifted his gaze back to Daniel only to pause. Daniel was pale and his hand shook, the phone bouncing against his ear. It didn't take much to deduce who was on the other end of the call. Without saying anything, he sat next to Daniel.

"You will gather four million into an account number that will be texted to you, and then you will transfer the money. Details will be sent separately." The voice was male and deep, kind of sinister. "It's that simple. You do what we want and you'll never hear from us again. But if you fail… let's just say that there are plenty of ways that we can make you pay, and we'll start with your son. Make no mistake, we get what we want."

"But… the bank systems have a ton of checks and balances. It's not going to allow me to do all that," Daniel said. "Even if I had master access, it isn't going to allow it."

"That's your problem. Unless you want a demonstration of what we can do?"

The threat left Richard chilled, and he understood what these assholes were doing. Everything they said was designed to unnerve Daniel, and it was working.

"Maybe your boyfriend will get a visitor some night…."

"That isn't necessary," Daniel said, his hand shaking even more. Richard took his other hand and entwined their fingers to let him know that he was there.

"We'll be in touch." The call ended, and Daniel practically dropped his phone.

"What am I going to do?" Daniel asked. "I can't do what they want." He got to his feet and went down the hall. Richard followed and reached the bedroom as Daniel began pulling suitcases from under the bed. "I don't have a choice, Richard. I can't do this. They want me to break into my father's banking systems and transfer money to an offshore account. There are so many safeguards against that kind of activity that it will send up alarms not only at the bank, but with the Federal Reserve." He sighed. "My dad talked about banking and its systems every damned night as I was growing up. I know all this shit. Some of these systems were put in place to stop the exact things they want me to do."

"Okay." He put his hand on Daniel's to stop him before helping him to his feet. "Think about what you're doing. You aren't going to get away."

Daniel set the suitcase down. "But he threatened you. How can you think so clearly and be so fucking reasonable?"

"Daddy, bad word," Coby said as he wrapped his arms around Daniel's leg.

Daniel lifted him up. "I know. I'm sorry." He held Coby close, and Richard left the two of them alone for a second while he retrieved Daniel's phone. He smiled as he brought it to him.

"Look. They blocked their number on the call but not on the text." Fucking amateurs. "Can you trace that number and see where it came from? It's probably a disposable phone, but maybe we'll get lucky." If they made one mistake, maybe they'd have made another. He showed Daniel the number, and his eyes widened. "Do you think you can trace the number back?"

"I can try," Daniel said and set Coby on his feet. He took a deep breath. "It's probably a dead end."

"But what if it isn't?" Richard offered as he took Coby's hand. "What do you want for breakfast? Daddy has something he needs to do, so let's us make something, okay? You can help."

"I a good helper," Coby said, skipping along happily down the hall.

Daniel went to his bank of computers and started working, typing quickly while Richard messaged Gerome.

"It's a Miami area code," Daniel said as he continued working and typing. "This used to be so easy, but now everyone wants to sell you this kind of information, so you have to pay for it, and even then, it isn't always accurate." He continued working as Richard opened the refrigerator door.

"Grapes," Coby said, pointing. Richard got them out. He got a bowl as well and set Coby to work picking the grapes off the stems. Then he got out some eggs and bread, figuring scrambled eggs and toast would work. He wasn't much of a cook, but he could manage something as simple as that.

Richard's phone vibrated, and he answered Gerome's call.

"What's up?"

"It's not good. They contacted Daniel this morning and told him what they want. I think they made a mistake, and we're seeing if we can exploit it. But I think this is bad, and I don't know what to do. Things are different here. It's like my hands are tied behind my back."

"You want Terrance and me to come over?"

"No. I'll be back in an hour or so. Can you have Terrance watch the place here as best he can?" He knew he had scant resources and that he had to use them wisely. He talked as he cracked the eggs and got them mixed.

"I'm not sure getting involved is a good thing," Gerome began. "But if you're asking for help, I won't turn my back." He sighed. "I sure hope this guy is worth the risk."

Richard turned away. "You met him and Coby. Why don't you tell me?"

Gerome sighed again. Richard smiled, knowing he had won.

"Okay. You got it. We can talk when you get here. I have to be to work at noon, so get here before then if we're going to hash this out." He paused, and Richard lowered two pieces of bread into the toaster. "I wish we had the resources we had… before. This isn't going to be very easy."

"Got it," Daniel said from his computer, and Richard looked over with a grin. "Harry Jensen. The area code is from Miami, but it seems the bills are being sent to a Tampa address." He smiled, and Richard wondered how he got that information and then decided that maybe Daniel's skills weren't as rusty as he'd thought they might be.

"I done," Coby said.

Richard finished with the eggs and brought his makeshift breakfast to the table. Coby took his seat and began eating once his eggs were cool enough, though he seemed to stuff himself with the grapes.

"I make grapes," Coby said as he reached for some more from the bowl.

"Have another bite or two of eggs first," Daniel told him and moved the bowl away.

Coby pouted but took a couple more bites of egg.

Daniel added a few more grapes to his plate. At least Daniel didn't seem quite as upset as he had been earlier. "What do we do?"

"We finish breakfast," Richard said as a plan formed in his mind. "We'll make a few phone calls after we eat." He ate his toast and a few grapes along with his eggs. Once he was done, he took his dishes to the sink and then waited while the others finished.

Daniel washed up Coby, who then scooted to the floor to play, and Richard motioned Daniel to the sofa. Then he had him unlock his phone to get the number. He called the number on a burner phone, which he kept as a precaution, and held it so both of them could hear. "Hello," Richard said in a fake voice. "I'm looking for Harry Jensen."

"This is he. What do you want?" The man was growly.

"I'm David with National Consumer Research, and your name was selected at random. Do you have two minutes to take a survey on toothpaste and mouthwash?" Richard had to keep from laughing.

"No. I'm busy." He hung up, and Richard ended the call.

"Was that the guy who called you?" Richard asked, and Daniel nodded. "Then we have a phone number and a name. Go ahead and find out anything you can about him. Let's see what this guy is up to and who we're dealing with. We may find something that we can use." He sat back, and Daniel kissed him before jumping off the sofa to his computer. He worked furiously, and Richard shifted to the floor to play with Coby and his Legos.

"I don't know how much of this is relevant," Daniel said.

"Just gather what you can," Richard told him after he and Coby built a multicolored house. "I need to get home, but you and Coby can come with me if you like." He hated the thought of leaving them alone.

"I should stay here. I'll have a lot better luck with my computers and internet connection than I will at your place." He turned, biting his lower lip. "Will you be back?"

"Yeah. I have to go in to work this afternoon, but I'll be back in a few hours. You call right away if anyone contacts you or you see anything suspicious. Don't open the door for anyone, and if someone calls, agree to what they want and don't let on that we may know one of the people involved." He was pretty sure there were others behind this.

"Okay." He chewed on his lower lip, and Richard leaned over where he sat and shared a kiss that grew heated very quickly. "We can't," Daniel whispered.

"I know. I'll be back as soon as I can. Call me or the police if anything happens, and yell at the top of your lungs. I don't care what it is. 'Fire' works. People respond to that, and if there is anyone home around you, they will hurry to see what's happening." Richard kissed him again and hurried out and to his truck, keeping his phone close as he drove home.

TERRANCE RETURNED with him to Daniel's that afternoon once he was done with his shift at the store. "So you tracked one of them down?" Terrance asked. "That's good. You want me to find out where he lives and take him out? There are alligators down here. No one is ever going to find the body." He was dead serious.

"We'll keep that in reserve."

Terrance rubbed his hands together. "Come on. It would be fun, and if one of their ranks just vanished, it would put the fear of God into the rest of them and they would go to ground like rats."

"Yeah, and it would lead them to us, and who knows who else would follow?" It was tempting, though. Terrance was probably right—taking out this Jensen guy would scare everyone else, and he was pretty sure that Terrance could find a remote swampy area to dump the body. With all the creatures out there, it wasn't likely to be found. "Remember, we're supposed to be law-abiding citizens now."

"Fuck that. When someone messes with us, they deserve to feel the full force of our wrath. I'm tired of hiding out here like some scared little mouse. We're top-line predators, not food."

Richard wondered where that analogy had come from. "What have you been watching on television?" Their conversation drew off as Richard parked outside Daniel's condo. They got out, and Richard knocked as Coby's face appeared in the glass for just a second. Then the door opened and Daniel let them inside.

"It's been quiet and I've been busy," Daniel reported, leading them to his computer. "I found out quite a bit on this Harry Jensen. He lives in Tampa at the moment. Moved there from Miami about six months ago. He has connections down there, but it's hard to figure out how strong they are. His Facebook is bland, with little info, but I looked at some of his friends. He has a brother who has a LinkedIn page." Daniel smiled. "Mark Jensen works at my dad's bank. He's an assistant branch manager." He continued typing.

"And I bet he isn't willing to put in the work needed to rise through the ranks, so he's decided to jumpstart his prospects. Once this little game comes to an end, he gives his notice and is on his way," Richard said to Terrance.

"You think he's behind this?" Daniel asked. "I could call my dad and tell him what's going on." He paused and turned back to his computer.

"Would he believe you?" Richard asked.

Daniel shrugged. "I don't know. But I suppose if I did, my dad would have to deal with him, and who knows how fast that would get back to the others, and then…." He shivered, and Richard knew he was thinking of those threatening notes. "We have to be careful. Telling my dad would only show our hand."

Richard agreed with him. "Have you found out anything else?"

"There are other friends and associates of both of them, but I don't know who might be involved. And maybe Mark isn't involved and his brother just got this brilliant idea to rob a bank."

Terrance leaned closer. "How would these guys know about you?"

It was such a simple, perfect question. "Yes, how would they? Are there any connections between them and the guys in the hacking club in college? The blackmailers had to have heard about you from somewhere, and they are the most likely candidates. I bet someone talked to one of them or knows someone. Can you check their Facebook friends or LinkedIn contacts?" Richard offered.

Daniel nodded. "It's going to take a while." But he was already working away. "I don't get why one of the other guys in the group would need me."

"It's your dad's bank. Maybe they think you have a way in," Richard offered as Daniel continued working.

Richard stepped back, not wanting to look over Daniel's shoulder. Terrance sat on the sofa and turned on the television. Coby climbed up as well, and they ended up watching cartoons together. Coby definitely had his friends wrapped around his little finger.

Daniel, on the other hand, had Richard wrapped around his. Richard leaned against the snack bar, watching Daniel as he worked. He probably should have been getting ready for work, but it was nearly impossible to look away. Daniel was beautiful, with his dark hair and slim build, and Richard didn't have to look at his face to know how intently he was working. He approached and placed a hand on his shoulder for a second before leaving him alone. There was nothing he could do to help right now. Daniel was the internet and electronic systems expert, and Richard needed to let him do his thing.

"I'm going to need to go to work pretty soon," he told Terrance.

"I'm not on the schedule for tonight," Terrance said, and Richard nodded. "I'll stay for a while and watch things here. Don't worry about anything."

"Thanks. Just keep them safe, and we'll somehow figure things out." First they needed to gather as much information as they could. They knew one person who was definitely involved and had some ideas on who the others might be, but the picture wasn't complete.

The more they knew, the better their position was going to be.

"I will," Terrance said. "You go on to work." He smiled, and Richard returned to Daniel, kissed him once again, and then headed off to work.

ALL NIGHT he worried. The bar was busy, and yet somehow he managed to keep the patrons happy and not to spill drinks all over everything. His mind was elsewhere, though, and he wished to hell he could make this whole threat to Daniel and Coby go away. It would be so very easy for him to return to form—find out who these people were and make them disappear. He had done that sort of thing before, and he could do it again. In fact, it was so tempting to give Terrance free rein and let him just take out this Harry guy, scare the shit out of everyone else, and have it done. At least it sounded easy on the surface, but Richard knew it was impossible.

That part of his life was over, and he needed to remember that. In Detroit he had always done what was needed in order for his little family to survive and prosper. But just like his position in Detroit and in the family, that was gone. It was hard for him to accept completely. That way of life had been so much a part of who he was that when he was under stress, those old habits and behavior patterns surfaced. Maybe that was why those who failed in the program were discovered. They were unable to leave that life behind. The old temptations became too great, especially when he was revved up, and Richard was sure as hell stressed right now.

He made a round of the patrons at the bar and filled the server orders even as he mulled what their next steps might be. Richard was fairly sure these people had no idea who he was other than Daniel's boyfriend, and that could work to their advantage. But he needed to be careful, because if he gave away too much, Daniel might become suspicious. It was simply a matter of threading the needle so everyone remained in the dark about who was behind the events that unfolded.

The problem that kept coming up was that the more he got to know Daniel, the more he hated keeping secrets. That scared the shit out of him. Richard's life had always been about secrets and knowing more than everyone else. Knowledge could be the difference between life and death. The only reason he, Gerome, and Terrance were here was because he had found out one piece of information that led him to the understanding of what Junior was planning. A whisper overheard by one of his bartenders and passed on to him had set all the events rolling forward, and him on a path to Longboat Key and ultimately Daniel.

"Richard," Alan said as he passed behind him, and Richard pulled his mind out of his thoughts and back to the present. "What has you so preoccupied?"

Richard shrugged, finished pulling the beer, and got the orders at the bar up to date once again.

"You aren't usually like this. Is there something wrong?" Alan wiped his hand on one of the bar towels.

"No, I'm fine. Just a little preoccupied I guess." He turned to the older man. "Things are just very different here than I'm used to, and I'm trying to figure things out." It seemed a little roundabout, but Alan seemed to understand.

"One thing I know is that life is about change." He patted Richard on the shoulder. "I've owned this bar for the past ten years, and before that I worked on a fishing boat. I've raised three kids and had two wives. Change happens, sometimes whether we want it or not." Alan smiled and began mixing a margarita. "But there is one thing that I know. All that change and everything that I did combined to make me the person I am today… and I like him." Alan nodded. "This place is nice, and I have good people in my life. I can't ask for more than that." He patted Richard on the shoulder once more.

He liked that Alan thought he was good, and he smiled to himself as he filled more drink orders from the servers. It took a while for the deeper meaning in Alan's words to sink in. Everything that had happened to him, *good and bad*, made him the person he was today as well. Richard wasn't sure if he was happy with that person, but he hoped he was getting there.

Daniel made him happy and intrigued him. Heck, just thinking about him was enough to make him smile. Maybe he didn't need to rail against all the changes in his life but, like Alan, simply embrace them and then see what made him happy. "Thanks," Richard said as he passed behind Alan on his way to the other side of the bar. He wasn't sure if Alan understood what he was thanking him for, but he nodded and finished up the glasses he was washing, wiped his hands, and then asked Richard if he could handle things for a while and went back to his office. When he got a few minutes' break, Richard sent a message to make sure Daniel was okay. He smiled at the response, checked the time, and put the phone back into his pocket before returning to work.

At the end of his shift, before leaving, he knocked on the office door and poked his head in. "Do you have a minute?"

"What do you need?" Alan asked, looking up from his computer screen and then sitting back in his chair.

"Nothing." Richard had been mulling some things in his head. "But I had a few ideas and thought I'd run them by you." He stepped inside. "Business has been really good, and I was wondering if you ever considered building a patio and maybe a pergola onto the side of the building. There are trees there already, and if you designed the deck right, they could be used to shade it. The outdoor seating would be great most of the year. Our food is great, and that would give us a place that could be more family-friendly. People would come." Richard was sure of that.

"I've been thinking about something like that, but I haven't had the time to look into it." Alan sighed and tapped his finger on the desk.

Richard had done things like this back in Detroit. "I could look into some costs and get estimates if you like. Then we could work up a business plan to make sure it made financial sense." He really wanted Alan to succeed and the business to flourish. Alan had been really good to him, and he wanted to pay it back.

Alan tapped the top of the desk with his hand. "Sounds like a great idea. Go for it." He grinned, and Richard smiled in return before leaving the office to head out.

"DANIEL," RICHARD said after the door to the condo opened.

"Coby is asleep," Daniel said. Judging by the snores from the other room, Richard guessed that Terrance wasn't awake either. "And I apparently have a moose in the other room."

"I guess. Terrance always did snore loudly enough to wake the dead." He smiled and looked down at his friend, who was sound asleep on the sofa with Coby on his chest, the little boy's head on Terrance's shoulder. It was so adorable. Richard didn't want to wake either of them. Terrance opened his eyes, though, as Richard approached. "Thanks for staying to look after them."

Daniel gently lifted Coby up and carried him down the hall to put him to bed.

Terrance stretched. "You're welcome. It was fun." He yawned, and Richard didn't tease him. "The kid wore me out, though. All he wanted was horsey rides and airplane rides." He stretched, yawned again, and went to the door. "I'm heading home for some quiet. I'll see you later." Terrance left.

Richard turned to Daniel.

"He was wonderful with Coby, and yes… Coby wore him out completely. They played, and he ran Coby around here for hours." Daniel smiled. "Terrance is a great big kid, isn't he?"

Richard found himself nodding. He had never thought of Terrance that way. Hell, the things he had seen Terrance do in a previous life were anything but childlike. "I'm glad they had fun."

"I found out some more things." It was Daniel's turn to yawn.

"You should have rested." He felt guilty that Daniel had stayed up for him. Not that he was disappointed. Richard began turning out the lights and checking the doors. Daniel waited for him at the entrance to the hallway, and Richard met him, drawing Daniel into his arms. "I kept thinking about you my entire shift."

"You did?" Daniel breathed.

"Yeah. I was worried about you and kept checking my phone to make sure there wasn't a message. I take it everything was quiet."

Daniel nodded. "I kept thinking about you too. It was nice of Terrance to stay, but I couldn't help wishing it was you here with us. Terrance is nice, but I wanted you." He swallowed and looked a little nervous, and Richard tugged him closer.

"I want you too. We can talk about other things in the morning. Tonight, I just want to be with you, okay? The doors are locked, and I have the lights off. Coby is asleep. It's just you and me for a few hours." God, he had never thought how important this kind of time could be.

"Are you sure you're not sleepy?" Daniel asked and turned away, yawning. "Sorry." He smiled and tugged Richard down the hall. "I'm not going to wait any longer."

"I see," Richard said as he bumped the wall. "Or don't…."

Daniel giggled a little and got the bedroom door open. The light from the attached bathroom cast enough glow that Richard could see the rest of the way.

"I need to shower before I get in bed. I smell like grease and bar. Why don't you get ready for bed and I'll be right back?"

Richard hurried into the bathroom, stripped off his clothes, and started the water. He got under the heat and grabbed the soap, lathering up as the shower curtain slid aside and Daniel climbed in behind him, pressing right against his back. "I need to shower as well, and I thought we could save water." He ran his hands over Richard's back and down to his butt, squeezing a little. "Damn, you're something else."

"I know the package is pretty good." He looked behind him, grinning, but received a half scowl and a slap on the ass in return.

"And the rest of you is pretty amazing too. The exterior may have captured my interest initially, but it's the rest of you that kept me interested." Daniel turned him around, and Richard nearly lost his footing. Daniel helped keep him upright. "Don't sell yourself short."

Richard nodded as a wave of guilt, an unaccustomed feeling, washed over him. Daniel said he was attracted to him, but he didn't really know him. Was that fair? Richard was pretty sure he knew Daniel and he even knew one of his secrets. Daniel knew next to nothing about him.

"What is it?" Daniel asked. "What aren't you telling me?" He closed the distance between them, and Richard felt his walls crumbling. He actually thought of laying it on the line and telling Daniel everything. But he couldn't. It wasn't just his secret to tell. Fucking hell, how in the heck did his love life get so complicated that it actually felt like there were four people in it? This wasn't a four-gy, it was something that should be between him and Daniel.

"Nothing," Richard said, forcing a smile and hoping Daniel didn't press him. "I think it was your eyes that first drew me to you, and when you came in every Wednesday, I looked forward to that all week."

"You did?" Daniel smiled, gliding his hands down Richard's chest, only adding more heat to their warm shower. "I looked forward to Wednesdays too. Not only was it my only evening away, but I got to flirt with you. I spent weeks wondering if it was really me you were interested in. But you never acted that way with anyone else."

Richard shook his head, pressing Daniel against him, grabbing his perfect tight butt. "No, I never did. You were the only one I flirted with and the one I wanted to get to know, but you seemed preoccupied, and now I know why. You had someone at home who was a lot more important than… well, just about anything else." He reached for the soap and ran it over Daniel's back, lathering his skin before gently turning him so the water sluiced over both of them.

Daniel kissed him, neither of them paying attention to the water. At that moment, Richard wouldn't have cared what happened. Everything centered on Daniel, and each place Daniel touched seemed to come alive.

Daniel turned off the water, and they stood together, holding each other. Richard didn't want to move. This was just too perfect. But soon enough the air cooled and the humidity grew close in the small room. Richard backed away, grabbed the towels from beyond the curtain, and handed the first one to Daniel.

He was so lean, with smooth curves down his hips and legs. Richard held his towel, not drying himself but watching as Daniel wiped the cloth over his skin. Damn, he was beautiful. That was all there was to it. Richard loved watching him.

Daniel must have noticed Richard watching him because he blushed slightly. "What are you doing?" He paused and looked down at himself. "Is there something wrong with me?"

Richard shook his head. "Everything is perfect," he said softly.

Daniel smiled and then rolled his eyes. "You're still wet." He took the towel from Richard's hands and began drying him off. "Sometimes I wonder if guys are helpless at heart or something."

"No. Just preoccupied," Richard said and let Daniel finish. He hung up the towels and then turned around. Richard used those few moments to act, drawing Daniel to him. His skin was still damp, but soft, and Richard glided his hands down Daniel's backside and over the half globes of his perfect butt. "You make me want to forget everything else," Richard whispered as Daniel pressed to him.

He was already so turned on that Richard could barely think about anything other than the way Daniel felt against him. They fit perfectly, and Daniel felt so good. Richard reached between them, and Daniel groaned softly as he wrapped his fingers around Daniel's length, drawing out long, deep moans that filled the small room with the sound of desire. Few things had ever gotten Richard's heart pounding as fast as that little sound. "Should we go to the other room?"

Daniel nodded, and Richard reluctantly pulled back, his cock pointing directly at Daniel as though he were the center of everything. "Jesus," Daniel whispered, and before Richard knew it, Daniel sank to his knees.

Richard's eyes widened as Daniel took him between his lips, passion building so quickly that Richard held the counter for balance. His head spun as slick, wet heat surrounded him. It was stunningly hot, especially when he lowered his gaze. The sight of his cock sliding between Daniel's full lips alone was almost enough to send him over the edge.

Richard had had plenty of sex before, and he'd received blowjobs on multiple occasions, but none of them compared to the way this felt and the adoring look in Daniel's eyes as he raised his gaze to meet Richard's. Heat, humidity, and passion combined to threaten to pull the air from the room. Richard's leg bounced with energy as Daniel took him to the root, humming softly.

"Oh God," Richard groaned, his hips gliding forward and pulling back. Daniel only sucked harder, taking more of him, stripping away Richard's control layer by layer until he clamped his eyes closed. "Daniel… I…." He was at a near loss for words. He swallowed hard and then lost his breath again as Daniel sucked harder. Then he backed away, and Richard's mouth hung open as he pulled oxygen into his lungs. He had been so close, almost balancing on the edge of the knife, and now…. His body went nuts, begging for something that was no longer there. "That was mean."

Daniel stood. "I don't want things to be over too soon," he said with a quirky little smile.

"Come on." Richard opened the bathroom door and tugged Daniel into the bedroom. His heart was still racing, and if Richard didn't get Daniel into bed soon, he was going to fucking explode.

"Daddy."

Richard groaned as Daniel put on his robe. He climbed into the bed, hoping Daniel wouldn't be gone too long. Soft words and then maybe singing followed, and then Daniel appeared in the doorway. He closed the door and dropped the robe, gliding toward the bed. Or at least that was how it appeared to Richard.

Daniel slipped under the covers next to him. "He just wanted a drink of water."

"Is he asleep?" Richard asked, pressing Daniel back onto the mattress. Daniel nodded, and Richard covered his mouth, tasting Daniel's sweet lips. "Good. Because I want you, right now." He flexed his hips, sliding his cock along Daniel's, and they both moaned softly in each other's ear.

"I need you," Daniel whispered, and that was enough for Richard. "There's stuff in the drawer."

Richard nodded but didn't break his gaze from Daniel's.

Richard kissed Daniel again, running his hands down his flat belly before gripping Daniel's cock. He stroked it, and Daniel whimpered and vibrated with excitement. Damn, that was hot as hell. Daniel's innocence had been part of the initial attraction, but there had been fire behind his eyes, and Richard saw that clearly now. He had lit and nurtured that heat until it was about to burst forth and scorch him. Richard was more than ready. Seeing Daniel turned on, with his dark eyes and intense stare, was almost more than he could bear.

He pulled away, and Daniel huffed. "Now who's mean?" he countered.

Richard smiled as wickedly as he could before sliding down, taking Daniel between his lips, tasting his lover. Daniel whimpered as Richard took him deeper and deeper, sliding his hands up his thighs. Daniel parted his legs, and Richard slicked his fingers alongside Daniel's cock, teased at his entrance, and then slid a digit inside his body as he took Daniel to the root.

Daniel thrashed on the bed, moaning more loudly. Richard pulled back, giving Daniel a break to quiet him. The last thing he wanted was for them to have a little visitor once he had Daniel right where he wanted him. This was their time, just the two of them, and he intended to make it as openmouthed and eye-poppingly special as possible.

"Richie, I... oh God... I...." Daniel babbled and writhed under him, which was gorgeous. Richard was well aware that he was overwhelming Daniel with sensation, but that was the entire point. He wanted to blow his mind, and hopefully he would understand how important he was becoming to Richard. "Richie...," Daniel whined, and Richard backed away before he took Daniel too far.

Daniel heaved for air, and Richard reached to the side table and found the supplies. He got himself ready and then into position, his gaze boring into Daniel's deep eyes and down to his soul. Daniel's body opened for him, and Richard gasped and pressed deeper into the tight, wet heat. It felt as though Daniel pulled him in, and he had to hold back to keep from going too quickly. The last thing he wanted was for their time together to be painful. This was about pleasure, and fortunately, judging by the expression of eye-rolling bliss on Daniel's face, he was succeeding. Daniel pressed toward him, and Richard stopped to let his body get used to the sensation.

"Don't stop," Daniel whimpered.

"I won't," Richard breathed, kissing Daniel hard as he slowly pressed farther, the tightness around him as erotic and intense as anything Richard had ever experienced in his life. Richard panted and held still, Daniel's body clutching him.

Then he slowly backed away, and Daniel gasped, low and guttural. "Oh yes!"

He clutched at Richard's shoulders, holding him tightly as they moved as one. It wasn't him or Daniel, it was them... together. The pleasure and bliss between them was because of the two of them. Richard watched Daniel's deep eyes as they grew darker and his breathing shallower—small signs that were like road maps to Daniel's pleasure, and he understood them instinctively. But what shocked him most was how Daniel seemed to know just what Richard needed, heightening his pleasure with a firm touch or a kiss hot enough to melt steel.

For a second Richard wondered if he was that transparent, but none of the others he had ever been with brought him this kind of mind-burning passion or seemed to understand what he needed as readily as Daniel. "That's it, sweetheart, just let go. I'm here, and you don't have to hold off any longer." Richard was seconds away from tipping into release, but he was determined to wait, and Daniel gasped, arching his back and stilling as passion washed over him, carrying Richard right along behind.

Richard held still, not wanting to crush Daniel but completely wrung out as well. He kissed Daniel gently, groaning as their bodies disconnected.

Richard lay next to Daniel, taking care of the protection before tugging him closer, their kisses languid and gentle, an expression of tenderness that wrapped around Richard like a warm blanket on a winter morning. Was this something that could be open to him? Could he really have this forever? God, he hoped so… and pushed the alternatives out of his head.

Chapter 10

DANIEL WORKED as best he could, trying not to think too much about the threat that hung over his head. After a while he gave up and stared at the screen, thinking of what he knew and how he felt about the whole thing. What surprised him was the anger that built inside by the second, replacing the fear and making his heart race. He had done some research on the types of systems the bank used, and he'd developed a plan to do exactly what he was being pressured to do, but he hadn't told Richard any of that. He wasn't happy that he had made the decision to do what they wanted if it came to that. Daniel wasn't going to let anything happen to Coby no matter what. Still, there had to be a way to handle this.

He ended up pacing the room, thinking more and more. He was so tired of feeling like he was at their mercy. Hell, there had to be something he could do to take back some control. Right now he didn't have any, but he had gathered quite a bit of information on some of the people he thought might be involved, and he might even have found a connection between them and one of his friends back in college. The picture was becoming clearer, and the more he learned, the angrier he got.

His phone rang, and he tensed, looking at the display before answering it.

"We'll be sending you the detailed instructions on what we want," the now-familiar voice said, and something in the back of Daniel's brain snapped as his anger took over.

Daniel swallowed. "No," he spat with venom that startled him a little.

The line grew quiet. "You don't want to tell us no." The voice became more menacing.

Daniel thought about what he'd gathered and the notes. These people were cowards, hiding behind blocked phone calls and anonymous notes that were easy to make on any computer. Hell, he even pictured some idiot drawing red circles for a target with Magic Marker. "I'm not doing anything unless I get to see you. I don't care what your instructions say. You'll meet me to explain exactly what it is you expect. If something goes wrong…." He wondered where all this was coming from for a second as his brain told him to back off and just do what they wanted, the fear returning.

"It better not."

With that, he blinked as he realized the dynamic had completely changed. This person wasn't fixated on meeting him but on things going wrong.

Just like that, Daniel felt the balance of power shift. Whatever his big mouth had done to run away with things might have paid off. "Don't give me a load of crap," he retorted. "You need my skills, so unless you stop acting like a bunch of dicks, I'm not going to do anything, and I'll turn every note and piece of information over the police. They'll notify the bank, and you'll get nothing but people looking for you for the rest of your damned lives. I'm sure that call records and fingerprints, along with other evidence, can be retrieved." He had thought about how he wanted to handle this, and he was getting fucking tired of feeling so out of control.

A knock sounded on the door, and he got up, checked who it was, and let Richard inside.

"My father is an ass of epic proportions, so I may as well add a few million for myself while I'm at this. If I can hide the money for you, I can do it for myself too." Daniel winked, and Richard's eyes widened to saucers. "Like I said, you need me, but I certainly don't need you. I'm hanging up now."

"No," the man on the other end snapped, and Daniel caught Richard's gaze, grinning. "I'll let you know."

The line went dead, and Daniel put the phone on the counter.

"What in the hell did you do?" Richard asked.

"Scared the crap out of those chickenshits." His legs shook and he sank into one of the chairs, completely wrung out. "It occurred to me that you were right— they were using fear, and what's good for the goose is good for the gander. These people are amateurs. And the more I thought about it clearly, the more I got angry, and I shouted back at them. It seems they took the bait, and I bet they're scratching their asses right about now, wondering what the hell they should do." He smiled even as he tried to haul air into his lungs.

"They could try to hurt you or Coby in order to send a message," Richard said, and Daniel shrugged, knowing that was true. But slowly, Richard nodded. "But you gave them just enough of what they want to make them curious that maybe you were on their side after all and that you'll do what they want."

"Yeah. I thought that was pretty clever, if I do say so myself."

Richard sat down and took his hand. "But they aren't going to want to meet you, and I bet the threats are going to come back your way pretty heavy. Leaving notes is one thing, but looking you in the eye and having you identify them is something else. They have no idea that you may know who some of them are. That's your one advantage in this whole thing, and you can't tip them off to that." The phone rang, and Daniel hesitated. "Be strong."

Daniel nodded and answered the phone. "Hello." He kept his voice steady even though he was shaking inside.

"You think you're so smart. How will you feel if that son of yours gets a feeling of just how smart you are?" Yup, just like Richard had said. "We don't care how you enrich yourself in our little endeavor, but remember, we get what we want or you and your son will pay. The instructions will be sent. You have three days to get us what we want. Watch for our instructions."

The line went dead, and Daniel hung up and relayed the conversation to Richard.

"Then there's our time frame to figure this out." What shocked Daniel was the level of fear behind Richard's eyes. Daniel turned away and, not for the first time, wondered where Richard's insight into these people came from. Most of the time he was spot on regarding how they would behave and ferreting out what their motives might be. Daniel knew so little about him and where he came from, and he couldn't help wondering what Richard hadn't been telling him. Every time Daniel asked him questions about his past, he either got very bland information or Richard changed the subject.

"Yes." Now he wondered how he could make it seem like he was doing what they wanted, because Daniel sure as hell didn't want to break into his father's bank. Still, he might not have a choice, and then, unless he was careful and damn lucky, he had to hope that everything didn't lead back to him. Who would have thought that shit he'd done years ago would come back to haunt him after all this time? The fear that his anger had kept at bay took over once again, and he wondered if his little outburst had only put him and Coby in more danger. "But what do we do?"

Coby ran out of his bedroom, carrying his stuffed dog and his bag of blocks. He had been playing in there, but obviously decided that the living room was a much better place. "Mr. Richard, come play?"

"We're a little busy," Daniel said, his nerves now on edge. "Go ahead and play with your blocks." They tinkled as Coby dumped the bag on the floor and then sat down to play.

"Is there a way to make them think you've done what they wanted without actually breaking into the bank?" Richard asked.

Daniel paused a second, wondering if Richard had gone out of his head. "Sure. I could empty the trust fund that was left to me and give them all I have in the world." He snickered. "Not really, because I can't actually touch any of the principal, and there isn't that much in it. But I can't manufacture money."

Richard patted his hand. "I wasn't suggesting that. Just make them think they got what they wanted." He leaned closer. "I know you have no intention of stealing from anyone, and if you did pull this off, it could cripple people's trust in the bank and hurt innocent people. I've done a lot of things that…." He paused and cleared his throat. "I was just wondering how we can make them *think* they're getting what they want." Richard rubbed his chin.

"I have to call my dad," Daniel said. "Regardless of anything else. I could probably pull this off, but…." He was so damned conflicted. Part of him wanted his father to suffer, and yet… he was his dad. Regardless of how cutthroat his father could be, that wasn't Daniel. "I don't know if he'll even take my call."

Richard nodded. "All you can do is try."

He stood, and Daniel extended his hand. "Don't go," he whispered. "My dad always manages to turn everything around so it's about him and what he wants and needs." He relaxed a little when Richard sat back down. For a second Daniel wondered how Richard was able to make him feel calmer just by being there. He went through his contacts and dialed the direct number to his dad.

"First Florida, Mr. Upton's Office."

"Karen, it's Daniel Upton. I need to speak to my father. It's important," Daniel said.

She sighed. "Oh, honey. Are you okay?" She was always so nice.

"I think so. But Dad might not be." He made his message cryptic in the hope that his dad would take the call just out of curiosity.

"He's not on the phone. Let me see if he's free." She put him on hold, and Daniel drummed his fingers on the counter. The last time he'd spoken with his dad, things had not gone well at all. Lionel Upton rarely listened to anyone.

"What have you done now, Daniel?" his father asked in a stern voice.

"Jesus, Dad. I didn't call to ask you for anything, but to warn you. Maybe I should just hang up and take down you and your entire bank." That would get his attention. "I need you to call me back on a line that can't be overheard by anyone. Call me back on your cell… please. It's important." Daniel hung up, and his heart pounded. Richard scooted closer and hugged him. Daniel had no idea if his father would do as he asked, but then his dad's private cell number appeared on his phone.

"Do you want to tell me what's going on?" his father asked gruffly as soon as Daniel answered.

"Look. I have been approached to hack into your bank systems and steal four million dollars. And I could do it." The time for being nice to the old asshole was over. "Do you understand? Coby has been threatened, and I won't let anything happen to him." He stopped his drumming fingers and waited for his father.

"How could you…?" His dad suddenly seemed confused and maybe a little unsure of himself.

"I could get in through your international wire transfer system and then piggyback into your home systems. It wouldn't take me long before I could have access to your entire private network, and then I could wreak havoc through every system you have. Hell, I already have one of your fingerprints that I could use for executive-level access." He paused a second. "Are you scared half to death yet?"

"Daniel…." He was clearly shocked.

"I've never done it, and just because I could doesn't mean I would. But there are people who want me to, and the threats are frightening. I need your help to stop them." Daniel squeezed Richard's hands.

"How do you know how to do all of this?"

"Because it's what I did in college. It was a game back then, but someone found out what I did, and they are trying to get me to hurt you." He swallowed, and Richard began writing.

Tell him about his potential mole, Richard wrote on a scrap of paper.

Daniel nodded.

"Are you kidding me with all this?" his dad asked.

"No, I'm not." Daniel growled softly. "Look, talk less and listen. I know it's not one of your skills when it comes to your children, but give it a try. Okay?" He was getting pissed off. "One of the blackmailers accidentally left a slight trail, and I have been able to follow it through the internet and social media. One of the guys I think might be involved has a brother who's one of your assistant branch managers. Mark Jensen. I don't know if he's involved, but someone has a real bone to pick with you. They even knew that you and I don't speak and told me I could take whatever extra I wanted for myself."

"Daniel!!"

"I'm on the damned phone to you, aren't I?" Daniel said. "I'm telling you about it because you're my dad. It may be the last familial thing either of us does, but I'm letting you know, so don't get all high and mighty." That was enough. He was about to hang up.

"Okay. Point taken. What are you going to do?"

"I need your help, Dad. We need to work this from both ends, I think." He was still trying to formulate a plan. "A theft from the bank or even an attempted breach is not going to be good for you. And these things have a way of coming out. Then customers run for the hills, and poof, no more bank. I don't know enough on these people to go to the police, and what I have is mostly conjecture and feelings. But know this: I have been threatened, and so has your grandson. We need to figure out a way to get them what they want and for the path to lead right to them."

"What am I supposed to do, just give them the money?" his father blustered.

"No. But maybe there's a way to make them think they're going to get it," Daniel said. "I'm working on it. They have given me three days. Then I don't know what I'm going to do. I've thought of calling the police, but there are four of them on Longboat Key, and what are they really going to do? They manage traffic, but they don't handle extortion. By the time they acted, we could be dead." He felt his voice breaking and swallowed hard.

"Okay, son," his dad said. "I'm going need to get authorities involved. But I have to ask you again, could you really break into the bank?"

Daniel steadied his voice. "Yes, I think so. I've looking into your systems, and given time, I could get access. Maybe when this is done, I could show your people how to close the holes that I'd use. Right now we've got to figure out how to fool these guys so we can get them caught and sitting behind bars." Only then would he be safe.

"Okay," his dad said. "I'll alert my security people, and we'll see if we can arrange something to throw these guys off the scent. I'll call you no later than tomorrow morning. We'll have a plan on our end, and you can tell us what you're thinking. I'd ask you to come to the house, but that would only tip our hand." At least his dad was thinking the same as him.

"I'll be in touch."

His dad hesitated. "Stay safe." He ended the call, and Daniel set the phone down, resting his head on the counter as he tried not to shake from head to toe.

"He believed me," Daniel said. "He listened to me. I didn't think he would. Dad said he would get with some of his people to see what they can come up with."

"They're going to try to safeguard the bank," Richard said, and Daniel nodded. "That's going to be their first duty. Ours is to make sure you and Coby are safe." He checked the time and groaned. "I'm going to have to go in to work in an hour. I don't want you here alone. Gerome and Terrance are working too." Richard sighed. "I need more resources and don't have them." He gripped the edges of the counter, and Daniel wondered again what Richard was taking about.

"We'll be fine," Daniel said. "I'll keep the doors locked and the windows shut. I won't let anyone in."

Richard picked up his phone, texting out a few messages. "Gerome says the store closes at six and he'll be over afterwards. Call if you hear or see anything. I'll figure out a way to get here." He brought Daniel close. "I hate the thought of anything happening to you… either of you." Richard hugged him tightly. "You're becoming my world, and frankly that sort of scares me."

"Why?" Daniel asked.

Richard released him and backed away, looking anywhere but at him. It was strange, and yet Daniel understood it. Richard was just as nervous about whatever was between them as he was. But this time he didn't intend to let Richard off the hook. He held his gaze and waited, determined to get him to say something.

"I guess because it's new for me. I haven't done relationships very well in the past." He shifted his weight from foot to foot. "Maybe I should just pull on my big-boy boots, stop worrying, and put my heart where it belongs."

"New things are always frightening for all of us. But if we don't try something new or different and if we don't take a chance, then we never grow—and we never find something that could make us very happy." Daniel half smiled. "I need to let you go to work. I'll call if anything happens, but I don't want you to be late." He swallowed hard. He knew how difficult it was for Richard to say what he did, and for some reason, Daniel kept his declarations to himself. He wasn't sure why, other than Richard's evasiveness, but he needed to look deeply into his own heart and figure out his feelings. It wasn't going to be difficult, because he knew he was falling for Richard. There hadn't been many people who had offered him the kind of support when things went to hell that Richard had. But it went beyond that. Richard made his heart race just by walking in the room. He was sexy as hell, but there was a gentleness and a heart in him that Daniel thought not many people got to see. That made what Richard did show him special.

Daniel walked Richard to the door and said good night. They shared a kiss, and then Coby raced over. He seemed to want one of his own, and Daniel kissed him on the forehead and held him as he waved goodbye to Richard. Then Daniel closed and locked the door.

"We play now?" Coby asked as he squirmed to get down.

"Why don't you play with your toys and I'll play with my computer?" he asked, and that satisfied Coby. Daniel had work to do and plenty to think about. The threat, his father, the bank, and most of all Richard.

Daniel made sure all the doors were locked and pulled all of the curtains. No one was going to see in, and Coby and he weren't going outside. Now he just had to make it through a few hours in one piece before Gerome arrived. For the millionth time, he wondered what he would do if Richard and his friends hadn't entered their lives. For the past few weeks, regardless of other things, some part of his life other than Coby actually made him happy.

Daniel peered out the front curtains and let them fall back into place before sitting at his desk to try to figure stuff out.

Chapter 11

RICHARD'S PHONE vibrated in his pocket. He pulled it out and read the message from Gerome that he was at Daniel's and that Coby was apparently allowing him to take a break from giving horsey rides. He breathed a little easier knowing that Daniel wasn't at home alone, but he felt jealous because he wasn't there. It seemed his friends were almost spending more time with Daniel than he was.

"Is everything going okay?" Andi asked as she put in her orders for two of the tables. "You still seeing the Wednesday fish and chips guy?" She smiled slightly and winked.

"Yes. Though I don't quite know what's happening." He wasn't going to complain either. "Daniel has a young son, and...." He pulled a beer and then another, lining them up before mixing a rum and Coke.

"And you can't decide if you want to be with someone with a kid?" she asked.

"No. Coby is great," he said without thinking and realized that he did like the thought of being a dad. That didn't bother him nearly as much as he thought it would have before Coby had come bounding out of Daniel's place and scared him half to death. No, what bothered him was something he couldn't talk to anyone about, including Daniel. "And things with Daniel are good."

Andi leaned on the bar. "So it isn't the kid, and yet you seem jumpy. Are you waiting for the other shoe to drop? Because it always does, and then it bites us in the ass." She loaded her tray as she watched him. "You know what the other shoe is. It's written all over your face." She leaned a little closer. "You have a secret you haven't told him."

Richard tried to clear his expression but swallowed anyway and hated himself for it. "Everyone has secrets," he said blandly and started pulling another beer for one of the ladies farther down the bar.

Andi picked up her tray, pausing before moving away. "Of course we do. I have things that I keep close to my heart. It's natural. But it's the ones we keep too closely that come back to bite us." She winked and left, and Richard wondered if he had suddenly taken to wearing his heart on his sleeve.

He delivered the beer before washing some glasses with more force than necessary. He was lucky he didn't break a glass and cut his hands all to hell. But she was right. Still, his big secret wasn't one he could share, and it wasn't his alone, so he had little choice but to hold it where it was and learn to live with a past he couldn't share with anyone.

His phone vibrating pulled him out of his thoughts. *There's someone in back watching Daniel's place. Coby and Daniel are safe, but should I go after them? Terrance is on his way.*

Richard answered, stabbing at the phone in his anger. *Once he gets there, see if you can get whoever this is to talk.* Richard wished to hell he was there, but he was stuck at work. The guys knew how these things should be done.

HIS PHONE remained quiet for the next few hours until finally he was done with work and left the locked-up bar. Richard drove right to Daniel's, not sure what to expect. He parked and knocked on the door, half surprised that Daniel opened it. "What's happening? Where are Terrance and Gerome?"

"They headed out a few hours ago and haven't come back." Daniel seemed on the edge of his nerves.

"Did they say why?" Richard asked, but Daniel shook his head.

"Just that they had something to do." Daniel closed and locked the door.

Richard sent messages to both the guys and received a quick response that they were watching the condo from outside. It seemed they had been unable to apprehend whoever had been watching. Still, this felt a lot more like the way he and the guys had done things in Detroit, as a team.

We sent a clear message, Terrance said in his text. *We're heading home now that you're here.*

Richard thanked both of them and drew Daniel into his arms. In a way it felt comfortable, like they actually had some control over something, but Richard knew they were playing a dangerous game and the inclination would be to go too far. They had to avoid that. "Is Coby in bed?"

Daniel nodded. "And I have some ideas on the bank front," he said. "I think it could work, but I'm going to need my dad's help."

Richard leaned closer. "You don't trust him."

"No. But it's not because of a specific reason. Just that I need to be careful. Right now our interests align, but that could change quickly." Daniel shook in his arms, and Richard did his best to comfort him. "So I'm going to be careful."

"What's your idea?" Richard asked.

"Well, the bank is going to have systems, duplicates to the production system, that they use for testing and development. I'd like to mirror the actual environment, move the money around in there, and then provide the thieves with a false screen where they can move their money offshore. It's that simple. Those transfers take days, and the bank folks will know where and the account that it's to be sent to. We should also be able to trace their connection back to their location, and then we have them and law enforcement can scoop them up." Daniel did that adorable thing with his lower lip. "But I can't call the police here. They aren't going to be able to handle this kind of thing, and it needs to be discreet and kept quiet to keep me and Coby as well as the bank out of the spotlight."

Richard knew just the person to call, but he didn't want to step forward for fear of giving away more than he should. Elizabeth had been responsive the last time he'd called her. But this was so different and definitely bigger. A call to her might result in their getting moved again just to get them away from the illegal activity. "I agree. The police here aren't really going to be able to help us much. This is going to need a delicate touch. We could try calling the FBI…."

He had clearly already thought about that. "I don't know how seriously they're going to take this. If my dad were to call them, they might be willing to listen, but then they would be all over the bank and I'd be a suspect." He grew pale. "I don't want Coby to go through that kind of scrutiny." He sighed loudly. "I just want to be able to go back to my life."

"Your dad was going to speak with you in the morning?" Richard asked, and Daniel nodded. "So then let me check that everything is secure and we can go to bed. I know that you've been working a lot, and I've had a long day." He hugged Daniel tighter. "Unless you want to me to go."

A knock startled both of them, and Richard told Daniel to go to his room as he checked through the curtains. The he opened the door and let Gerome inside. "We almost had him," he said softly. "The guy is wily, but we chased him off. I doubt he's going to be back soon. Terrance and I checked the area once again, and we're going to head on home."

"Thanks. One way or another, this should be over soon. They gave Daniel three days, and he's called his dad at the bank. So hopefully the bank and Daniel can figure out a way to make these people think they're getting what they want and yet lead the authorities to them. I just want him to be safe."

Gerome patted his shoulder. "I know. And I think Daniel has been good for you… all of us." He nodded slowly. "Before, we were living for us and what we want. Maybe those two have shown us what it feels like to live for someone else."

Richard had to agree with him. "That still doesn't mean…." He couldn't say any more. But Gerome knew what he meant. Explaining about who they were was taking a huge risk.

"Yeah." He turned to leave the condo, and Richard held the door, wondering as Gerome left how long they could keep their secret. Richard was pretty aware that they could stay silent as they had to. All three of them had kept quiet enough that there should be no need for them to leave. However, there were no guarantees, and Richard wondered more and more what he would do if he had to relocate.

"Daddy!"

The cry had Richard sitting upright in bed. It took him a second to parse what he had heard, but he was up and out of bed in seconds, pulling on his pants and running out of the room, with Daniel right behind him.

Coby was crying as they came into his room. "A man." He pointed to the window, shaking as Daniel comforted him.

Richard raced through the condo and out the front door, tearing off after a figure at the end of the driveway, running barefoot along the road and not feeling it under his feet.

The man tried to cut across a lawn, and Richard leaped for him, bringing him down in a roll of bodies. He hoped to hell the fucker didn't have a weapon.

"What the fuck were you doing?" Richard asked, yanking the guy to his feet, shaking him.

"I wasn't doing anything… I…," he stammered.

Richard tugged him back toward the condo. "You want to try again? We can go down to the ocean and take a little swim that you won't return from. The sharks and other sea lovers can pick you clean." He kept his voice low but put all the menace he had pent up inside him into those few words. "I'm tired of whatever is going on. You are going to give me answers."

"Or what?" he blustered.

Richard stopped, moving them into the darkness. "Let me think. There are plenty of ponds with alligators. This is Florida. Why don't I just throw you in and let them have at you? I doubt anyone will ever find anything." He tugged the man closer. "It will make me very happy to watch you as gator chow." He met the guy's gaze, and damned if an acrid smell didn't pierce the humidity. He'd pissed himself. Perfect. In this case, fear would work for him. He led Mr. Soggy Pants to the tiny yard of the condo and up to the porch. "Any other fantasies you want to tell me?"

He shook his head, and Richard let him go. "I was paid to watch the place. This guy came into the shelter and said I could make two hundred bucks and have a cell phone if I watched the place. All I had to do was make sure the guy and the kid were here. He said it was some kind of custody thing with the kid, and I needed the cash." The guy fumbled in his pockets and pulled out some wadded cash with shaky hands. "I don't want no trouble."

"Well, you found it." Richard pushed the money back toward him. He obviously needed it. "What did the guy look like?"

"Tall, kind of chunky," he stammered. "I don't know. I didn't look at him too good. He gave me the money, and that was all I cared about. I can eat for a month on that much."

Richard got a closer look at his half-vacant eyes and ratty clothes. He wasn't going to get anywhere with this guy, and whoever had hired him had to know that. This was just another way to try to put fear into Daniel… and it had to stop.

"Keep the money." Richard reached into his pocket and pulled out some cash of his own. "Here's a little more to add to it. I suggest, strongly, that you make yourself scarce and don't go contacting anyone." He took the phone out of the guy's hand. "This is what I'm paying for. Not that it's going to work for very long. He probably prepaid the minimum, and it will stop working soon." Richard slipped the phone into his pocket. Maybe Daniel could get something off of it that could help them. "I don't want to see you around here ever again."

The guy actually saluted and turned before hurrying off the drive and then out to the road, running down the side until he was far away. Richard smiled that he hadn't lost his touch and slowly ambled to the end of the drive, turning to watch the guy. Putting his hands on his hips, Richard stared after the man until he disappeared around the bend in the road. Then he lowered his arms and sighed. Back home he would have made sure the guy carried a few bruises with him. That was behind him, and maybe he was better off for it.

He went back inside and found Daniel in the living room with Coby sprawled out on the sofa right next to him. "Is he asleep?"

Daniel nodded. "I tried to put him to bed, but he wanted Uncle Richard to do it." His eyebrows shot up.

"Did you tell him to call me that?" Richard asked, but Daniel shook his head. "He came up with it all by himself?" A nod. "Well, shit." Richard gently lifted Coby into his arms, and Coby put his around Richard's neck. "It's time to go to bed."

"I sleep wiff you, Uncle Richard. I be safe then." He placed his head on Richard's shoulder. "No bad men come then." He yawned, and Richard barely made it to his room before Coby was sound asleep. Damn it all, he was not going to let his eyes fill with tears over a little boy who just wanted to be safe. Shit…. He swallowed around the lump in his throat and laid Coby in his bed.

"You go on in. I'll sit here for a little while in case he wakes up again," Richard offered.

"Come on back out. I'll make some herbal tea and we can talk a little." Daniel looked wiped, but he followed Richard to the living room. "What the hell was that?"

"Another fear tactic." Richard pulled out the phone. "This was on the guy. He's probably homeless and was paid to watch you for some imaginary custody issue. I believe he didn't know anything, but his phone might. It was given to him by the guy who paid him. Maybe there's another number in it we can use."

Daniel put water on to boil and then sat on the sofa. Richard joined him and put his arm around Daniel as he leaned against him. "What's going to happen after this is over?" Daniel asked and turned so they could see each other. "Are you going to disappear into the night like some dark hero in a movie? Like the Lone Ranger or Zorro from the old movies, never sticking around when the job was done?" He swallowed, and Richard wanted to kiss the spot on his throat.

"Danny, I…." The nickname just came out.

"I know you have a past that you don't talk about. You say things but don't tell me anything about it. I know you grew up in foster care with the guys, and after that, you survived on the streets somewhere in the Midwest…. After that, all of you ended up in Iowa and then here. There are a few things in between, but that's about all you've told me." He got up when the water began to boil and made the tea before returning to the sofa with two mugs. "I know you feel like you can't tell me whatever it is." He sighed, lowered his gaze, and sipped his tea. "I'll see you when you come to bed."

Daniel walked slowly down the hall.

Richard knew this had been coming. It had to eventually. He stood and took his tea into Coby's room, sitting in the light blue wingback chair in the corner, setting the tea on the dresser next to it. He watched as Coby slept.

What the hell had happened to his life? Richard closed his eyes to try to control the circling thoughts that didn't seem to want to end. His life had changed so much, and he had hated it—part of him still did. He didn't understand how in a few weeks, after meeting Daniel and Coby, he could suddenly want to hold on to the life he had here with everything he had. If he had the chance to return to his old life… right now… he had no idea what his choice would be. That was frightening. Since he was eighteen years old, Richard knew who he was and where he belonged. For months he had been fighting the change in his life, trying to figure out how to retain some of that person. Now all he wanted to do was let that man go and become someone new. But who would that person be?

Shit, Terrance would tell him to quit acting like a teenager and thump him on the side of the head… or worse. But he couldn't help it. Richard had thought the relocations with Witness Protection were the toughest things he'd ever done, but this was worse because Daniel made him happy in a way he never thought he could be… and it could all be ripped away from him. A little boy and his dad had wormed their way into his heart. He hadn't been looking for it or intending for that kind of relationship, but it had happened…. Richard smiled. No, it had been gifted to him for some reason, and he wanted to be worthy.

Worthy…. He mulled the word as it ran through his head over and over. How could he possibly be worthy? He had done things that would have Daniel racing for the hills if he knew. The intimidation—granted, that was directed at people who'd tried to cause trouble in his clubs. He was a racketeer, a man who helped launder money and fronted for organized crime. Hell, he had been part of it, on the inside, a vital portion of the family business. He'd had people eliminated and roughed up on occasion. There was no way he could show any weakness or else he would have been out. And Richard had been happy, or at least he thought he'd been happy. The irony of it all was that he now knew what happiness was, true happiness. And what he thought had made him happy—his life before—could take that all away, and there was nothing he could do about it.

"Coby is sound asleep, and he isn't going to wake again," Daniel whispered from the doorway.

Richard slowly, and as quietly as he could, rose out of the chair and took Daniel's outstretched hand, letting him lead to the bedroom.

Richard got into bed and closed his eyes, Daniel lying next to him. "Night," Richard whispered into the quiet, and he received a soft hum from Daniel, who was most likely already asleep.

Secrets and lies killed healthy relationships. That was probably why most of the men in the family had mistresses and a whole different life outside of their home. They all dealt in secrets and lies. It was only a matter of time before Daniel grew tired of Richard's secrecy and evasiveness.

R ICHARD MUST have slept late. He woke to an empty bed and then a thump as a body landed on top of him. "Wakey-wakey," Coby said with a smile, about two inches from his face. "Pancakes!"

Daniel's voice drifted in from the other room, and Richard got out of bed, thankful he was wearing shorts. He pulled on a T-shirt and scooped Coby into his arms. "We have to be quiet."

Coby nodded and put his fingers over his lips as Richard carried him toward the living room.

"Stop it, Dad. I came to you, remember?" Daniel said, sounding pretty frustrated. He rolled his eyes even as he flashed Richard a smile. "Okay. … That will be awesome. I only need the name of the system so it looks like the real thing and I can take it from there. … Yes. I will tell you all the holes I find so you can close them. … No, I won't actually take anything or cause harm. You are my father—unlike you and Mom, I don't want to hurt either of you."

Wow, that was a little snippy, but knowing what Daniel had told him about his relationship with his parents, it was probably justified.

"Yes, I'll be in touch. … Look, Dad, you're going to need to trust me on this. You and I may see things very

differently, but I have never lied to you and you know it."
Daniel listened for a minute more and hung up.

"Tough call?"

"Just Dad being Dad," Daniel explained and tickled Coby's belly. "Let's get some pancakes into this empty belly." He bounded into the kitchen and got to work.

Richard set Coby on his feet, and within ten seconds, the entire floor was covered with blocks and toys. "I think I know what Harry's doing, and I have a plan, but I think I'm going to need some help," Daniel said.

Richard came right up behind him, sliding his hands around his waist and under his T-shirt, right above the waistband of his sleep pants. Damn, his skin was hot and smooth, luxurious under his fingers. "Let me call the guys and see if I can find a time for them to meet so we can talk things over."

Daniel nodded. "Were the three of you in a gang or something?" he asked softly. "You always do things together, and I've noticed that all of you seem to have these complementary skills. Maybe you should go into business together or something."

Richard said nothing, knowing how close Daniel was to making the last mental leap to what really happened. "The guys and I are friends." Which was very true. "After all this time, we know each other very well." He leaned a little closer while Daniel mixed the batter and finally backed away so Daniel could get out the griddle and start cooking.

Richard got on the phone right away. Terrance and Gerome weren't working until noon, so after Daniel's okay, he told them to come over. Daniel made some extra batter.

"Mr. Terrance and Mr. Gerome are going to have pancakes too," Daniel told Coby, who smiled and went right back to building something important, judging by his concentration.

"What kind of pancakes does Daddy make?" Richard asked. "Like mouse pancakes or cactus pancakes?"

"Mouse pancakes. I want mouse pancakes." Coby ran over, jumping up and down. "Daddy, make mouse pancakes."

"I'll do my best," Daniel said.

Richard joined him at the stove. "It's easy. Terrance's mom used to make them when we were kids." He made a main circle and added two ears on it. Richard winked at Daniel, who made some more mouse pancakes. Richard then showed him how to make cactus pancakes, and soon enough Coby sat at his place with one of each, happily eating away.

Terrance and Gerome arrived, and they got regular pancakes, with Coby crowing in delight about his "special" pancakes.

Once Coby was done, Daniel wiped him up to get the syrup off just about everywhere and then set him down to play.

"I'm making a dinosaur," Coby pronounced, and Richard watched him play, concentrating on getting his Legos just right.

"What's going on?" Terrance asked once Richard turned back to the table.

"I have a plan of sorts to deal with our friends who want me to steal for them." Daniel folded his hands. "I didn't steal anything when I was in college, even though I could have lined my pockets many times over, and I won't do it now." He spoke clearly, but there was underlying worry. "I think I can fool these guys by transferring some fake money into their accounts. Basically, it will go nowhere." He sighed.

"But that means that Daniel is going to be vulnerable once they find out they've been fooled," Richard added.

Terrance and Gerome both nodded.

"What if we can't actually locate these guys? I'm a geek, not a detective, and I can make a computer sing, but I don't know how to find people. My dad doesn't want to go to the police, but I know he will if anything goes wrong."

Terrance turned to Gerome, and Richard did the same. He was the planner and the one who developed the intricate business schemes and forecasts that they had used to hide all the mob money they had been laundering back in Detroit.

"Okay. Contrary to popular belief, funds don't get electronically transferred at the drop of a hat. It takes a while for things to process and for them to ensure that everything is correct," Gerome said, and Daniel nodded. "I take it you are going to use that play in the system."

"They want *me* to transfer the money, but I don't want to do that. I can provide them access to the mechanism, and I thought I'd let them enter the information and actually transfer the money. That way the actual felonious act is being perpetrated by them."

Richard thought about what Daniel was saying. "I get it. But how do you get them to do it and not just have you make the transfer?"

Gerome smiled. "Greed." He turned to Daniel. "When they contact you, tell them that you altered the bank system so they can steal money almost at will."

Daniel raised his eyebrows. "I can make them think they can use the link to transfer money in the future when they need it."

Gerome grinned. "You can tell them that you tested it already a day or so ago and that it worked. Even doctor up an account screen for yourself at an overseas bank as proof."

"We know who one of the group is," Richard explained.

"Then we lean on them. Add pressure to make them think they have to do this fast. It will help them throw caution out the window. Figure out a way to freak them out so their greed gets the better of them." Gerome turned to Daniel. "And you remain unflustered and confident in your abilities. That is going to scare them even more and make them start to think that their plans may be unraveling."

"Are you sure?" Daniel asked and turned to Richard.

"I think Gerome is right. But don't seem too confident, just sure of your abilities. They are going to question you, even try to fluster you. Don't be surprised if they make another play to get close to you. That will give them the illusion of power."

Terrance leaned over the table. "We'll be here to watch your back."

Richard was so proud of his friends he could burst.

"Why are you doing this?" Daniel asked Gerome.

"Because you're important to Richard, so you're important to us. It's that simple. The three of us are like brothers. We always have been." Gerome finished the last of his pancakes and took care of his dishes. "I will say this: just be careful, and whatever you do, don't break the law. Keep good records of everything and why you're doing it." He leaned a little closer, and Richard wondered what Gerome was getting at. "Do you trust your father?"

Daniel swallowed. "I'd like to think so. My parents don't understand who I am and why I've made the decisions I've made. But I doubt my father would lie about anything to do with the bank. It's his passion, and he's lived to build that business and his career. He isn't going to do anything to jeopardize that."

"Maybe," Richard said. "But that also means that if it comes down to the bank or you, he'll choose the bank. So if he tries anything, you'll want to have proof that you talked to him." He smiled, and Daniel finally seemed less scared than Richard had seen him since this all began. There was, of course, no guarantee that this plan would work. A million things could go wrong. But they were going to try.

"Daddy, come see," Coby said, and Daniel left the table.

"Call Elizabeth," Terrance whispered. "Not sure what to say, but we need to get her help. It's way beyond what the cops here can handle."

"She's going to freak," Gerome said softly.

Richard nodded, but they were going to need more help than their group could provide. He was also well aware that Elizabeth was going to be suspicious as hell of their motives, but at this point, he didn't care. If they pulled this off, they were going to need someone in law enforcement to help mop up the mess, and she was the one person Robert knew he could trust. She hadn't given up on them after the incident in Iowa, and she'd come through as far as the bar was concerned.

"You know this entire idea is crazy, don't you?" Daniel said when he returned to the table. "We don't know what these people are up to or how far they'll go."

Richard opened his mouth to say that he understood these guys, but he paused, because Daniel was right. Richard and the guys had been thinking of these people like the men they had worked with in Detroit, but they weren't there, and these guys could be thinking differently. What if they were wrong?

Daniel's phone rang, and Richard tensed. He nodded and answered it as everyone else grew quiet.

"Yes. It's progressing well." Daniel looked at the others. "I'll have what you want tomorrow and I'll have tested the application." He grew more and more tense. "Yes. … You can transfer whatever you want when I'm done. I'll have a link tomorrow. Where do I send it?" He waited again. "Then you'll leave me alone, right? No more calls and my son will be safe? You promise?" The nervousness in Daniel's voice was perfect. He was doing what they wanted as far as they knew and setting up their plan. It took Richard a second to realize that there was no acting involved right now. The confidence that Daniel had exhibited only a few minutes ago was gone, ripped away by the voice on the other end of the phone. "I understand… but you promise to leave me alone."

Daniel hung up the phone. "They bought it, but—"

"What did they say?"

Daniel swallowed. "That if anything goes wrong, I won't see anything or anyone before they blow Coby's head off." His hands shook.

Richard turned to where Coby was playing. Fortunately he hadn't been paying attention to what they were talking about.

"I don't know if I can do this."

"You can. Remember what we told you. This is part of it." Richard tried to calm him, but he could feel Daniel losing control. Not that he blamed him in the least.

"Terrance and I are going to take off. One of us is going to be around to watch things for a while." Gerome met Richard's gaze. Richard gently patted Daniel on the shoulder and followed the guys outside.

"Call her as soon as you can. This could go south so damned fast. Give Elizabeth all the names that we know and see how much she can help. We can try to protect him, but if these guys decide to make good on their threats, there is only so much any of us can do." Gerome turned to leave, and Richard went back inside.

Daniel sat at the table, his hands still shaking. "What else did they say?"

"They said that my boyfriend and his friends better not interfere in any of this or they would take you out as well." He lifted his gaze. "What the hell is happening to my life? I put you and Coby in danger, and all because I was stupid in college and had to be cocky and better than everyone else. Now it's all coming back to haunt me, and you too." Daniel got up and took care of the dishes. "I think I should just get out of here. Take Coby and go north. If I leave tonight, I can be out of this area of the country by tomorrow, and they are going to have to hunt to try to find me." He dropped a plate, and it shattered in the sink. Coby began to whine, and Daniel stood still like he had just short-circuited. "I don't know what to do."

Richard tugged Daniel gently away from the sink, pulled out the broken pieces of the plate, and threw them away. "It's going to be okay." They had a plan, and that was half the battle. Their quarry seemed to be falling into line. He wished he could have talked to them himself to assess their state of mind, but they were behaving as Richard would have expected. "They went for what you dangled in front of them—the chance to take whatever they wanted. It's almost too good to be true, and that's going to be their downfall." He tugged Daniel into a hug, and Daniel went right into it. Coby came over and hugged his legs, and Daniel bent down to pick him up.

"Don't be sad, Daddy." Coby patted Daniel's cheek.

"I'm okay," Daniel whispered and leaned against Richard's shoulder. Coby squirmed, and Daniel set him back on his feet. He returned to playing, and Richard held Daniel a little tighter. "I need to get to work so that the app is ready to gather the information we need from them." He slipped away, his steps unsteady as he went to his computer.

Richard finished cleaning up the dishes and put the washed and dried things aside for Daniel to put away later. Then he stepped outside to make a call.

"IS THIS going to become a habit?" Elizabeth asked a few minutes later, after Richard explained the basics of what was going on. "You're treading on dangerous ground."

"We haven't done anything other than try to help," Richard told her defensively.

She scoffed. "And you're trying to tell me that you're walking away from the chance to steal millions and then disappear into the night with no trace? Maybe skip the country?"

Richard growled. "Yes, and if I were going to do that, the first person I would call is you."

"Sarcasm isn't appreciated."

"All we want is to be safe and to have a chance at a life, but we seem to run across people who have other ideas." Richard settled his frustration and decided to try being calm.

"Okay. Let's say I believe you. What is this Daniel to you?" she asked. "Why are you helping him rather than just walking away and not getting involved?"

"I like him." He had to be honest.

"I see."

"And he has a kid. The notes they sent him were frightening, even for me. I don't want anything to happen to them. So the three of us can handle things here, or you can be involved and get law enforcement in here to mop up. We have a plan to get you the names and even location of the perpetrators. We can turn over the notes, and Daniel will give you everything that they've said. His father is president of the bank, and he's working with him to make sure that nothing is actually stolen."

Elizabeth grew silent, and Richard wondered what she was up to. "What the hell has happened to you guys? I can understand the shakedown at the bar. But this?" She groaned. "I'm very concerned that you are going to draw attention to yourselves regardless of how careful you try to be. How involved have you been?"

"Other than chasing a few people away from the condo, we haven't come in contact with them. Daniel has been the only one in contact. We have a name, and with a quick phone call we were able to confirm one identity, and he has a relative who works at the bank."

"How did you gather this information?"

"Daniel did through social media. He's really smart and knows how his way around the internet." He was pretty proud of how he had done that.

"Does he know about you? Has he guessed or found out about your old life on the internet?" she demanded. "Because you know you can't blow your cover. If that happens, we'll have to step in and relocate you. And you should be aware that the heat isn't off of any of you. Just this week Junior managed to release a series of orders from behind bars, and the three of you are at the top of his hit list. Just because you're away from Detroit doesn't mean that what happens there can't influence you."

Shit. Richard was shocked at how easy it was to become complacent.

"No. I haven't told him, and I haven't talked about our background." He sighed softly. "Look, we have done nothing illegal up to this point, and we've been careful not to. As hard to believe as you may think that is. As I said, we will pass you all of the information as long as you can help us. Once these guys realize they've been had, they're going to come after Daniel, and we need them taken out before that." He was getting tired of this conversation. "Think about it and call me back, but don't take too long, otherwise we are going to have to make other arrangements that you aren't going to like nearly as well." He ended the call to add gravity to his words. Elizabeth was going to have to decide for herself if she was going to take the chance that what he was telling her was true.

Richard turned as the curtain next to the window fell back into place, and he knew it hadn't been Coby watching him. Slowly, trying to come up with a cover story, he pushed open the door.

Chapter 12

"WHAT DO you think you're doing?" Daniel
hissed. "Are you in with them? Is that what this is? You
show up and start coming over as the notes were sent. I
should have known better than to fall for this. You have
all these secrets and avoidances. Now it makes sense."
He stood in front of Coby. "What is it you want?" His
insides churned at the thought of how close he'd grown
to Richard and the fool he'd been. All Richard had had
to do was pretend to help, and then Daniel had gone
right along with him and let him lead him down the gar-
den path. "Just get out and keep your friends away from
us too." Daniel pushed Richard back toward the door.

"None of us is in on this," Richard said, but Daniel wasn't buying his excuses this time. He finally saw

things clearly. He had to get Richard out of the house so he and Coby could get away. "You have it wrong. I was trying to get us some help."

Daniel rolled his eyes. "And you couldn't get the help with me in the room? Nope. I don't think so." He was so angry and humiliated he could barely see. Daniel had trusted Richard, and now he had put both Coby and himself in danger. "Just get out of here and leave us alone."

"Daniel, I am not working with the people behind this. I was calling for some help because we're going to need it."

Daniel put his hands on his hips. "Then who were you calling?" He leaned forward. "Does this have something to do with your secrets? Are you guys some undercovers cops or something?" Man, he was all over the board. His head ached. "Maybe you were supposed to set me up somehow." And here he had told them about the things he'd done in college. If they were undercover law enforcement, then he was already in enough trouble and he was going to lose Coby and.... He'd been so stupid through this whole thing. A trusting dupe. And he was going to pay for it with his son and God knew what else.

Richard seemed pained. "Will you let me explain?" He swallowed hard.

"Sure. You explain all you want while I pack our things so we can get out of here before someone comes after Coby and me."

"Daniel." Richard seemed so calm. "I...." He stepped back. "Look, I'm not an undercover police officer, and I'm not in league with the people who want to hurt you and Coby. You need to trust me. I've been trying to help you."

"Then who were you talking to? I saw you out there, and you were arguing with whoever it was."

Richard's shoulders slumped and Daniel knew he was either going to get some answers or Richard was going to clam up. When no answers were forthcoming, he pointed to the door. "Just go."

"What are you going to do?" Richard asked. "You need to keep Coby safe, and running away isn't going to do it." Daniel put his arms up as Richard came closer. "Look, I can't tell you what you want to know because it isn't just mine to tell." His gaze grew softer, and Daniel felt his resolve weaken before he remembered how he'd been played, and he turned away.

"Just go. I don't want any more stories from anyone. I should have known you were too good to be true. Everything turns out that way." Daniel went to the door and opened it. "Just leave. I have plenty of things that I have to do, and I don't need you. Just leave us alone. I'll figure out what I need to do on my own. I've been doing that for years, and I'll keep doing it one way or another."

As soon as Richard stepped outside, he closed and locked the door. Leaning against it, he wondered what he was going to do now.

"Uncle Richie?" Coby asked as he hurried over. "He didn't say bye."

Daniel lifted Coby into his arms. "I know. But it will be okay." It had to be okay. Not that he knew what he was going to do. Coby put his arms around his neck, and Daniel stood still. No matter what he'd said to Richard, he didn't know what he was going to do, and his heart… well, the shards of plate in the sink were nothing compared to the tiny pieces his heart had shattered into. But he had things he had to do to protect both Coby and himself.

AN HOUR later Daniel hurriedly picked up the suitcases he had packed for both of them and got ready to carry the bags to the car. He was ready. As soon as he got their things and Coby into the vehicle, he'd be gone. But as he opened the door and turned to get Coby, a man raced inside and slammed the door behind him.

"What the hell?" Daniel asked. "What are you doing?"

He glared at Daniel, and Coby tried to hide behind him, whimpering softly. "I'm here to make sure you do what you're supposed to do. I had to wait for your friend to leave." He smiled, showing a few dark spaces where his teeth had been. "Now I suggest you get to work."

The man saw the suitcases and growled, backhanding Daniel hard enough to have him seeing stars. Pain bloomed on his cheek, spreading through his head.

"Next time you try anything, it will be the kid that gets it. Now get on that computer of yours and get busy." He reached around and grabbed Coby, who screamed at the top of his lungs.

"It's okay," Daniel said, trying to calm his son as he struggled, hoping the intruder didn't hurt Coby, even as the ringing in his ears continued. He lifted Coby and did his best to calm him down. "I was doing what you wanted."

"And there was a fucking parade of people through this place, so I need to make sure you're working and not just stalling." He pulled back his jacket to give Daniel a look at the gun in his waistband. "Just so you know how serious this is. Now get to work and don't try anything funny. I got me plenty of leverage."

Daniel nodded. "Go play with your blocks while I have to work." He knew from the pictures he'd seen that this was Harry Jensen and that he was in some serious trouble. He needed to finish developing the application that would fake out the thieves, but he couldn't do that in front of Harry. It would only raise suspicions. Shit, he was in real trouble, and from the way Harry watched Coby, he was well aware of Daniel's weakness.

He wished to hell that he hadn't kicked Richard out. And damn, he had jumped to some pretty wild conclusions that were obviously not true. He turned to the computer and then proceeded to pretend to try to break into the banking system.

"You need to hurry the hell up," Harry told him after maybe half an hour of sitting there, watching Coby as well as staring at what Daniel was doing. It was unnerving and made him more nervous by the second.

"I'm on track to have everything you wanted tomorrow. I've already gotten into the system and have left bots that will allow me to put hooks in the system when I need them." He forced his voice to stay level even as he lied through his teeth. "I just need to put the finishing touches on everything so that tomorrow, right before the bank closes, the transfers can be made and will process that night." He turned to watch Harry. "They will go through without any trouble. I've identified the accounts that we can use to support the transfer." He returned to what he was doing and hoped to all hell that he could keep up this charade long enough to figure out what the hell to do.

He was in some hot water, and the temperature only climbed by the second. His heart raced and his ears rang as he forced his fingers over the keyboard, all the while watching Coby and hoping to hell that Harry didn't get too impatient and that Coby stayed calm and quiet. He needed a chance to think, but he wasn't getting much of one with every stroke of his keyboard being scrutinized.

He tried to work, but nothing was going to come to him. His fingers had minds of their own and didn't want to press the right keys. Still, he somehow forced his mind onto the work, glancing at Coby every few seconds.

"I'll fucking break his neck if you don't get back to work."

Daniel swallowed and for the millionth time wondered how he had gotten himself into this. His big mouth and stubbornness had pushed Richard away, and it seemed that he had been the one thing keeping the real threat at bay. Daniel sighed and continued working, or at least pretending to work. He set a program to run. It would put on a display but not really do anything. At least it would give him a few minutes to think.

"Daddy." Coby walked up to him, keeping an eye on Harry the entire time. "I have to potty."

"Okay. I'll take you." He got up. "This has to run for a while anyway." He took Coby by the hand and went down the hall to the bathroom, feeling Harry's gaze on them the entire time until he closed the door and silently flipped the lock. Not that it would keep Harry out if he was determined, but Daniel felt better with a door between them. He turned on the light and pulled the curtain aside to peer out into the backyard.

He nearly screamed, but swallowed it when Richard appeared in the window. Daniel opened it.

"What's going on? I saw someone in one of the windows, and I recognized him from some pictures you showed me."

Coby flushed the toilet and pulled up his pants, then saw Richard and smiled.

"Take him and get him out of here. Harry Jensen showed up a few minutes after you left, and he's watching me." Daniel lifted Coby. "Go to Uncle Richie and be as quiet as a mouse for me. Promise?" He took the screen out and handed Coby through the opening. He stayed quiet, and Richard took him.

"Get the hell out here!" Harry called, and Daniel flushed the toilet again.

"Get through here," Richard said quietly.

Daniel climbed up to the window and scrambled out into the yard. He reached in and pulled the window closed again as the door exploded inward. He dropped down, and they raced down the small yard and out the gate, scampering across the front yards of the other condos. Richard's truck was parked on the street, and Daniel dove into the passenger seat, taking Coby from Richard, who made a call through voice command. "I got both of them," Richard said as soon as the call was answered.

"Okay." Terrance's voice came through Richard's phone speaker. "We're going in, and this guy is going to sing or I'll rip his nuts off." The line went quiet, and Richard set the phone aside and continued driving.

"Terrance and Gerome followed me over, and they are going in to mop up."

"He has a gun," Daniel said hastily.

Richard chuckled. "Not for long." He pulled off the road, sent a text, and then continued driving. "We're going on into Bradenton for a little while, staying away and giving the guys a chance to take out the trash. Then we'll see what information we can get from him."

They were about to cross the bridge when Richard's phone chimed, and he pulled to a stop and then turned around.

"They got him?"

"Yes. Gerome says for us to go back," Richard explained and picked up speed, heading back the way they had come.

Daniel hesitated as they pulled into the drive. Gerome met them out front.

"What's the deal?"

"This guy's an amateur. He thought he could talk big and be a real thug." Gerome rolled his eyes, acting like this was no big deal. "I sent a message to our friend, and arrangements are being made. Terrance is getting the trash ready to move, and we'll have our friend meet us and make an exchange." He lifted his gaze and met Daniel's. "You're going to have to do a little cleanup as far as the bathroom door, but we got him." He flashed a smile before turning to Richard. "I suggest you take Daniel and Coby to your place. We'll get some things and bring them over once we're done."

He turned away. Daniel wasn't very interested in going back in there right now anyway. Richard drove quickly and got them to his place and inside. The cool air felt good, and Daniel settled on the sofa with Coby on his lap, holding him tight. "Do I want to know what the others are doing?"

"No. It's best you don't," Richard said, looking out the windows and then pulling the curtains. "But at least this should convince you that I'm not in league with the blackmailers."

"I'm sorry. I jumped to a bunch of conclusions."

Richard shook his head. "You did, but you were right about one thing. I haven't been honest, and I need to be." He began pacing a little in the room. "Like I said, what I needed to say wasn't just my story to tell. I had to talk to the guys first. Terrance went by your place on his way home and saw this guy go into the condo. He called me, and we all raced over as quickly as we could."

"So you saved us even after I was an ass?" Daniel asked, feeling even worse.

"I've been an ass plenty of times in my life, so you don't have a monopoly on it." He sat down, and they waited for a while. Richard put on some cartoons for Coby, but basically they just sat quietly, waiting to hear the next development in a saga that seemed to be taking more turns than Daniel could ever have imagined. Daniel wondered what was going to happen next, and then Richard's phone rang.

"What's going on, Gerome?" Richard asked. "I see. They are going to take him into custody? The feds?" Richard smiled, and Daniel's eyes widened. Wow, it seemed they weren't taking any chances. "Yes, they're going to want to talk to Daniel." He sighed and continued listening, his shoulders slumping. "We can't...." He groaned and sat back. "I see. I suppose that's something." He continued his conversation. Daniel tried not to listen in, but it was hard because he was curious. "I'll have them there in ten minutes." He ended the call.

"I take it we have to go back to my place," Daniel said.

Richard nodded. "Yes."

"And what do I tell them about you and Gerome and Terrance?" Daniel asked. "I know you aren't cops, and you aren't part of the bad guys. I can't figure out what the three of you are… or were. None of it makes much sense to me. You seem to understand people in ways most of us don't." He held Coby closer, staring into Richard's purple-flecked blue eyes and wondering what he should say so this man didn't disappear into the night, because Daniel had a feeling that was a real possibility. He didn't know why, but his gut twisted at the idea. It had been bad enough when he thought he might have lost Richard for an hour or so, but….

"Whatever you think is necessary. Show them everything and tell them all about your plans with your dad and how you were going to try to lead them down a path. Say anything you like…." Richard swallowed. "Just make sure you and Coby are safe and that nothing is going to happen to you. I'll tell you everything as soon as I'm able." He stood and gently cupped Daniel's cheeks. "I don't know what happens next. That is probably out of my hands, but I have to tell you this… I came back because I love you, Daniel. It's that simple." He kissed him. Daniel's heart leaped at the words.

Richard didn't move for a few seconds, and it felt like he was memorizing him. Daniel's curiosity rose once again, but it didn't matter right now, not in the grand scheme of things.

"I fell in love with you a long time ago," Daniel whispered and then stood, clutching Richard to him. He wished he knew what was going to happen next, and that this cold pit of fear that had settled in his belly would go away. But it seemed there were plenty of unknowns on both sides, and he was just going to have to see what happened. They both were.

"Come on, we're going home," Daniel told Coby gently.

They made their way out, and Daniel buckled Coby in as best he could. Richard drove the short distance as though he were carrying a load of fragile eggs. Once they arrived, Daniel got Coby out and walked to the driver's side. He kissed Richard hard, his heart aching the entire time as though it knew the threat and had neglected to tell his brain.

Coby gave Richard a hug as well, and then Daniel and Coby went inside, Daniel wondering if that was going to be the last time he saw him and not understanding why.

Chapter 13

RICHARD SAT in the truck, watching Daniel as he went inside. He waited until the guys came out and got in the truck as well, and then they all drove home, not saying a word the entire trip.

"Where is he?" Richard finally asked once they were inside his apartment.

"We trussed him up like a pig and dumped him outside the police department. Then we made a call to say that a suspect that the feds were interested in was outside. He wasn't going anywhere. And now we wait to find out what's next." Gerome sighed. "I'm going to go back to my place and pack up my shit. There isn't much there, but we might as well be ready for when the marshals march in here and move us to the next location." He left, and Terrance shrugged and followed him out. Richard thought they were right. He had figured if they could somehow help Daniel without drawing attention to themselves, they could stay. He should have known that wasn't possible.

Richard slowly got up and wandered the drab apartment. He didn't have the heart to actually pack, because that would be like giving up. The thought of moving away ripped his heart to shreds. He knew he should just accept reality. He had messed up. He should have stayed back and let Daniel handle things himself. But he couldn't allow him to go through this alone. Turning his back on Coby and Daniel just wasn't something he could do.

Richard sat on the edge of the bed, staring at the empty walls. Unlike Daniel, he had never put out anything personal in his space. It was a government apartment. When he'd moved in, it hadn't felt like home; nothing here had. That was until a certain dark-haired angel had walked into the bar for dinner a few months ago. But it wasn't until that man and his son had gone boating with them that things had started to change, and this place, this little area of the country, had begun to feel like it could be home. Now that was gone, and Richard needed to face it.

Richard had to keep busy, and he was scheduled to go to work. He wasn't sure if he should go in. His life, the one that had been given to him, could be ripped away. Richard could deal with that. He had gone through that twice before, and doing it again seemed insurmountable, and yet very likely now. The unbearable part was that his heart had hung itself on Daniel, and now he might have to let him go too. Richard wasn't sure he could actually do that.

A knock on the door pulled him out of his thoughts. He left his bedroom and pulled it open.

Two men in suits stood on his doorstep. He didn't need to see their badges to know they were marshals. They had that look. "We need to speak with you. All of you," one said as he flashed his badge.

"Come on in," Richard said, figuring it was time to pay the piper. "I'll message the guys and have them come over." He pulled out his phone, and soon enough the other two came in and sat down.

All three of them sat on the sofa, staring at the two agents, who sat in the chairs across from them. "Who wants to go first?"

"Do you want to introduce yourselves, or should we call you Agent One and Agent Two?" Richard asked, and they both blushed a little.

"I'm Reg Thompson, and this is Donald Marquart."

"Richard, Gerome, and Terrance, though I think you know that already." Richard figured he might as well start. "What do you want to know?"

"It seems Mr. Upton knows nothing about your backgrounds, though I suspect he's curious. How involved have you been in this episode?" Donald asked. "And why wouldn't you just call the police like you should have when he received the first note?"

Richard shrugged. "The police aren't our first go-to when there's trouble. I'm sure you can understand that. Besides, there are maybe four police officers on the entire force here. They hand out tickets and deal with shoplifting and such... hardly extortion and death threats." He was determined not to get upset. "None of the perpetrators have actually seen us, and they know me as Daniel's boyfriend. We have no indication, unless you know something we don't, that they think we're anything other than just friends of his." Richard leaned forward, watching both of them for some type of information, but these guys would make stellar poker players.

"That's true. We have kept our profile as low as possible," Gerome explained. "But you can't expect us not to live our lives. Richard and Daniel have grown close, and he isn't going to let anyone hurt someone he cares for. Any more than you would." Gerome sat back while Terrance folded his arms over his chest and stared daggers at them.

"We've supported someone who needed our aid," Richard said. "And we called you for help."

"You've apparently done that before," Donald said, narrowing his gaze. "It seems you three have a magnetic relationship with trouble."

"Hey. You know our background, so we know shit when we see it going down. The police have put a protection group out of commission, and you're going to be able to stop this group of thieves before they try to hurt someone else again. You're welcome." Richard crossed his arms over his chest the same way Terrance had.

"Yeah, you guys are Robin Hood." Reg rolled his eyes. "What did you get out of this? Were you promised a cut of the action?"

Richard growled and narrowed his gaze. "Do you want to walk out of here in one piece? There are only two of you." He was so angry.

"Knock it off," Donald told his partner. "And you settle down. His job is to ask questions."

"But not to be a jackass," Richard added. "And no, we were not going to be cut in. Daniel was working with his father so that a duplicate system would be used and the thieves would be fooled so the information they entered could be captured and recorded. As far as I understand, Daniel was going to trace their connection back to the blackmailers as well so law enforcement could trace everything." He leaned forward. "Daniel is honorable and gentle. He cares for Coby more than anything else in the world. I saw the notes he was sent and heard some of the phone calls. They were designed to scare him to death. Have you seen them?"

Reg shook his head. "The FBI is handling that piece of the case. We are here to assess your vulnerability and determine if you need to be relocated." They shared a brief exchange of looks and then turned back to them. "Mr. Upton has been very quiet about all of you. He says you've been his friends and support."

"So…," Richard prompted.

"The decision has yet to be made. But I suggest you be ready to pack up if necessary." They stood.

Richard saw them to the door and let them out.

"Well, that was helpful," Terrance said as soon as he closed the door.

"Sorry, guys," Richard told them. "I…."

"Don't you fucking dare," Terrance said. "We all did what we needed to. It's what we do for each other, and none of us was about to let that little boy be hurt." He glanced at Gerome, who nodded. "We may have given you shit at the beginning, but hell, we're probably a little jealous of you."

"But what if we have to move and are split up?"

Gerome shrugged. "Then we have to move and go our separate ways. But it will be relatively easy for us. The real question is for you. If we have to move, will you be able to leave Daniel behind?"

"I may not have a choice. If we stay, what do I tell him?" Richard asked, leaning forward so he could see his friends.

"The truth," Gerome answered, and Terrance nodded. "We'll help you deal with any potential fallout. Just put your cards on the table, and if he doesn't take it well, then we'll end up relocating anyway." He stood and headed for the door. "We all need to get ready for work. Regardless of anything else, we have jobs and need to pay the damned rent." He smiled. "Do you remember when we used to call workaday people schmucks?" He pulled open the door. "Welcome to schmuckhood."

He closed the door behind him, and Terrance got up to go as well. "We'll talk once they let us know."

Terrance left, and Richard sat in the quiet apartment, wondering about his future and what the hell it was going to look like. One thing was for sure—he had little control over it now. It was either in the hands of the marshals service or Daniel. Probably both. He was well aware of the fact that it was most definitely not his to determine anymore. Richard hated that, but he was starting to get used to it.

Terrance's mother used to tell them that if they wanted something badly enough, they should pray for it. Richard had always just gone on to figure a way to get it. But he was out of options, so he slowly bowed his head.

Chapter 14

DANIEL WAS exhausted. He had spent hours going over everything with the FBI agent in charge. At one point he was afraid he was going to be charged with a crime, but he hadn't done anything, not really. And in the end his father had vouched for him, and Daniel had turned over all the notes he had received.

"What happens next? Can you protect us?"

"We're following the path you started," Agent Padron told him. "His associates will be tracked down and rounded up. I also understand that Mr. Jensen is talking to try to save his own skin."

"That's good." At least it sounded like Daniel wasn't going to have to worry about people coming after him after all.

"You should have called us right away, especially after you might have identified one of the people involved. We could have intervened and stopped things from progressing this far," Agent Padron explained.

Daniel didn't argue with him. Up until a little while ago, all he'd had were some notes and a threat, which wasn't going to be high on anyone's priority list. Still, it was best to go along and not make waves. This was their investigation now, and Daniel could step back and hopefully just go on with his life.

"Where do we go from here?" Daniel asked.

"We will be speaking with your father in more detail and with the people from the bank, but it doesn't seem like things have progressed far enough for any of their systems and data to have been put at risk. Though I suspect they will be looking into some of their employees and the kind of access they might have."

"So we're done?" Daniel asked as Coby climbed on the sofa next to him.

"I'm hungry," Coby said.

"Almost," Agent Padron said. "How much help did you get from your three friends, and what role did they have in all this?"

"They're my friends, and they had no role other than to support me and help keep the two of us safe. They didn't meet with anyone and they didn't speak with anyone involved."

Agent Padron cleared his throat. "Then what I'd really like to know is how a blindfolded, trussed-up Harry Jensen, who doesn't remember anything, managed to find himself outside the Longboat Key Police Department, and who notified them that he was there?" He raised his eyebrows.

Daniel shrugged. "I don't know. I didn't see any of that. Maybe it was the cop fairy making a delivery?" Daniel was determined not to smile.

"Do you really expect me to put that in your report? We know you couldn't have done it." He lowered his gaze. "I think that needs to be explained."

"Why? Was he harmed? Did the police not get the man they wanted? Sometimes it's best not to look a gift horse, or a gift criminal, too closely in the mouth." He was determined to keep Richard and the guys out of this as much as possible. In the end, they had cleaned up the mess better than all of the plans he might have come up with. "I have to get him something to eat." Daniel was grateful for Coby's interruption, because it gave him an excuse to bring this long interview to an end.

"We'll be in touch if we need anything more," Agent Padron said.

Daniel escorted him out, closing the door and locking it right away. The police and FBI were working to get the rest of the people associated with Harry and were watching the building, but he wasn't going to take any chances. It seemed this was over and the thieves were being rounded up. Daniel should be relieved.

He made dinner for Coby and wondered about Richard most of the time he spent doing it. Daniel hadn't had a chance to speak with him. Richard was probably at work, so he wasn't going to get a chance to find anything out on his end. The FBI had asked a few questions about him, and Daniel had downplayed his role, figuring it was best not to get him too involved. But he wanted to see him and talk to him.

Daniel still felt like a fool for jumping to all those conclusions, especially since even after that, Richard had been the one to save them in the end.

I NEED to speak with you. Richard's message came through a few hours later. There was no explanation, and Daniel immediately worried that bad news was to follow.

Of course.

I'll be over in ten minutes, he messaged.

Daniel acknowledged the message and picked up the apartment to give him something to do. He was jittery and nervous, not that anyone would blame him after the day he'd had. But things with Richard were still up in the air, and he needed to understand what had been going on. He had gotten the toys put away when a soft knock came. He checked and opened the door before letting Richard inside.

Richard moved rigidly as he stepped inside the apartment, and Daniel closed and locked the door and put on a pot of coffee. "Have you eaten?"

"Yes." Richard seemed so serious. "I'm fine." He went to the table and sat down, pushing out one of the other chairs. "It's good that Coby is asleep, because the things I have to tell you, I don't want him to hear." He swallowed hard, and most of the usual confidence he exuded was absent.

Daniel nodded and sat as well. "It's that bad?" Daniel asked with a grin, trying to make light of the situation, but Richard simply nodded. Daniel settled in the chair, placing his hands on the table. "Then why don't you tell me."

Richard cleared his throat. "It's not something I'm supposed to talk about. So I need you to listen and let me get this out. But I have to ask you to promise me something first." He took Daniel's hand. "You have to promise me that regardless of what you decide to do in the end, that what I tell you will never be repeated to anyone." He sighed loudly.

"Why don't you just say what you need to?" Daniel whispered, and held Richard's hand in return.

"You know a little of my story, and what I've told you about my background is true, but it's only a small part. I did grow up in foster care, and Gerome and Terrance are like my brothers. But we lived on the toughest streets in Detroit. And the three of us learned to survive, and we did that by being part of a family. We were tough kids, and no one messed with us. It didn't matter that we were gay. The three of us were formidable. You have to understand that there was no opportunity for us, so we made our own. Up until a year ago, the three of us were part of the Garvic family in Detroit. We basically ran the gay vices in the city. Clubs, escort services, things like that. We were damned good at it, and we made a lot of money."

Daniel swallowed hard. "You're mobsters?" The words came in through his shock, and he pulled his hand back.

"We were. The old man didn't care what we did as long as we returned money to the family. And that we did, a lot of it. Gerome is a real idea man, and Terrance was the muscle, as you could probably guess. I managed the business and saw to it that our commitments to everyone were met."

Daniel swallowed. "Did you kill people?" He watched Richard's reaction very closely.

"I didn't personally, like that really matters, but it was just business. I like to think that innocent people and our customers were always safe in our establishments. Being tough was part of doing business, otherwise you were *out* of business." He put his hand up as Daniel was about to ask another question. "That part of my life is over, and it has been for a while. I have a new life here, one that I'm starting to like and care about." The pleading in his eyes was almost enough for Daniel to forget about the rest.

"Why are you here?" Daniel asked.

"The old boss, Garvic Senior, he didn't mind what we did as long as we returned the money we were supposed to. But after he died, Junior decided to be a real dick. He didn't want to be associated with anything gay, so he decided he was going to take us down and get rid of us. We got wind of it, so the three of us turned him in. We gave evidence against dozens of people, and they're all in jail because of us, with more trials scheduled as the police follow the trails through the organization. After we testified, the marshals put Terrance, Gerome, and myself into the Witness Protection Program, and they eventually moved us here."

It took Daniel some time to process all of this. "You're a witness?"

"Yes," Richard answered flatly.

"And the three of you turned yourselves and the people you worked for in to the police?" Daniel asked. "You did what was right in the end?" He was putting the pieces together. "At least that explains how you knew all those things about what the people who were pressuring me were trying to do. You had been on the other side?"

"In a way, yes. See, we've had people try to pressure us too. We know how they act, and I tried to help. I've done stuff that isn't exactly nice, a lot of it. Before I got here, I wasn't a good person. And I may never be a good person; that's just a fact. And I certainly won't be someone like you. But my life is different than it was, and I'm not the same person I was in Detroit. Back there, Harry would have been taken out and fitted with cement shoes and never seen again."

Daniel smiled. "Instead, you guys trussed him up like a pig and delivered him to the police. The FBI guy was wondering how that happened. But I don't think they want to look too closely. A gift horse, and all that."

Richard nodded. "The person I was on the phone with was my contact at the marshals. I was asking her for help when you saw me." He leaned forward. "More than anything, I wanted to keep you and Coby safe. That's all that's mattered to me for weeks now. I know I'm not good enough for you, and I probably never will be. But I'm a different person—a better person—because of you, because I love you. I wasn't looking for it, but it happened. I fell in love with you, probably on that damned boat ride." He took a deep breath, and Daniel waited for what Richard had to say next.

When Richard didn't continue, Daniel asked, "Do you have to move? Is that why you're telling me this?"

Richard shrugged. "I don't know. If you decide you don't want me around, then yeah, the three of us are going to have to relocate somewhere else. So if you want me to say goodbye and you don't want to see me anymore, then I can make that happen. You won't have to worry about any retaliation or even seeing me on the street. The three of us will be gone in a day or so if that's what you want." He swallowed hard. "It's all up to you." He paused, folded his hands, and seemed to wait. "You have to have questions."

"If I want, you'll just leave, and I'll never see you again?" Even as he asked the question, the idea hurt deep down, like it felt so wrong it would physically hurt him. The thought of not seeing Richard ever again scared the shit out of him. But so did the things Richard said he'd done. Daniel's mind went to all the mob movies he had seen and the images they conjured up.

"Yes. Me telling you this is against the rules. They have decided so far that we can stay because basically no one knows who we are. But you do, so they'll move us. All I have to say is that you have become suspicious and then we'll be gone. If that's what you want, just say so." His gaze shifted to the tabletop.

"What about us? What if something happens in the future and you have to move? Will you just be gone some day and I won't know what happened or where you are? Will I have to move with you?"

Richard shrugged. "I don't have those kinds of answers. If you and Coby were in danger, then you'd probably have to relocate with us." He slumped in the chair. "I know this is a lot for you to take in all at once."

"And you're a gay mobster?" Daniel asked yet again, because that was almost too much to take in.

"I was one, yes," Richard explained. "But I'm not anymore. I'm just a guy like you who has a past that could put him and anyone else around him in danger if the family ever found out where I was. I'm told that Junior is still trying to find us from prison. So far they haven't found us, and the more time passes, the harder it is going to be for them to locate us. But it could happen, and if it does and you're with me, then you and Coby could be in danger." He pushed his chair back.

"I thought you should know what's been going on and why I've been acting the way I have." He patted Daniel's hand. "I honestly don't expect you to be willing to give up your life for me… for us. Coby is too precious for that."

Daniel thought for a few seconds. "So you don't want us in your life?" he asked. It seemed pretty clear that Richard was using this as an excuse to walk away. Richard usually went for what he wanted, so this was his way of backing out. "Is that what you're trying to say?"

Richard shook his head as he stood. "I want you more than I've ever wanted anything or anyone in my life. There is no doubt about that. But staying with me has risks, very real ones." He came around behind Daniel and slipped his arms around his shoulders. "This is your decision. It can't be mine no matter how much I want you and Coby. If I could, I'd whisk the lot of us away to some island where we could live away from everything and everyone to keep you safe. But I can't." His voice broke, and Daniel knew that was real and something rare and special. "This has to be something that you decide." Richard straightened up and his arms slipped away.

"They may never find you," Daniel said. "You've been here for months and you haven't been found."

"Nope. And the three of us are determined to stay under the radar. But it seems that keeping a certain little boy and his daddy safe was more than worth any risks to ourselves. But I don't want to risk the safety of the two of you. I can't." Richard backed away.

"You aren't," Daniel said softly. He closed his eyes and imagined the family he wanted. His mind conjured up a picture of Coby smiling in Richard's arms. They were at the playground, and Richard stood next to him as Coby grinned up at both of them before Daniel put him down and he raced over to the swings. "Uncle Richie, push me." He could hear Coby's voice as clear as a bell. That would make Coby happy, but it was also what Daniel wanted. A chance at a family of his own.

Shaking his head, he pushed the image away and tried to think of what his life would be like without Richard. All he could come up with were lonely and dull thoughts. His heart ached at the thought of never seeing Richard again, and he couldn't visualize it. The images that kept pushing their way back to his mind were ones of the three of them. In a short time, it was apparent that Richard had become an integral part of their lives, and Daniel didn't see a happy way forward without him. His heart wanted Richard, and it was more than willing to take whatever chances were required to have him in his and Coby's life. The thought of letting him go was too dark a well for him to drink from.

Daniel rose and turned as Richard stood still.

"You don't have to choose anything right now." Richard looked toward the door. "I should let you do what you need to do. Think about what it is you want and—"

Daniel lunged and caught Richard in a hug. The thought of being without him was more than he could bear. He hugged him so tightly. "I want you too." Richard knew the good and the bad about him and he still loved him.

"Are you sure? Even after you know the things I did?"

"Like you said, you aren't that person any longer. You've changed, and believe it or not, you've changed me." He laid his head against Richard's chest as muscular arms encircled him. "I think you showed me that I'm stronger than I thought I was."

"I always knew you were," Richard whispered.

"So what happens next? Do I have to do something?" Daniel asked.

Richard nodded and gently tilted his head upward. "Yeah. Kiss me."

Daniel did, with delight that turned heated within seconds. He pressed against Richard, holding him tightly, knowing he would walk through fire for this man, just as Richard had put his own future and life in jeopardy for him. "I love you," Daniel whispered between kisses as Richard guided him down toward the bedroom.

"I love you too." Richard teased his lips with his tongue and broke their kiss, walking backward. Daniel followed because the thought of being separated from Richard was too great of a loss at the moment.

As soon as they passed through the doorway, Richard closed it and sat on the edge of the bed, drawing Daniel forward between his outstretched legs. "You're mine, just as I'm yours." Richard brushed Daniel's hair away from his face. "I will do anything I can to protect you and care for you… and I will try to be the man you deserve." Richard's hands shook, and Daniel placed his own on top of them.

"All you need to do is be yourself. That's all I ask. Be the man I fell in love with. The one who takes Coby to the park, the one who sits with me and watches television, and the one who makes sure to keep us safe from harm. That's the only Richard I will ever need."

Richard smiled and drew him onto the bed. "Are those the only things you need?" Heat rolled off him, and Daniel pressed right into it, taking what Richard had to give and holding each gift in his heart. He knew their life wasn't going to be perfect and that uncertainty hung over them, but that weighed nothing in balance with the incredible man who loved him. Richard's care would always tip the scales.

"No," Daniel moaned softly. "I want this Richard too. The one who gives himself to me, who loves me and isn't afraid to show it." Daniel kissed away whatever else Richard was about to say. He had what he really wanted, and that was all that mattered.

Epilogue

RICHARD CHECKED the time and smiled to himself as he let Alan know that he was going to be taking his break.

"Of course you are. It's Wednesday," Alan said with a smile. "I'll be out to watch things for a while." He locked his computer and followed Richard out of the office and into a construction zone. Alan had been thinking of stepping back, and Richard had wanted more of a place of his own, so he was managing more of the business and Alan had made him a partner. Part of the deal was to enlarge the bar a little and expand the restaurant portion of the business.

Alan went behind the bar, and Richard got their table prepared so when Daniel and Coby arrived at six, their place was ready, including the booster seat for Coby.

"Uncle Richie," Coby said as soon as he passed through the door, running over to Richard, who picked him up and swung him into his seat.

"What do you want for dinner?"

"Fishies!" Coby said.

Richard already knew what Daniel wanted, and he put in three orders of fish and chips. He got their drinks from Alan at the bar and then sat down with the family, only to have Gerome and Terrance join them a few minutes later. They sat at the far end. "I got fishies coming," Coby said, squirming to get out of his seat and climbing onto Terrance's lap.

"You guys spoil him rotten," Daniel lightly scolded all three of them, and they didn't argue. They did spoil him, because none of them had had anyone to spoil them, and Richard figured they were making up for it. Richard knew it was true for himself. Coby wasn't going to want for anything and would have the best chance in life possible.

"How was work?" Daniel asked the guys.

"Good," Terrance answered. "They want me to be an assistant manager." He sounded thrilled about it. Daniel chuckled, and Richard sighed slightly. Over the past six months, the mantle of respectability had landed on all of them. It meant hard work and sometimes drudgery, but they were settling in.

Daniel leaned over the table. "I got a call from my father today."

"What did he have to say?" Richard asked as Andi come over to take Gerome's and Terrance's orders.

"He asked if the three of us could come over for dinner next week. He wants to see Coby and talk about what I can do to help beef up the bank's security." A thaw had developed in Daniel's relationship with his folks. "He also said that the police rounded up the last person involved in the incident." That had become their code word for what had happened, when Coby was present. The assistant branch manager had been involved, and he'd tried to run. Richard had to give him credit, the guy had managed to lie low for six months.

"Have any of you heard anything from… you know?" Daniel asked very quietly. All three of them shook their heads. Richard knew that no news was good news as far as the marshals went. They didn't make contact unless they heard of a threat, so the three of them went on with their lives unless they needed something. "Good. Same as last week. Now we can talk about something more fun. Like Coby has been asking for another boat ride."

"Dolphins. I wanna see the dolphins."

Richard smiled. "We can see if we can go for a ride." He met Gerome's gaze.

"Well, since his birthday is coming up, we already arranged for a boat ride and a party," Terrance said, tickling Coby and adding his giggles to the overlapping voices, making the place that much happier. "Is that okay?"

Coby nodded and hugged Terrance before doing the same to Gerome and coming around to give Richard a hug as well. "Big party with cake and boat, and dolphins and bouncy castle." He gave an example of how he could bounce, and Richard grinned.

"You can have whatever you want for your birthday party," Richard told him. "So you and Daddy make a list, and the three of us will see what we can do." Coby's eyes were wide, and he nodded, like his little mind was conjuring up flying carpets and magic wands. "It looks like Andi has our food, so you need to sit down so you can eat."

Coby hurried back to his place and climbed into his booster seat, digging in to his food as soon as she set it down. "I like fishies."

Richard shared a smile with Daniel as they started eating. The past six months had been eye-openingly happy for him. He had always thought that running the business and living on the edge the way he had in Detroit had been good and made him happy. He'd had no idea. Here, his life was simple and he was helping raise a kid, but damn, he was happy, and he fucking grinned as he took his first bite of flaky white fish.

"Do you ever wish you could go back?" Daniel asked, and Richard shrugged. Yes, there were times when things got slow and predictable and he wished he could go back to the action and excitement, but then something would happen, like he'd return to their home. The condo would be quiet, and Coby would be in bed, the lights would be off, and he'd push open the bedroom door to see Daniel's bright eyes, his intense smile, and his body laid out on the bed just waiting for him. His life in Detroit had nothing on the kind of heat and excitement Daniel could deliver when it was just the two of them.

"I would never go back if I could," Richard whispered and leaned over the table. Daniel met him part of the way, their lips touching briefly. "I have everything I could possibly want right here." Back in Detroit, Richard would have been classified as a bad man. He'd done things he would just as soon forget. But Daniel made him want to be good, to be the man Daniel deserved, and Richard strove for that every day.

"Me too," Daniel said, and slipped his hand around the back of Richard's neck, pulling him closer to kiss him again.

Keep reading for an excerpt from

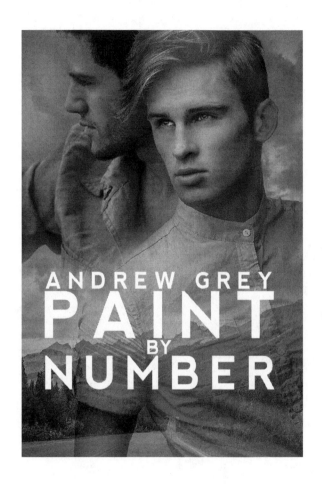

Can the Northern Lights and a second-chance romance return inspiration to a struggling artist?

When New York painter Devon Starr gives up his vices, his muses depart along with them. Devon needs a change, but when his father's stroke brings him home to Alaska, the small town where he grew up isn't what he remembers.

Enrique Salazar remembers Devon well, and he makes it his personal mission to open Devon's eyes to the rugged beauty and possibilities all around them. The two men grow closer, and just as Devon begins to see what's always been there for him, they're called to stand against a mining company that threatens the very pristine nature that's helping them fall in love. The fight only strengthens their bond, but as the desire to pick up a paintbrush returns, Devon also feels the pull of the city.

A man trapped between two worlds, Devon can only follow where his heart leads him.

www.dreamspinnerpress.com

THE CITY was unusually quiet, but Devon's brain wasn't. Three in the morning and he wandered the loft, pacing like a caged tiger and not knowing what to do. Normally he would paint, but the damned review hung in his head, and the thought of picking up a brush scared the shit out of him. So he left everything where it was and simply paced.

Devon closed his eyes and tried to bring up an image of something worthy, anything at all that might inspire anything. He stood in front of his windows, looking out over the street, but nothing came to him. It was like the well that had bubbled up with feeling from his soul had run dry. But Devon knew it was worse than that. His soul had starved itself and was dying. That was the only explanation.

Maybe he was done and the gift, as so many people called it, was gone. Maybe it really had come from a bottle. And if that was the case, then it was no more, and Devon would need to find his way without it.

A single bang sounded on his door, reverberating through the loft like a gong. Devon went over and unlocked it, then pulled the door open. "Don't you ever fucking sleep?" Devon asked as he stepped back.

His friend Stephen waltzed into the loft, carrying a bag in one hand and a case of Coke in the other. "I saw the review and figured you would be up standing in front of those windows, wondering what you were going to do." Stephen was a ray of sunshine, and right now that was what Devon needed. "I brought mint chip and Mississippi Mud ice cream, so sit your butt down and we can pig out until we lapse into a sugar coma and wake up in a whole new world."

Devon plopped down on the sofa. "Have you been watching *Sex and the City* again?" He took the mint chip and pulled off the top.

Stephen went to his kitchen and returned with spoons, then popped open a couple cans of soda. "Don't be bitchy. I'm here with libations and comfort, so don't get your panties in a wad." He grabbed the deep, dark, fudgy chocolate ice cream and sat next to him. "I got you caffeine-free soda. I figured after all this sugar, the caffeine would make our heads explode."

Devon shook his head. "What does it matter? If the damned thing exploded, I wouldn't have to read any more reviews about how uninspired I am."

Stephen took a huge bite and then set the carton on the table. "You've been complaining for months that you feel empty, and yet you went on painting. Now when someone calls you on it, you mope and go all Debbie Downer on me." He snatched up the carton as soon as Devon reached for it. After they each took another bite, they switched flavors. "So things are hard right now. So what? Find something that inspires you and go out and paint it. You've been successful and you have some money, so get the hell out of the city, change your scenery, and find something to replenish your soul."

He made it sound so easy. Devon took a bite of the chocolate ice cream, humming at the intense fudginess and closing his eyes. "That's easy for you to say." He drank some of the soda. "You know, this is a lot like college. Remember?"

"Yeah, except I am not going to end up climbing into bed with you, and we are not going to wake up tomorrow with you all mopey and my backside sore as hell from that baton between your legs." Stephen giggled. "Been there, done that… nearly ruined our friendship."

Devon joined him. "I doubt my dick had anything to do with that. It was more like the fact that we thought we might be in love and actually tried to be boyfriends." God, what a disaster that had been. Devon loved Stephen with his entire being, but they were not in any way meant to fall in love with each other.

"The harder we tried, the worse it got."

"We weren't that bad," Devon said, feeling petulant and a little picked on.

"You snored loud enough to wake the dead," Stephen complained.

"I had a deviated septum, which has been fixed, thank you very much. And don't forget that you talk in your sleep." Two could play this game. "And you never picked up anything. That dorm room was small enough without walking your dirty-drawers obstacle course."

"And you were anal about where everything goes." Stephen pushed out his lower lip in a pout that would have been cute… ten years ago.

"Only so I can find it without tearing everything apart," Devon explained.

"And yet you still managed to lose your key at least three times a week." Stephen broke into a grin. "Yeah, there was definitely a reason things didn't work out between us. But as soon as we stopped the whole boyfriend thing… and I moved back in with my regular roommate… everything returned to normal."

"Except your unnatural fascination with my dick," Devon pressed with a grin.

Stephen rolled his eyes. "Okay. There was one thing that always worked. You and I were great in the sack." They had done the friends-with-benefits thing a few times over the years, and it had worked out. No long-term stuff, no commitment, just a night with a friend that ended in mind-blowing sex. Yeah, that part of things they had down pat. The rest of it… no way in hell.

Devon took one more bite and yawned. "Come on, we should put this stuff away and get some sleep. Do you want to go home?" Fatigue was setting in.

Once Stephen shook his head, Devon put the ice cream in the freezer, and he and Stephen got into bed.

It felt nice not to be alone, and soon enough Stephen rolled over and was asleep, with Devon following after him.

HIS MOUTH felt like he had spent the entire night drinking. Devon smacked his lips and climbed out of the bed, leaving Stephen to sleep. He paused at the bedroom door, looking back and smiling. His friend was sound asleep, and Devon wondered for the millionth time why they just couldn't seem to make it work.

Then Stephen rolled over, farting loudly, and Devon chuckled to himself, heading to the bathroom. He definitely had his answer.

Brushing his teeth made him feel more human, and he shaved and returned to the bedroom, where he dressed quietly before leaving the room, letting Stephen sleep for as long as he wanted.

In front of the huge windows, his work waited for him, a canvas on the easel. He looked at it and shook his head, taking it down. The piece was another just like the ones in the exhibition, and it needed to be set aside. He thought of painting Stephen, but even that idea came up short. There was nothing at all that he wanted to do; nothing lit a fire in his belly and made him feel anything.

"Just lie around and watch television for a few days," Stephen said as he came out of the bedroom in his boxers, scratching his butt.

"You know, you could have a boyfriend or maybe a husband if you didn't act so much like an old married straight guy."

Stephen flipped him off and started a pot of coffee. "Ass."

"Maybe, but I'm not the one scratching his like he's got the damn clap." Devon turned away from the window and blinked a few times. His phone began to ring, and he picked it up, recognizing the 907 area code from home, but the number wasn't immediately familiar.

"Hello?" Devon answered skeptically, half expecting it to be a telemarketer masking their number with one he was familiar with.

"Devon?" the voice questioned, and he recognized it immediately.

"Mrs. Fitzgerald? Oh, it's good to hear your voice." He closed his eyes, and images of home—the one he'd left years ago out of emotional necessity—came flooding back.

"Honey… I wish I had better news. It's your dad." She sounded sad in a way he had never heard before. Mrs. Fitz was one of those people tragedy followed, but she just continued on with the same "the sun will come out tomorrow" outlook.

"What about him? I just talked to him last week, and everything was fine," Devon said, worry spiking inside.

"He isn't fine. Your dad had a mild stroke two days ago. He's okay, and the doctors say that if he rests and eat right, he can recover, but he sits alone in that cabin all day and night, or he goes down to the Trading Post and eats their food and drinks way too much. That's what caused this, I know it. All that awful, fatty food."

"Where is he now?" Devon asked.

"Your dad is at the hospital in Anchorage. Joe and I will go down there and pick him up in a few days. They want him to rest, but they're sure he won't once he gets back to the house here. That combined with the fact that the nearest doctor is forty miles away in Wasilla. So they want to make sure he's stable and on his way to recovery. He can move in here for a few weeks, of course, but I thought we should let you know what was going on. Lord, that man is as stubborn as a mule."

"That explains why he didn't call to say what happened to him," Devon said a little bitterly.

"Quite possibly." She paused and said something away from the phone. "Is there any way you can come up here and stay with him, at least for a little while? He needs some family. Joe and I understand if it's too much for you and if you're busy, what with your life and success and all." The words might have sounded snappish, but her tone was anything but.

Devon took a few seconds to look around his space and sighed. He felt empty and as down as he could ever remember. The only things keeping him from going down to the local liquor store and buying a bottle were his friends and supporters, who loved him and would kick his ass from here to kingdom come if he so much as had a single drop, Stephen and Roz among them. They loved him enough to intervene if he needed it.

"Let me look into some things and see what I can do, okay?" It was the most he could do in his unthinking and uncaffeinated state. "I'll call you back before the end of the day, and thank you for telling me."

"Sweetheart, of course I'd let you know. You're family, and he needs you. The old goat just doesn't realize it."

"Thank you." He said goodbye and hung up the phone.

"What is it… a call from the frozen north? God, you'd never get me up there. I'd freeze my little butt off, and I like it where it is, thank you." Stephen actually turned to try to get a look at his own ass. "You don't think it's getting saggy, do you? There is nothing worse than a guy getting older and not realizing that his butt is about to meet the backs of his knees."

"Focus a little," Devon said as he took the cup of coffee Stephen offered him. "My dad had a mild stroke. He's in the hospital and apparently doing okay. They're going to send him home soon." He sipped from the mug and sat down, growing number by the second.

"Do you want me to help you make travel arrangements? I can watch your place for you while you're gone."

Devon shrugged.

"Come on, it's your dad. He needs your help." Stephen sat down right next to him, hip to hip. "If my dad told me he needed my help… well, that would be once hell froze over. After I picked myself up from a dead faint, I'd be there for him. It's my dad."

"Even after all those years of fighting?"

"Sure. I have my trust fund, thanks to Grandpa, and Dad can't do anything about that now. Besides, if he had to ask for my help, it would be like swallowing his pride and his balls at the same time." Stephen threw his head back and laughed.

"That's what I thought."

"Yeah, okay, stuff with my dad is shit. But it isn't that way with yours. You love the guy. So get on a plane and fly all the fucking way to Alaska and take care of him for a few weeks. He had a stroke and he could have died. Do you want the phone to be the only way you talk to him…? I didn't think so."

Devon groaned. "Things are… complicated."

"They always are, but you deal with them." Stephen pulled out his phone. "There's a flight leaving first thing tomorrow morning from LaGuardia. You change planes in Seattle and then fly up to Anchorage." He began pressing buttons like crazy.

"What are you doing?"

"Buying you a ticket. First class all the way, baby." He continued working. "Okay. I got you a truck in Anchorage so you can drive to that tiny town where your dad lives. And a car will pick you up in the morning right out front to take you to the airport. Now call that nice lady who told you what was going on. I emailed you the details and your itinerary so you can send it to her." Stephen put away his phone and crossed his arms over his chest.

"Were you always this pushy?" Devon asked.

"Yes. Pushy is my middle name." He got up off the sofa, heading to Devon's bedroom. "Where do you keep your luggage? Under the bed? And do you have clothes for the frozen north, or do we need to go shopping?" He turned back, a smile of delight crossing his lips. The man loved shopping as much as the guys back home loved to shoot stuff.

"I have plenty. Thank you." There wasn't going to be any stopping him, so Devon went along. Swimming up a waterfall was easier than going against Stephen when he set himself a task. In the bedroom, Stephen dressed and then opened the closet and began pulling things out, pausing with a handful of hangers.

"Why are you so scared to go back?" Stephen asked the one question that Devon had never answered in all the years they'd known each other. He'd always managed to avoid the question. "Did you corrupt the star of the ice hockey team or something?"

Devon growled. "No. I fell in love with the local golden boy."

"And...."

"He didn't love me back." Devon shrugged. "He was also my best friend. And he's straight, with two kids and an ex-wife, and is apparently courting wife number two. Not that it matters. I'm over him." It was the man he'd never managed to get over that he'd stayed away from for a decade.

"Are you really?" Stephen asked.

"Yeah. It's been ten years, and he has his own life. Not that it matters. Craig is straight, and...."

Stephen sat on the edge of the bed. "There's more to this than you're telling me. A lot more. Did you and Craig ever get together? Did he shatter your heart into a million tiny pieces?"

"No and no. The whole heart-shattering thing was someone else entirely. Someone who didn't even know how I felt about him back then." He shifted and figured he might as well share the rest. "Anyway, things got bad after that."

Stephen leaned forward. "Who was it?"

Devon shook his head. "That's the whole thing. There were all these rumors, and I was pretty sure Enrique was gay, but I couldn't turn the town rumor mill on him. And I was such a mess I didn't think I was good enough for him, and then things got even worse." God, baring all this shit made him want a drink.

"I'm sorry. I...." Stephen drifted off.

Devon sighed as images of those dark days flooded his mind. He fought to keep the darkness from overtaking him. "I don't talk about my mother much, but I should." He blinked as the memories hit him hard. "After the crap with Craig, rumors of me being gay started in town, and it got ugly for a while, with a lot of whispers and parents holding their kids tighter. Until Mom put a stop to it. She took on all of them, including my dad, like the champion she always was." Devon wiped his eyes. "You know my mom passed away just before I left."

"You told me it was a car accident," Stephen supplied.

Devon nodded. His AA sponsors had told him that he needed to deal with the underlying cause of his drinking, and he had shared his story in a meeting, but nowhere else until this moment, and his heart pounded in his ears.

"Mom had gone to Anchorage to attend a PFLAG meeting. She was determined to understand what I was going through." Devon swallowed around the lump in his throat as the loss he usually kept at bay welled like a tsunami. He breathed deeply through it, wanting a drink but accepting the glass of water that Stephen pressed into his hand. "The accident was on her way back." Logically he knew it wasn't his fault, but losing his mother and champion, the town rumors, Craig—all of it had been too much.

And now he was going to have to deal with all the baggage from a decade ago heaped on top of everything else. God, and all he needed to do was navigate the remains of his tattered heart and keep himself sober. It was going to take a fucking miracle.

ANDREW GREY is the author of more than one hundred works of Contemporary Gay Romantic fiction. After twenty-seven years in corporate America, he has now settled down in Central Pennsylvania with his husband, Dominic, and his laptop. An interesting ménage. Andrew grew up in western Michigan with a father who loved to tell stories and a mother who loved to read them. Since then he has lived throughout the country and traveled throughout the world. He is a recipient of the RWA Centennial Award, has a master's degree from the University of Wisconsin–Milwaukee, and now writes full-time. Andrew's hobbies include collecting antiques, gardening, and leaving his dirty dishes anywhere but in the sink (particularly when writing). He considers himself blessed with an accepting family, fantastic friends, and the world's most supportive and loving partner. Andrew currently lives in beautiful, historic Carlisle, Pennsylvania.

Email: andrewgrey@comcast.net

Website: www.andrewgreybooks.com